The T

THE THIRD GIRL

S.C. SHANNON

JOFFE BOOKS

Joffe Books, London
www.joffebooks.com

First published in Great Britain in 2025

© S.C. Shannon

This book is a work of fiction. Names, characters, businesses, organizations, places and events are either the product of the author's imagination or are used fictitiously. Any resemblance to actual persons, living or dead, events or locales is entirely coincidental. The spelling used is American English except where fidelity to the author's rendering of accent or dialect supersedes this. The right of S.C. Shannon to be identified as author of this work has been asserted in accordance with the Copyright, Designs and Patents Act 1988.

No part of this book may be used or reproduced in any manner for the purpose of training artificial intelligence technologies or systems. In accordance with Article 4(3) of the Digital Single Market Directive 2019/790, Joffe Books expressly reserves this work from the text and data mining exception.

Cover art by Nebojša Zorić

ISBN: 978-1-80573-124-5

*For those who prefer their stories dark, their plots twisted,
and their nights sleepless — this one's for you!*

CHAPTER 1

Before
Christina

The day before my seventeenth birthday, I was kidnapped.

The air was crisp but had a stale odor because of the lack of ventilation. Loud music rattled the walls — a sound I'd heard since the day I was captured. The handcuffs and chains tightly secured me to the old, rusty metal frame bed. Even the slightest movement caused my wrists and ankles to ache. With a tear streaming down my face, I shifted onto my side, my eyes fixated on the wall.

Suddenly, an ear-piercing scream shattered the silence. I covered my ears as I repeatedly hummed the "Itsy-Bitsy Spider" nursery rhyme — anything I could do to get my mind off my impending doom.

The screaming stopped, and heavy footsteps grew louder in my direction. I attempted to curl my legs in a ball, but the chains prevented me. The door crashed open and slammed against the wall.

I didn't look. I never looked. They trained me not to.

Looking always resulted in discipline.

I knew better.

I heard his stomping feet coming toward me. I tried not to cry. *Be strong.* My skin burned as he placed the rough cloth around my eyes. Slowly, he unlocked my chains as the nausea set in. He yanked on my arm as I struggled to pull it away. I dragged my feet through the dirt on the wooden floor, kicking up dust as I struggled to resist. I had no more strength in me to fight.

Suddenly, a loud crash from down the hall caused him to halt. Thunderous footsteps grew louder, and I held my breath as I tried to determine what we were waiting for. The rumbling stopped, and an ear-piercing howl emanated from my left. Unexpectedly, I was yanked to the floor as my brain registered what was happening. I removed my blindfold, and she hovered above him, repeatedly stabbing him.

"Run, Christina, run!" she screamed. "Go get help, now!"

"I can't leave without you," I pleaded.

She continued struggling with him — a blur of limbs as she groaned. "Christina! Go!"

As I ran toward the door, I cast a glance at her, fighting him on the ground. "I'll come back for you! I promise!" I screamed.

"I know! Go! We don't have much time!" she yelled back.

The pounding in my chest was like a drum, making it difficult to breathe as I navigated the dark halls of this place. I expected someone lying in wait, ready to grab me at every turn.

This was my one chance. I had to save her.

The front door was in sight, and freedom was within my grasp. Not much farther now. I reached for the doorknob and was relieved when it turned freely. As I quickly burst through the door, the aroma immediately engulfed me; I'd forgotten what the fresh air felt like in my lungs.

After a quick look around, I sprinted toward the opening in the woods, hoping that the thick tree trunks would hide me long enough to get away.

The sun was setting on the horizon, and I would soon be out of daylight. With each stride, the breeze cooled my cheeks as I raced down the trail, chasing the sinking light. I ran for what felt like an eternity — my legs throbbing with pain, my muscles twitching uncontrollably, and my lungs burning for air.

With each step, my mind insisted I couldn't go any further. I kept trying to reassure myself that the pain was temporary, because Penelope's life was at stake. I had to fight through it. Right as my mind was ready to give up, I saw an opening in the woods beckoning me into the unknown.

One final look behind me, and then I sprinted into the clearing.

Relief overcame me as I realized it was a house. I ran to the glowing windows as the sun had crested beyond the mountains.

Please be a good guy!

I darted toward the front door and banged my fists as I screamed for help.

The porch light turned on, and I observed a man through the door's glass.

He cautiously cracked it open, only revealing a tiny sliver of his faded blue baseball cap and flannel button-up shirt. "What can I do for you, miss?"

I tried to speak, but my mouth was so dry that it felt like sandpaper scraping my throat, forcing a painful cough to escape. My body buckled, and I placed my hands on my knees as I gathered my composure. "I'm Christina Johnson!" I paused like he would know what that meant. After a brief silence, I continued, "I escaped! I've been missing for weeks! My friend Penelope is still back there!"

The man's mouth was agape as he opened the door wide. "Honey!" he yelled. "Call the police! It's one of those girls that was kidnapped!"

He let me in, placing his hand on the small of my back. I was shaking from the cold, and the fading rush of adrenaline caused me to collapse in his embrace. He escorted me to the couch as I watched his wife on the phone, looking at me sorrowfully.

She walked over to me and placed her palm on my shoulder. "Don't you worry; the police are on their way to find your friend."

I sat there anxiously waiting for the police as the guilt set in for leaving Pen behind. The woman grabbed a blanket and covered my shoulders as the shaking continued. My thoughts were filled with the horrible things that could be happening to her at that house. What if he got the upper hand and took the knife from her? What if she's dead already?

I stared at the large black-and-white clock hanging on the wall.

Tick. Tock. Tick. Tock. What was taking so long?

How could I leave her behind? I buried my head in my hands and cried.

In the distance, sirens pierced the air, and I felt myself exhale, knowing it would all be over soon.

I glanced to the doorway just as a police officer approached. He had a youthful innocence about him, with a crisp uniform and a face free from the wear of long years on the job. I watched as he whispered to the residents who had opened their door to a stranger without question. He looked in my direction and waved for me to come to him. For the first time in weeks, I felt like everything was going to be all right. I was safe.

"OK, let's go find Penelope. Think you can help us?"

I nodded yes and followed him to his cruiser. "I ran down the trail until I made it here," I said, as I pointed to an opening in the woods.

I jumped into his car and forced a smile at the couple who helped me. The woman raised her hand as her husband placed his arm around her shoulders. I watched them vanish into the reddish glow of swirling dust kicked up by the tires. As he navigated the path with urgency, I realized the distance I had traveled to get here. I stared out of the window as we passed the trees — the darkness absorbing them. The headlights created shadows along the trail, causing me to see things that didn't exist — imagining them out there, waiting to take me back into the torture room.

The trees opened, and before us was a neglected, off-white, one-story house with broken shutters and chipped paint. The yard was overgrown and not maintained. Trash littered the space, with empty beer bottles collecting dust.

I glanced in the side mirror and realized a string of cop cars had joined us, forming a long line like an unbroken chain. The silence was broken by slamming car doors, startling me as the sea of tan uniforms washed over the yard toward the house.

"Stay here. We're going to find your friend," the officer said.

I hunkered down, terrified of seeing those responsible for what has happened to me the last few weeks. The cop ran toward the house with his arms stiff in front of him and his gun out. The cops sprinted to all sides of the structure in a choreographed mass. My hands trembled as they kicked the front door and rushed into the property.

Please be alive, Penelope!

I sat there patiently as the light seeped through the wooden slats covering the windows. Anxiously, I observed their movement from one side of the structure to the other as deep voices yelled, "Clear!" every few seconds.

What's taking so long?

Then silence. The house was dark again.

A few moments passed and they all walked out, looking defeated and alone as they whispered on the porch.

Where was Penelope?

The officer approached my door and opened it. "Where is she?" I asked before he could speak.

He hesitated, as if he couldn't find the right words. "She's not there. They . . ." He paused. "Everyone is gone."

CHAPTER 2

Present
Christina

"In the shadows of ordinary life, people vanish without a trace. Families left in agony, questions unanswered, and a haunting mystery that lingers long after the search ends—" a deep voice says on the TV show.

My heart races, and I shut my eyes.

When I regain consciousness, the darkness engulfs me, but the sound of an engine's roar and the tangible vibrations of tires on the road are impossible to ignore. Something shrouds my head, making it difficult for me to breathe — a rough adhesive bites my lips, muffling my desperate attempts to call for help.

Desperately, I thrash my arms and legs, but the restraints grip me. Is this really happening? The realization sets in — I'm being kidnapped. Panic engulfs me as a spiral of terrifying thoughts blow through my brain. Am I going to die?

My eyes shoot open. I look — computer, glass, rug. I listen — water dripping from the sink, the gentle purr of my dog's breathing, the hum of passing cars. I move — wiggle my fingers, ball my fists, tap my feet. *You are safe. It was just a memory.*

I reach for the remote and change the channel. Welcome to my life. When I least expect it, a flashback will emerge, and

I use my simple tricks to adapt to the anxiety. Name three things I can see, three things I can hear, and move three parts of my body. Follow up with a reminder that I am safe and the feelings subside. It wasn't always manageable, but I have had decades to master it.

"That's enough TV for me," I say, looking at Thor with his head cocked and one ear flopping slightly. "No more bad memories for me today."

I place an earbud in my right ear while keeping the left ear open to listen to what is happening around me. Ever since that fateful summer, I have been overly cautious in every aspect of my life. I avoid leaving home and have been grateful that everything can be delivered to my front door. The only complication, however, is openly inviting strangers to my house, but even that doesn't concern me now. The benefit of being American is the nearly unlimited access to guns, as long as you can pass the background checks. At any current time, there are at least seven pistols hidden but easily accessible in every room. They are concealed in compartments that only I know how to reach, and while that makes me feel safer in this world, no one is out of danger, with evil lurking around every corner.

I log onto my laptop and pull up the project I have been working on. Being a freelance transcriptionist wasn't the career I had planned for myself when I was younger, but it allowed me to work from home at a decent salary.

Currently, I'm enjoying my assignment. My client is an author who writes his entire novels by hand on yellow legal pads, records the audio, and then has someone digitize the work from there. Set in the aftermath of the Civil War, the story I'm transcribing follows a disfigured boy and his life as part of a traveling sideshow. I just started the first draft, but it is a welcome break from the usual law-related depositions, meeting minutes, lectures, and speeches I usually work on. Every person has their own creative process, and I found his approach exciting, and the story great, which is a bonus.

Thor nudges my thigh with his nose, and I pet him softly. He stretches his legs and exposes his belly to be scratched as he lets out a long sigh. "Oh, life is so hard for you, isn't it, buddy? What could you possibly be sighing about?" I ask.

Most people are fearful of rottweilers; their fierce loyalty and protective nature can be intimidating, but he is the epitome of sweet and devoted. He serves as much more than a therapy dog; he's a faithful companion. After experiencing the trauma I did as a kid, I swore I'd never have children of my own. So, it has been a pleasure having something that somewhat fills that void.

A message appears on my computer: *I don't think Mom is doing too well.* It's my sister Nicole.

"Shit," I say to myself, pulling the phone out of my pocket to reply.

Why do you say that?

She's been lying about going to doctor's appointments.

You sure? You think it's back?

If it's not already, then they are concerned it's not gone.

Is she doing OK? She took it pretty hard last time.

Eh. As good as anyone can, I guess.

Should I head out there?

No, I don't think so yet. Her next appointment isn't for a few weeks.

Well, keep me posted. I was planning on visiting next month anyway.

I will. Everything good with you?

Yeah, just the usual stuff. You?

Nicole responds with a thumbs-up emoji, which is her way of letting me know she's done with the conversation. We were close when we were younger, because our mom was constantly working to support us. She was a registered nurse and worked as many shifts as possible to make ends meet, so I cared for my little sister. But once I turned eighteen, I left town, everything, and everyone behind with it — including my family.

Looking at the clock, I realize it's time to wrap up work and fit in a workout. I jump on the treadmill and start my usual routine — a short warm-up, one mile as fast as I can go, and finish with about twenty minutes of jogging to maintain my endurance. I keep the mindset that you never know when you would have to run for your life. The only way to survive the unknown is to prepare for it, and this is part of my routine now. I hate that I always think like this, but I had to learn the hard way. I only escaped because I was lucky. I don't want to be caught in that situation ever again.

I finish my workout and hop in the shower. When I get back to the kitchen, I make Thor his dinner, which he scarfs down in minutes. Despite having a full stomach, he follows me around like a giant 100-lb shadow, waiting for me to drop some of the ingredients I'm using to make spaghetti and meatballs for myself.

Taking both hands, I scratch behind his ears. "You already ate an entire bowl, fatso! You can't have any of my dinner," I say to him. His entire rear body shakes as he wiggles his tail and licks my face.

"Yes, I love you too, baby. You're such a sweet dog, aren't you?" I say, patting him on the head.

The smell of ground beef and garlic fills the kitchen, making my stomach growl in anticipation. I sip on Cakebread Cellars Cabernet Sauvignon as I watch Thor clumsily chase a ball around the island.

As I bring the wine glass to my lips, I'm startled by a knock at the door. I'm not expecting anyone today — I glance at the clock: 7:20 p.m. I open my phone and look at the security camera. A man is standing there. It is too late for visitors. My breathing becomes labored as my palms become clammy. *Don't worry; it's probably just a solicitor. He'll go away.* But my knees tremble, making it difficult to stand.

Knock. Knock.

I sit on the floor and crawl slowly to the window. The knocking continues as Thor runs to the door, ferociously barking and alerting the stranger to his massive presence.

Just breathe!

Silently, I unlock the hidden compartment beneath the window and uncover a concealed black Ruger 9mm pistol. The stranger remains undeterred, despite Thor's loud barking.

Knock. Knock. Knock. Knock.

I stay quiet. No one can know I am in here. I look — door, window, curtain. I listen — door-knocking, Thor barking, my heart beating. I move — tap my thumbs to each finger, wiggle my toes, lift my arms. *You are not in danger. He is not here to hurt you.*

Cautiously, I peek through the curtains, my eyes darting from the window to the pistol. I don't recognize this man. He is medium height, with dark brown hair and caramel skin. He is wearing a blue-collared shirt and slacks. I watch as he looks around, which immediately arouses my suspicion. What is he looking for? He knocks again — this time louder and more forcefully. *Just go away already! No one here is opening this door.*

I breathe in deeply and exhale. *Just breathe. You're not in danger.*

I look out the window once more. The man glances around again, removes a white envelope from his pocket, and quickly scribbles something on the back. Then, he places it underneath the doormat. He pivots and strolls toward the street. Standing up, I watch him get into a small black sedan, possibly a BMW. Once he drives away, I lean against the wall, relaxing my shoulders as I exhale. Thor trots over to me and sits beside me as I pet him.

"Thanks for the assist, buddy! You are a good guard dog!" He jumps on me and starts licking my cheek. "Good boy!"

I shut the compartment with the pistol inside as I walk over to the door. I carefully open it and survey the area before reaching for the envelope.

I quickly close and lock the door. I read what the man wrote on the envelope aloud: "I'm Emily's husband. She was in a terrible car accident and passed away. She instructed me to give this to you if anything ever happened to her."

"Emily?" I say to myself. "Emily Henderson? What does he mean, 'if anything happened to her'?"

My heart drums in my chest.

I open the envelope as it flutters in my grasp. I gasp as my mind processes what is written on the piece of paper.

She's still alive — find her!

CHAPTER 3

Before
Christina

A piercing scream startled me from behind.

When I turned around, there was a young girl thrown over a boy's shoulder as they laughed together, almost colliding with me.

"Dude, watch where you're going!" I said.

The boy looked at me and smirked but kept walking.

"Dickhead," I mumbled, rolling my eyes.

I was more than ready for the school year to be over. I walked across the quad, threw my backpack on the table, and sat down. "Can this day be done already? I'm so ready for summer!"

Penelope and Emily looked up at me. "Seriously, I can't wait for the school year to be over and never see this place again. This place is so lame," Penelope said and then blew a giant bubble with her gum.

"Pen, you realize we have to come back after the break, right?" I asked.

"I don't want to think about that!" Penelope muttered. "I'm officially in summer mode! All that's on my mind is sleeping in, getting a tan, and lots of boys!"

Before I could respond, a group of guys with oversized T-shirts, JNCO jeans, and chained wallets hanging from their pockets walked toward us, directing their attention to Penelope.

"Heard there's a party tonight," one boy with spiky blond hair said.

Penelope rolled her eyes. "Already have plans," she said.

"C'mon. It should be fun," a boy with dark brown hair added.

"No. We're busy!" she barked, spitting her gum at them, causing them to turn and walk away. "As if!" she said. "Like we'd ever be into them."

"I think they're freshmen," I said.

"Freshmen? Ew! Even worse," Penelope scoffed.

"We're only sophomores," Emily muttered.

"Practically juniors, Em. We'll be outta high school in no time," Penelope replied.

Penelope and Emily started having a side conversation as I pulled out the newest edition of *Cosmopolitan* magazine from my backpack. These girls were my lifeline. I couldn't fathom navigating high school without them. We had all been friends for as long as I could remember. I met Penelope on the first day of kindergarten. I recall being terrified of being away from my mom, and I was trying to be brave like she told me to be when this random girl with a ponytail on the top of her head approached me. "I like your pigtails. We're going to be best friends."

A few weeks later, Emily came into class and Penelope walked over to her and said, "Your dress is pretty. Be best friends with us." And we *have* been best friends for over a decade now. Which, in girl time, seems like an eternity.

Now, as I looked at them, I realized how much history we have together. The three of us couldn't be more different from each other, though. Had we not met as kids, I couldn't imagine a universe where we would become friends now.

With her popularity and sociable nature, Penelope possessed a confidence that seemed to invite gossip behind her back. It was usually harmless, but at times, it could appear callous. In contrast, Emily was the polar opposite. She often relied on Penelope's exuberant charm to take the spotlight, making her quiet and shy demeanor less noticeable. I found myself stuck in the middle, switching between introversion and extroversion. My biggest fault was my need to make people laugh, and I wasn't very good at it. I constantly wanted to maintain peace and make people happy, but it was almost impossible with teenage girls.

"Is that the new edition of *Cosmo*?" Penelope asked.

I showed her the cover. "Yeah, just got it yesterday."

She ripped it from my hands. "Oh, I have to check out these survey results! Mind if I borrow it for next period?"

"You're gonna read that in class? Won't your teacher take it?" Emily asked.

"Mr. Teague is so old, he'll think it's my textbook," Penelope said.

Emily asked, "But it's *Cosmo*!" she paused. "Everyone will think you're reading about sex in class."

Penelope laughed. "Will you ever stop being a prude, Emily?"

"I'm not a prude," Emily protested. "You know that."

"Get off her case," I mumbled. "She's not a prude."

Penelope closed the magazine and rested it on the table. "Emily, when was the last time you made out with someone?"

Emily's eyes shifted from right to left as her cheeks flushed. "Uh, a few weeks ago."

"Who did you kiss?" I demanded.

"It doesn't matter," Emily whispered.

Penelope blew a bubble in her gum. "You're right. It doesn't matter."

"Wait! I want to know!" I persisted.

The class bell disrupted the banter. "All right, losers, I'll see you after class." Penelope got up and walked away.

Emily and I started walking toward our class. "So, who's this mystery guy?" I asked.

Emily started biting her nails. "It's complicated."

"Are you going to tell me what's going on? You've been so weird the last couple of weeks. You've been way quieter than usual."

"I just, I don't know — I'm feeling confused," she said.

"Confused about what? Boys?"

"Something like that."

"Em, I don't know what's going on, but you can tell me. You know that, right? I'd never judge you."

"I just—" another bell rang, stopping Emily from finishing her sentence. "Oh shit! We're late!" she said.

"Who cares? It's the last day of school."

"I do, but thanks, Chris. I appreciate you listening," she said. She turned and jogged toward her class without acknowledging my question. As I walked toward my classroom, her statement was replaying in my head. What had Emily so twisted that she felt like she couldn't tell me?

CHAPTER 4

Present
Christina

I feel faint, so I walk to the sofa and sit down. I re-read the note. How could Penelope still be alive? There have been no signs of her since the night I escaped. Why would Emily want me to find Penelope after all these years? Why did Emily only want to tell me this if something happened to her? It doesn't make any sense.

I grab the laptop from the coffee table. "Do I really want to do this?" I say aloud.

Thor's paws echo as he trots in my direction. He sits in front of me, and I gently touch his massive black-and-brown head. "I think this is a terrible idea."

His butt wiggles, and he scoots closer to me.

"Am I making a mistake?"

Thor rests his massive paw on my leg, panting heavily with his tongue lolling out.

"You're such a good boy! Mama loves you," I whisper as I place my hands on his face.

He jumps up and begins licking me.

I chuckle as I try to push his massive upper body off me. "Yes, I love you too, baby. Now get down. I have to look something up that may make me a psycho again. I really shouldn't be doing this, but I have to," I say as he tilts his head from side to side.

He lays down by my feet as I consider the task I am about to take on. My hands hover over the keyboard, trembling with anticipation. All moisture has evaporated in my mouth, leaving a dry Sahara Desert in its wake. It has been years since I dared to search for information regarding the life-changing incident. Suddenly, the sensation of being smothered overwhelms me, and I can't catch my breath. I shut my eyes.

Darkness surrounds me. The air is cold and damp, causing my muscles to tremble. Beyond the door that confines me in this room is a muffled echo of voices. I can't decipher what is being said; it is boisterous, even joyful. Someone out there is enjoying that I am locked in here.

So far, nothing has happened. They dragged me into this room, chained me to a bed, and didn't answer any of my questions. I begged to be released, but they refused to acknowledge my cries. Now, I am left in this dark, decaying room, terrified of what awaits me. It is not knowing what's coming that is eating me alive. Will I be raped? Tortured? Murdered?

I look at the wall, drag my thumbnail across the decaying plaster, and leave a thin, jagged line. It's the only way to tell how long they have kept me here — day one.

My eyes shoot open; terror ripples through my gaze. I look — computer, couch, fireplace. I listen — howling wind, ticking clock, Thor panting. I move — wiggle each finger, roll my shoulders, tap my feet. *You are safe. There is no danger here.*

The anxiety subsides, and I type "Christina Johnson Kidnapping" into the search engine. It feels strange writing Christina Johnson after all this time; it doesn't come naturally anymore. Something about it feels foreign, as if that person was just a figment of my imagination and not someone I spent eighteen years of my life as.

A flood of results appears on the screen. I scroll through the various sites, forcing me to remember what I had spent the last few decades trying to forget. I can't breathe. I sit there staring at a photograph of Penelope and me. Somehow, it captured us during that phase of our lives — innocent with our entire future still filled with uncertainty — our mouths opened wide in cheeky smiles, eyes crinkled with joy, and no clue of our impending doom. We were kids. How could anyone survive that ordeal? Especially alone?

I click on the link, not ready to return to the white house in the woods.

TWENTY-FIVE YEARS LATER: WHAT HAPPENED TO PENELOPE SOLACE?

Most people can recall the story that made waves across the country: two girls went missing, but only one returned. Who could ever forget the news of teenagers Penelope and Christina? What seemed like an innocent night of adolescent amusement turned into a nightmare when the two girls never came home.

Their young, beautiful faces covered the front page of all the newspapers — a reminder of the dangers of teenage freedom. Night after night, the community and volunteers from out of town scoured the woods, searching for the missing teens. One question kept repeating in everyone's minds: why would someone take these girls?

Tranquility Ridge, California, was a town in its infancy back then, with a population shy of 10,000 people. It was a short drive from Lake Tahoe and ideal for whatever outdoor explorations your heart desired. Bad things didn't happen there, at least not within the last hundred years. The only shadow on its past was that Tranquility Ridge was somewhat near the site of the infamous Donner Party, back in 1846. Other than that, the area had been peaceful until the kidnapping of the girls.

Adding to the mystery of the entire incident, Penelope was the only child of the newly elected mayor of the town, Bonnie Solace. There was one general theory floating around: was the kidnapping related to her mother's political affairs?

This led to more people questioning the safety of the family members of politicians.

Approximately three weeks after the girls disappeared, the community and the nation were shocked when Christina Johnson escaped her captors and returned safely home, albeit battered and bruised. The news footage put Christina on display for all to see — broken, vulnerable, pleading for help to find her friend. She credited her escape to Penelope's bravery, deepening the intrigue regarding this story. Why did she leave her behind? Was there a possibility that Christina had something to do with the disappearance? Was she a suspect, or involved somehow?

Slowly, with every passing news cycle, their story was replaced with fresh faces, a new location, and a breaking sad tale to be told. It was not long after Christina returned the headlines shifted to the breaking news of the Widowmaker Serial Killer hunting down married men in Northern California. As the months passed, with no leads in Penelope's disappearance, life moved on. While several documentaries and podcasts have kept this tragedy alive in the minds of curious internet sleuths, the story itself has become one too common — a teenage girl goes missing, only to be replaced by the next teenage girl missing.

So, as we check in twenty-five years later, what are your thoughts on the matter? Did Christina have something to do with the disappearance? Is Penelope still out there? Or is she just another casualty of the mountains of Tranquility Ridge?

A tear rolls down my cheek. Somehow, it still feels fresh. Now I remember why I always stayed away from reading articles about what transpired that summer. I loathe the way the incident was reported. It would've been nice if, after all these years, people had exonerated me from being involved. Instead, there has always been this cloud over my head.

I never understood how callous people could be about my return. Rather than being relieved that one of us survived and was safe, they made me a suspect. I was victim-shamed into believing I was responsible for what happened to her somehow. They accused me of being a coward for leaving her behind. Everywhere I went, whispers followed.

My life was never the same after that. How could it be? There was no way I could go back to school that fall, because I feared everyone, and the trauma I endured was real. With the investigation ongoing and perpetrators still on the loose, there wasn't a single person I didn't suspect of being involved. I didn't feel safe anymore.

When I turned eighteen, I begged my mother and my sister to leave Tranquility Ridge with me. While supportive and understanding, my mom couldn't abandon her career, and Nicole didn't want to part with her friends. Knowing I would never have a normal life, I left town, changed my last name, and never looked back. I thought I had escaped my past. *Why now, Emily? Why, after all this time, do you want me to find Penelope?*

CHAPTER 5

Before
Emily

Emily kicked the empty beer cans from her path as she approached her front door.

For as long as she could remember, her father had been a deadbeat alcoholic, and put it on display for the entire neighborhood to see. He was constantly disheveled, with stained clothing, reeking of old liquor and body odor, and he was abusive to her mom. She had only seen her dad strike her mom a few times, but Emily knew it was a frequent occurrence, because of the constant fresh scrapes and bruises.

She entered the small, one-story house she had lived most of her life. On the outside, it was a regular home, but what happened within the walls was far from ordinary. Her family moved to this side of town when the bank foreclosed on the nice house in the pretty neighborhood where her friends used to live. It was the result of her little brother's untimely death.

No one expected her family to recover after her father ran over her little brother in the driveway. The damage was irreversible. Rather than taking accountability for his actions,

Emily's father blamed her mother for not watching her baby brother more closely. He'd opened the door and run outside without her knowledge. Her dad stormed in, grabbed her mother by the throat, and threw her against the wall. Before she even realized what was happening, he dragged her by the hair to the front yard to show her what he felt she caused. Emily had never seen her father strike her mother until that day, and he hadn't stopped since.

Since then, Emily and her older brother were forced to grow up too fast. She had often questioned her mother's decision to stay, but her father's manipulation had convinced her mom that she was to blame, and this was her way of atoning for her perceived sin.

Emily threw her bag on the table, causing several empty cans to fall with a clattering, metallic rattle on the linoleum floor. Her dad snorted, looked in her direction from the couch, turned on his opposite side, and fell back asleep without acknowledging her.

"Hi to you, too, Dad," she mumbled.

She opened the fridge, not surprised that all that remained inside was a white Styrofoam takeout container, a six-pack of beer, and a random bottle of hot sauce.

"Where's Mom?" she asked Ryan, as he walked into the kitchen.

"How the hell would I know?" he remarked as he looked into the fridge. "Dude, what the hell? How is there no food in this house?"

"How the hell would I know?" she retorted sarcastically. "What's up with your attitude?"

"None of your business," he snapped.

"Sheesh. I'm sorry for asking," she muttered.

He rolled his eyes. "Good. I'm gonna get food. You want Taco Bell?"

"Sure. Two tacos and a quesadilla would be great," Emily said.

"Two tacos and a quesadilla? You letting yourself go already?" he snickered.

"Oh, shut up!" She struck his arm with her fist.

"You hit like a girl!" he joked.

"I am a girl!"

"Shut the hell up in there!" her dad screamed. "I'm trying to sleep in here!"

They both rolled their eyes, mocking him. "All right, I'll be back," Ryan said, grabbing his keys and walking out of the kitchen. "Don't call the police or anything if Dad chokes over there."

"Wasn't planning on it," she said.

The door shut with a loud bang as she walked to her room. She threw herself onto her bed, feeling the comfort of the familiar mattress. Lying there, she stared at the ceiling and thought about Penelope pressuring her about her recent hookups. Penelope knew about everything, so why would she act like she had forgotten?

She turned on her side and looked at the collage of pictures on her wall. She knew she was lucky to have two amazing friends, but there was the sting of jealousy whenever she looked at them. Penelope embodied everything that Emily desired to be, while Christina had a kindness she wished she was capable of giving. As Emily got older, she felt like she was losing herself as she tried so hard to fit in with them. They had been friends first, and somehow, it made Emily feel like she was always tagging along.

Over the last few months, the crack between the three of them seemed to grow. Emily felt lost. High school was more complicated than she thought it would be. She was expecting how it was portrayed in the movies, but she felt like she was constantly treading water, barely holding her head above instead. Penelope and Christina were so confident in who they were, and they didn't try to be anything different. Not Emily, though. She didn't know who she was anymore, and it was all Penelope's fault.

Outside, an engine rumbled so loudly that it rattled the window. She peered outside and saw her neighbor sitting in the driver's seat of his Ford Mustang. He looked toward her and smiled. His mahogany complexion, angular jawline, and almond-shaped brown eyes radiated warmth. He motioned with his hand for her to come out, and she jumped up to meet him.

"Hey, Eric. How's it goin'?" she asked, as she hugged him.

"I'm good. I'll never get over the purr of that engine, you know? Damn, that sounds sexy," he smiled, looking at the car. "You always look like you're being held captive in there," he grinned. "I figured you needed a jailbreak."

She smiled. "It feels like that sometimes."

"Wasn't it the last day of school?" he asked.

"I didn't know you still paid attention to that since you're in junior college now," she said.

He laughed. "Oh, that's right. I'm a cool college kid now. Why do I even waste my time with you high school girls? Especially the pretty ones, 'cause they are bad news."

She chuckled as she felt her cheeks flush. Was he flirting with her? Eric had been her neighbor for at least a decade, and while they were close, they crossed no boundaries, even though she had always felt drawn to him. He had this nurturing, protective character, and whenever her dad was having one of his tantrums, he would sneak her into his bedroom and let her take his bed for the night. She'd be lying to herself if she said she didn't have feelings for him, even if she wasn't sure what those feelings meant.

Emily could recall the first invitation as if it happened yesterday. She was hunched over, sobbing with her head buried in her knees. Inside the house, her father was breaking and throwing pans. To avoid her father's wrath, she was hiding in the shadows along the house. Eric came running to her, and escorted her back to his room where she cried for what felt like hours. He didn't pry about what led to the breakdown — she sensed he already knew and had heard the commotion. As her emotions calmed, he lightened the mood by making her laugh and bringing snacks until she fell asleep. It built a bond that she never really understood, that got more complicated as they got older.

"So, any plans to kick off the summer?" he asked.

She looked away. "Eh, I don't know. I think I'm just going to stay here and chill for the night."

"What? No plans with the girls?"

Emily walked over to the planter and sat down, with Eric close behind. "Things have just been weird."

He sat next to her. "What do you mean?"

"They just seem to get closer and squeeze me out. Not to mention, Pen's been really off. She's so popular and outgoing, and I'm just — well, I'm just me. Maybe she doesn't want to be friends with me anymore."

He placed his hand on her shoulder. "I'm sure it's not what it seems. But you can't just lock yourself in your room, either. Remind them how fun you are. That won't happen if you just pull away. Get out of your comfort zone! You have a lot to offer."

She started fidgeting with her hands. "The problem is I don't know *how* to get out of my comfort zone. My life would be so much easier if I could have Penelope's personality."

"You don't need her personality; you have your own. And honestly, from what you've told me, if she didn't like you, I don't think she'd keep you around. She doesn't seem like the charity type."

"I know, it's just complicated, I guess."

"How complicated can it be?" he said, smiling. "You're sixteen! Stop taking life so seriously! Go out there, make mistakes, and be a teenager."

She chuckled. "I don't know how just to be a teenager. You know why."

"Yes, you do. Just stop caring what everyone thinks. I know it's easier said than done, but now's the time to do reckless shit, you know? Stay out late, drink too much — go streaking for all I care! Enjoy being sixteen!"

"No way you will ever catch me streaking!"

He smirks. "I bet Penelope would go streaking."

A loud crash sounded from her residence, causing them both to look in that direction. "Looks like shitbag is up," Eric said.

"One day, I'll be long gone from this place, and I'll never have to see that man again."

He wrapped his arm around her shoulder for comfort. "Well, until then, you're always safe here."

Something about the sincerity in Eric's chocolate-brown eyes made Emily believe him. Maybe it was time she got out of her comfort zone and acted with less regard for the consequences, like he'd said, and perhaps he was the perfect person to help her figure this out. Maybe this would be the summer that changed her life forever. After all, what else did she have to lose?

CHAPTER 6

Present
Christina

In my room, underneath my mattress, is a box filled with memories. Contained within are photographs and mementos of a childhood taken from me too soon.

I throw the box on the top of my bed with the note Emily left for me. With my hands on my hips, I stand there staring at a past I swore I'd never go back to. I should rip up Emily's letter and never look back. I should burn the contents of this box and try to erase all memories of these girls and that place.

She's still alive — find her!

"Dammit, Em. Why did you have to be so fuckin' cryptic? You didn't think to leave a hint? Maybe a GPS location, or how you want me to find her?" I say. "What the hell am I going to do with this?"

There's a sudden gust of wind as Thor rushes past me and flies onto the mattress, bowing his front legs with his rear high in the air. "Not now, baby. Get down!" I reach for his collar as he quickly bounces to the left. "Seriously, get off!" He shifts to the right, but I'm able to grasp the collar and pull him down.

"Stay off!" I say, as he licks my hand. "Lay down," I tell him, and he complies.

When I look back at the mattress, the comforter is tangled with the box's contents scattered. "Did you do that, so I'd be forced to look inside?" I ask, looking down at him as his tail wags. "Well played, buddy."

I hold the container, covered in a collage of pop-culture magazine cutouts, memorializing all my interests from back then — No Doubt, Blink 182, Green Day, Alanis Morissette, Nirvana, Ben Affleck, Matt Damon, Leonardo DiCaprio, *Buffy the Vampire Slayer*, *Clueless*, and *Sex and the City*. I don't even recognize the girl who liked all those things anymore.

I grab the miscellaneous items to throw back into the box and chuckle when I find my long-forgotten and dead Tamagotchi pet. "This dude was way easier to care for than your 100-lb ass," I say, looking down at Thor. "Maybe I should switch you for him!"

I continue grabbing more items scattered on the sheets. There were movie stubs for various movies, including *The Craft*, *Clueless*, *I Know What You Did Last Summer*, *Titanic*, *Romeo + Juliet*, and *Scream*. A flood of memories comes back to me of us in the theater, giant tubs of popcorn with our different flavored slushies. "Why did I keep these?" I mumble, rolling my eyes.

I reach for a snap bracelet and place it on my wrist, and it takes me back to when the girls and I won them at the carnival. I grab the Gelly Roll Pens, which I used to write my daily letters in class rather than listening to the lecture like I should have been doing. Finally, I throw the remaining items in the box: a couple of mood rings, beanie babies, and a Delia's catalog with my dream outfits circled.

"Thankfully, Mom never let me buy those clothes," I say to Thor. He barks in return as if he is agreeing with me. "They were ridiculous! Although I hear '90s fashion is making a comeback."

I look down and see CDs on the ground that I had burned with our computer. I pick them up, recalling how much effort and time it took to make them and how they captured each of our musical phases as we grew from kids to teens. "I don't even have a CD player anymore. I should get rid of these. I'm sure the sound quality is shit, too, since they were all downloaded from LimeWire anyway."

As I turn to throw them in the box, I pause when I recognize the vibrant pink Lip Smacker chapstick in the folds of the comforter. I saved it as a tangible reminder of the first time Ryan kissed me. I remember the anxious feeling as I applied it to my lips moments before it happened. I was so nervous, and he was so handsome. It was a forbidden relationship that should have never taken place, much less go on for as long as it did. I could never have expected what our future would hold that day, and all the bad that would result from the secret union.

I stand to straighten the comforter when I notice a few pictures I missed. I inspect each photo, bringing it close to my face, taking everything in as a gush of memories overwhelms me. "Who are these people?" I whisper, throwing them into the box.

We were just kids, and we had the world at our fingertips. Penelope always knew what she wanted to do with her life, but Emily and I were still trying to figure it out. We were like all the other teens our age — dreaming of something bigger and better.

The three of us were links in a chain, bound and unbreakable. Looking back, however, I can't help but recognize the rust that had been forming on that chain — the structural integrity more compromised with every secret we kept from one another.

I place the box back under the bed, not quite ready to get rid of it yet. I walk out of my room with Thor trotting behind and went to the kitchen, grabbing a bottle of wine from the cupboard.

The wine instantly soothes me as memories swirl in my mind. Life was never the same after that summer; I was never the same. While anthropophobia isn't a clinical disorder, it was what my doctor said described my condition best. My fear of people had reached a point where it paralyzed me completely. The thought of being around strangers would always send waves of severe anxiety crashing over me.

I never understood what caused Emily to withdraw from me when I needed her the most. When everyone accused me of seeking attention and being responsible for Penelope's disappearance, she could have been there to help drown out the noise. But she was gone. Physically, she was there, but our friendship was never the same. I continued trying to accomplish some feeling of normalcy and friendship to be myself again, but there was always something hidden in her eyes, as if her secrets were trying to claw their way out.

When I left after I turned eighteen, we kept in touch, checking in with each other from time to time. I had planned to leave everything behind, but my mother insisted. She was one of the few people who knew where I had gone. But we never experienced genuine friendship again. So why now? None of this makes any sense. *What happened to you, Em?*

I grabbed my laptop and typed *Emily Henderson Car Accident* in the search tab. When nothing popped up, I remembered she got married, so I erased the last name and replaced it with *Easton*.

Thor jumps on the couch and rests his head on my thigh. I pet him as he growls happily. "You're the only dog I know that growls when he's happy," I say to him, causing him to rumble louder. I lean down and kiss his giant head. "What would I do without you, buddy? You're the only person, er, animal that I trust."

I draw my attention back to the screen and see that several news websites from Northern California display articles regarding the traffic accident, so I click the first one from the *Tranquility Ridge Gazette*.

HIT AND RUN CLAIMS LIFE OF NEW MOTHER

On Thursday, tragedy struck when passersby saw the body of a woman in the street near the intersection of Maple Lane and Birch Street.

The Tranquility Ridge Police Department (TRPD) estimates this happened between 9:00 a.m. and 9:20 a.m.

on Thursday, April 9. TRPD said they located her car in the parking lot adjacent to the intersection, and she may have been crossing the street when she was struck.

Police advised that surveillance footage of a possible suspect vehicle was taken from a block down from the location. TRPD Chief McCormack stated that a dark-colored, four-door sedan with tinted windows and damage to the hood was captured fleeing westbound on Maple Lane. McCormack could not provide any further information to the public.

They have identified the victim as Emily Easton, 43. Emily is survived by her husband, Thomas, and their newly adopted two-year-old daughter, Priscilla.

Police officials are asking the public to provide any information to assist with the investigation. They remind the public that they can provide information anonymously.

I shut the laptop, screaming with frustration. None of this makes sense. I haven't heard from Em other than to check in on holidays and my birthday in years. If she knew Pen was alive, why didn't she tell me before her accident? Why couldn't she find Pen herself? Why would she have her husband leave me this riddle? And how did she know she was in danger?

Shit. Was this even an accident? Sickness overwhelms me. *Emily, what did you get yourself into? Please don't tell me that, somehow, our kidnapping is the reason you're dead.*

CHAPTER 7

Before
Penelope

The burning tobacco cackled as Penelope inhaled the smoke.

She sat on the back stoop of her home, watching the curling wisps emerge from her mouth. Another school year down, and nothing to show for it.

"Well, isn't this the epitome of class?" a sharp voice said from behind Penelope.

Maintaining her gaze forward, Penelope didn't respond. The air shifted as her mother drifted closer to her, unhurried. "Aren't you so original?" she said, as she walked down the stairs. "Another wayward teen, smoking cigarettes in defiance. Life is so hard when you have zero responsibilities." Her mother stopped next to her. "Oh, are you too good to answer me?"

Penelope continued staring ahead, not acknowledging her as she blew out smoke.

"The minute you turn eighteen, you're on your own," her mother said.

Penelope refused to look as her mother walked toward her car, keeping any additional commentary to herself. Penelope watched as she drove off in her black Mercedes Benz sedan. She took the final drag of her cigarette and flicked it into the wind, wishing this place would burn down — her mother included.

Penelope and her mom had a complicated relationship, fluctuating between fiery arguments and icy silences. As Penelope transformed into a stunning woman, her mother's envy only deepened. It started simple — condescension, a subtle undermining that escalated into full-blown intimidation and abuse. As Penelope got older and mouthier, her mother had less restraint. Sometimes, she slapped Penelope so many times her face tingled with numbness. Whenever Penelope threatened to call the police, her mother would say with an eerie confidence, "The police work for me, dear. They'd never believe a piece of trash like you." The more she said it, the more Penelope bought into the manipulation.

Somewhere along the way, Penelope started believing the lies her mother spewed, that Penelope was nothing but garbage. It hardened her like drying cement.

Back in the house, she went to the computer and logged in to Instant Messenger.

She smiled when she saw *sn95lover* was logged on.

Babe! I've been thinking of that hot ass of yours all day.

Tell me more!

Penelope hunched over the computer and smiled.

I was thinking about how much I miss holding it in my hands. It's so perfect.

Tell me something I don't know already.

Lol. It's not just your ass that's perfect. You're fuckin' hot, too.

Once again, tell me something I DON'T know.

Lol! You wanna hang out later?

Maybe. I'm waiting to see what's up with the girls.

Penelope tapped her fingers on the desk, waiting for his response.

I wish I could come.

We have to wait. You know how bitchy my mom is. She'll make your life hell if she knew about us.

Call me later then?

I'll try

I guess I'll just have to picture you naked and handle myself :)

Penelope chuckled.

As long as you're thinking about me, handle your business!

Oh, come on, I miss you!

Lol. I miss you too. I'll try to stop by.

Promise?

I don't make promises I can't keep.

She closed the window before he could write back.

Damn you and your theatrics! I have so many questions. I already have the guilt of Pen's disappearance on my conscience, but now the possibility that your death is on my hands is too much to bear.

I can't breathe. I close my eyes. Deep breath in. I look — shadows on the wall, window, shutters. I listen — fan whirring, house creaking, cars driving by. I move — wiggle my nose, tap my fingers, roll my ankles. *You are safe.*

Wood cracks, and it echoes down the hall. I slowly remove the pillow from over my ears. What was that? I sit up, waiting for it to come again.

Crack. Crack. My heart drums in my chest. Is someone out there?

The silence is broken by Thor's ferocious bark, causing me to shriek. I jump out of bed and reach for the handgun in the drawer. As I slowly walk toward Thor, his bark quiets until it shifts into a deep growl — intensifying my fear. I'm not safe.

Each step is deliberate as I try to prevent my presence from being known. As I get closer, Thor's growl reverberates around me, vibrating my soul.

Crack. Crack.

The wind howls around the house.

I reach the opening of the hallway, breathe deeply, then hook the corner, screaming, "Don't make me shoot!"

My eyes scan the room as they take a moment to adjust to the darkness. Thor stands at the back door, his face turned toward me with a puzzled glare, as I see a trash bag dancing against the window.

"Are you fucking kidding me right now? You're barking and growling at a trash bag?"

He trots toward me as I lower the handgun, squatting down to meet his gaze. "You scared the shit outta me, buddy. I thought someone was in the house," I say, petting his head. "Come on, let's go to bed."

I turn, and he follows me into my room. I hate feeling this way. I don't want to be scared like this anymore. Maybe Em was right, and it's time to put this all to rest, finally.

CHAPTER 9

Before
Christina

"Nicole?" I asked as I entered the house.

Silence.

I threw my bag on the counter and saw a note.

I went out with Steve. I'll be back later.

"Oh, Nicky," I said to myself. "He is such bad news. I wish you'd see what a prick he is."

I opened the fridge, grabbed a Capri Sun and a Lunchables, walked to the couch, and sprawled out. I was lying there eating my snack when the phone ringing broke the silence.

"Hello?" My mouth was still filled with crackers.

"Hey, baby," a deep voice said.

No matter how often he called me that, it still gave me butterflies. "I literally just walked in! Are you stalking me, sir?" I asked.

"Do you like scary movies?" he said, distorting his voice.

I chuckled. "Stop it! That's not funny."

"I thought you loved *Scream*."

"I do!" I said, sipping my drink. "Now I feel like watching it! You wanna come over?" I ask.

"I wish I could, but I gotta work in a little bit."

"Booo! I guess I'll just have to ask my other boyfriend to come over."

He laughed. "Other boyfriend? Hopefully, he does a better job handling your multiple personalities than I do."

"Normal girls are boring. Be grateful I have so many personalities to keep you entertained," I said, as I shoved a cracker and cheese into my mouth.

"So, what are you doing? Besides missing me, of course," he said.

"Just got in. Nicole's out with dickhead, Steve."

"Why do you hate him so much?" he asked.

"I don't know. Just call it a sixth sense. He gives me the heebie-jeebies."

He laughed. "Really? The heebie-jeebies? Better call the cops and make sure everyone is on high alert!"

"Hey! Don't be an ass. I'm just saying he's creepy. The way he looks at her and me — all females, for that matter. It's like he's always undressing us with his eyes."

"No shit? Well, that's a different story. You need me to kick his ass?" he asked, his voice echoing concern.

I laughed. "Not yet, but we'll reassess at the end of the week," I said. "So, what's up with you, besides having to work?"

"Not much. You think you'll be free when I get off?"

I rolled onto my stomach and kicked my feet in the air. "Pen wanted to go see a movie tonight. *Armageddon*, I think."

He sighed. "I wanted to see you. Is Emily going to be there?"

"She should be. I don't know why she wouldn't, but she's been kind of weird. Has she said anything to you, Ryan?" I asked.

"Whoa, now I'm just Ryan? Am I in trouble?"

I laughed. "Sorry, baby. Has she mentioned anything to you?"

"Not really. She's been in her room a lot, though. But when she isn't, I always see her outside talking to Eric. I think she has a thing for him."

"Eric? Your neighbor? She's never told us anything! That brat is keeping secrets from us!"

"Well, don't accuse her of anything, but it's pretty obvious she has a little crush. But considering you're keeping me a secret, I think it's only fair she has hers, too."

I rolled my eyes. "I just don't want it to be weird."

"Won't it be more weird that you've kept our relationship from her for . . . how long now?"

He had a point. It had been almost a year since we'd been together, and I couldn't bring myself to tell Emily that not only was I dating her brother , but that I was in love with him, too. "I'll tell her when the time is right."

"Well, I wish you'd hurry, so I could spend time with my girlfriend instead of running around behind my sister's back all the time."

He had been my rock, patiently guiding me through the maze of our forbidden love. I never imagined it would develop into what it has become today, and that's the only issue. The weight of keeping this secret from her was crushing. "I'm just afraid that once she knows about us, she'll accuse me of only being friends with her to be with you."

"You know that isn't true. You were friends long before you even liked boys."

I chuckled. "You got me there."

"Please let me see you tonight. I miss kissing you, CJ."

My cheeks warmed, and I smiled. "OK, I'll figure something out. I miss kissing you too."

"Good!" he exclaimed. "I love you!"

"I love you too, babe. Talk soon."

After we said our goodbyes, I laid on my back and let my eyes wander to the ceiling, its plainness contrasting with the buzzing thoughts in my mind. With each passing moment, the anxiety of confessing to Emily intensified, like the impending sting of ripping off a band-aid. Lately, she had been struggling with Pen and feeling like an outsider. I didn't want to do anything that would further isolate her. But we were growing up. Maybe it was good that she had a crush on Eric. Perhaps that was what I needed, for her to understand how I could fall for her brother. It would never ruin our friendship. Would it?

CHAPTER 10

Present
Christina

As I navigate through the giant blue-green Jeffrey Pine trees, breathing becomes more burdensome. I have this nagging sense of uncertainty while driving along this stretch of highway, inching closer to the town that took so much away from me. There is only one way I will find Penelope. I have to go back to where it all started — regardless of how scared I am.

It took me a few days to muster the courage to come back. I packed my bag set it next to the door. It beckons me to do the right thing. It wasn't until I received an email from Emily's husband about her funeral that I knew I couldn't put it off any longer. My neighbor's agreement to watch Thor obliterated my excuses. I knew what I had to do. I had to face my fears and stop running.

So here I was — cruising the I-80 on a mission to find one dead friend at the behest of another. There is a sudden tightness in my chest as Tranquility Ridge appears. It is like a beacon against the backdrop of the dark green forestry behind it, luring weary travelers to what could be their final destination. I creep down the historic main road, the buildings standing like ghosts of a past I wish I could forget. Some stores may have changed, but the weight of my memories cling to every brick and wooden beam. My heart beats rapidly, and I know what's coming; I inhale as I try to fight it.

The ground is solid and frigid. They remove the chains around my wrists and replace them with rope. I don't know where I am or what time of day it is, because of the blindfold. I listen, and I wait for their return.

After a few minutes, a soft noise catches my attention. Thud. Thud. Thud. Thud. The loud footsteps resonate through the air, drawing nearer and nearer to me. My heart pounding, I retreat until I feel the cold, hard surface of the wall against my back. The murmur of voices is beyond the door. I reach for anything to protect myself using my hands, but there is nothing. The voices are getting louder, and I know I am out of time.

The door swings open, and it's too late.

There is a slight breeze in the air as they approach me. Every heavy footstep offsets the rhythm of my beating heart — deep breath in, deep breath out.

A deep, distorted voice breaks the silence. "It's been long enough. I think it's time we do what we brought her here for."

"Please. No!" I beg as my heart pounds in my chest.

Chills run down my spine as someone whispers in my ear. "I'd stop talking if I were you."

"Please," I whisper back. "Don't hurt me."

"Stop begging. It's unattractive," says the distorted voice.

"I—" as I spoke, a hand makes contact my cheek, sending spit from my mouth.

"Enough!" he yells. "There are rules here. You only speak when given permission."

I look — trees, road, car. I listen — music, passing car, engines. I move — licking my lips, tapping my fingers, tapping my foot. *You are safe. You will never go back to that house.*

The buildings become sparse as I reach the end of town. I glance at the GPS, and it's not much farther now. It has been a lonely life with my psychological issues and trauma. Who wants to be friends with someone who has trouble leaving the house? Unfortunately, until five or six years ago, almost all of that was out of the question. It took about fifteen years and a lot of therapy before I could leave my house. Now, the anxiety remains, and I struggle with strangers and small spaces, but it is manageable. I recognize my triggers and prevent myself from being in those situations. When all else fails, I do my exercises, and eventually, I get better.

I continue driving through the tunnel of towering trees, their branches forming a lush canopy overhead, barely allowing the sunlight to flow through. There is an opening on the right, and I turn down the gravel road. There is a clearing after, and the modern cabin before me is stunning. It is mixed with rich dark wood, contrasting light-colored stone, and oversized windows. It looked much larger in person than on the Airbnb listing. I park the car and just stare at my home for the next few days, unsure if coming here was the right choice.

* * *

I stand beneath a towering wrought iron archway with granite pillars on each side, coaxing myself to enter. Written in sizable gothic lettering, it reads *Tranquility Ridge Cemetery*.

I pass through the cemetery gates and proceed to Emily's graveside service. It is a small gathering, with only thirty people or less. I stand at a distance with an offset view of the podium. I don't recognize the woman speaking, but my heart shatters when I see Emily's husband holding their daughter beside her. She is so tiny, in a fluffy black dress, with curly brown hair and dark eyes. She reaches for a fluttering butterfly, unaware of the occasion that brought her here today.

She deserved to grow up with Emily as her mother.

As I gaze at the crowd of bodies in front of me, a wave of overwhelming emotions washes over me. I can't afford to have a panic attack now; my heart races and my palms grow sweaty. I look — headstone, tree, black coat. I listen — a woman's voice, leaves in the wind, lawn mower. I move — flare my nostrils, tap my forefinger and thumb, roll my ankle. *You are not in danger. No one here will hurt you.*

I regain my composure and focus on the eulogy. While the lady speaks about some of Emily's philanthropic endeavors, I study the crowd. Several people are hunched over with tissues in their hands. Others wipe their eyes as they nod in agreement. The woman tells the story of how Emily and Thomas met, and the long road to adopting their perfect little girl.

"Birdie!" Her daughter points, causing everyone to chuckle at her innocence, lightening the mood.

She doesn't know her mom is in that box next to her. All she knows is that a cute bird is flying around, and her dad is holding her. She doesn't realize that it will only be the two of them, that her mommy is never coming home. It breaks my heart.

Listening to the highlights of Emily's life, I can't shake the emptiness that settles within me. She is the last remaining thread to the girl I was before everything happened. Now it is all gone. I don't even know who I am anymore.

Emily got it right. She made something of herself. Why was she looking for Penelope? It was hard for me to move on, but after so much time she had to be gone. Right? Is that unwillingness to let go why I am standing here today? *I wish you would've told me what you were getting yourself into, Em.*

The group of people throws roses as her body is lowered into the ground, and the coffin fades away. I wish we would have never let that summer come between us. Goodbye, Emily.

Just past the group on the opposite side of the cemetery, I see a figure standing there. I can't tell if it is a man or a woman, but the person is wearing an oversized black trench coat and dark glasses, and holding an umbrella to ward off the sun. I squint to make the person clearer, but the group moves around the casket, blocking my view. I take a few steps to my right, but whoever was standing there is gone now.

As the funeral concludes, I walk toward my car, and the intense feeling of regret is devastating. How did it all go wrong that summer?

The air feels heavy as a slight breeze carries the faint scent of earth into my nostrils. I pass several crumbling headstones, weathered and decaying, long forgotten by the families that they belonged to. Rustling leaves fill the eerie silence, and I get the unnerving sensation that I am being watched. I reach into my purse, grab my keys, and walk faster.

I approach a large oak tree with its massive branches stretched outward like arms. A crow perched on the branch follows my movement, cawing as I walk below him. My body shivers and the hairs on my neck stand. It's as if the crow is warning me of what's coming.

I see the archway, but soft, muffled footsteps sound from behind me.

"Christina?" a deep voice says from behind.

I ignore my name and pick up my pace.

"Christina Johnson?" he says louder.

My breathing intensifies. I look — grass, trees, birds. I listen — blowing leaves, church bells, people talking. I move — legs walking, arms swinging, tapping forefinger and thumb. *You are safe. Just keep walking.*

I jump when I feel rough fingers against my arm. "Christina!" He pauses, "you walk so fast! I knew that was you."

My eyes meet his, and immediately, I am sixteen again. "Ryan?" Emily's brother. My first love.

I stop, and he wraps his arms around me. I melt into the warmth of his embrace. He pulls back and looks at me. "You still look the same. I recognized you immediately."

"Ryan. I don't know what to say. How are you? I mean . . . No. Not 'How are you'—"

He smiles. "I know what you mean. Hi, Christina."

"My condolences, of course. I don't know if you and Emily were still close."

He looks down at his shoes and then back into my gaze. "Thank you. We weren't best friends, but we were close, I guess."

"How are you holding up? Where's your mom? I didn't see her down there."

"Eh, she couldn't bring herself to come. She's having such a hard time. But me? I'm doing how you'd expect. It just feels so surreal."

"I can't even imagine what you're going through," I say. "And your mom. Poor woman."

"It hasn't been easy," he says, politely smiling at the funeral attendees as they pass us.

"It all seems unreal, and the way it happened," I put my hand to my heart, "it's just so tragic."

He places his hand on my elbow, causing me to flinch. "Thank you for being here."

"So sorry for your loss," a man says to Ryan while passing us.

Another gentleman approaches and puts his hand out to Ryan's. "So sad. Let us know if you need anything."

"Thank you. I will let you know, for sure," Ryan responds.

"So—"

Before I can finish, a couple approaches. "We are just devastated for you, Ryan," says a man with balding gray hair.

Ryan shakes his hand. "I appreciate it, really."

"Let us know if we can do anything," the woman says.

"I will. Thank you guys for coming. I know my mom will be happy to know you were here," he says. They smile and walk away.

"I was—"

Once again, someone interrupts me. A woman wraps her arms around Ryan as she sniffles. "Will you be back at the house? Can we do anything to help?"

"I will be there shortly. Just wrapping up stuff here, but we have everything taken care of."

"OK," she says, as she wipes her nose. "We'll meet you there."

He grinds his teeth. "How about we go get a drink or a coffee somewhere? I'd like to catch up without so many interruptions."

"Uh," I hesitate. "Don't you have somewhere to be? It sounds like you are having some kind of reception. I don't know if that's the right word for it." I avert my gaze.

There it is — the look. How could I ever forget it? Ryan always had this bewitching way about him that made him impossible to resist. There was something seductive about his eyes when he looked at me that way — narrowed and intense, and he's smirking, still confident. Truthfully, he hasn't changed much, either. He still wore his light brown hair in a tousled and disheveled style, giving him a carefree look. A pair of glasses highlight his eyes, which are a striking shade of blue. His formerly smooth, adolescent jawline is now covered with a sparse, light beard, and the flannels and baggy jeans are now replaced with a fitted black suit. He's grown into a very handsome man.

"I do, but I can see them any time. I have a feeling this will be my only chance to catch up with you. Come on! I know a place we can go. I want to catch up, given the circumstances. It would be nice to talk about her too," he says.

I came to town for Emily and to find Penelope. I did not come back for this. Seeing him here hadn't even crossed my mind. Of course he'd be here; it was his sister.

"Seriously, I wouldn't be that entertaining."

"Me either. But I'd rather be able to talk to you without everyone walking up and expressing their condolences. We haven't seen each other in, like, twenty years. Please?" His eyes plead with mine.

"I don't think it's a good idea," I say.

He caresses my shoulder. "Oh, come on. Are you in a rush to get home — wherever home is?"

"No, not really."

"Is there a . . . a man waiting for you somewhere?"

"No. Nothing like that."

"OK, woman?"

I smile. "No, nothing like that either."

"Then what's the hold-up?"

I cross my arms. "It's not really appropriate, is it?"

"What makes it inappropriate? I haven't seen you in years. Might as well take advantage of this fancy suit I'm wearing."

"I don't know, I really should be going."

"Please. Just one drink? It doesn't have to be alcohol. Hell, we can sit in the park for all I care. I just want to catch up before I don't see you for another twenty years."

Reluctantly, I acquiesce. "Promise, just one drink?"

He tilts his head with a cheeky grin. "Just one drink! I promise."

I sigh. "Fine, just one drink, and that's it."

"Yes!" he exclaims.

Deep in my core, I get this foreboding sensation that this is an invitation I should have turned down.

CHAPTER 11

Before
Emily

As Emily sat staring out her window, she could hear the escalating voices of her brother and dad arguing down the hall.

She attempted to tune out the commotion, like she always did. Her mind wandered, thinking about her friends, her desire to be loved, and how much she wished she could be normal. Emily brought her hands to her mouth, nibbling off each nail tip — a nervous habit since she was a child. She peered down to observe a tiny sliver of blood from where she'd bitten too far.

There was a loud crash followed by the sound of a bottle breaking. Emily's eyes raced to the closed door, and her heart pounded in her chest as she anticipated her father's drunken wrath.

The front door slammed with such force that the house shook. Her brother's car starting echoed through the air; its deep, rhythmic rumble filled her ears along with the sound of screeching tires as he sped away from the driveway. She wondered what caused the fight today. It was likely just another regular day, when her father was coming off a drinking binge.

Through the glass, she watched as Eric washed his Mustang. As the sunlight touched his honey-brown skin, it appeared even more radiant and silky, accentuated by his white tank top and the blue Dodgers cap backward on his head. His baggy jeans hung loosely, offering a small peek at his boxers as his body twisted and turned, sponge in hand. She was torn between the allure of his flirtatious behavior and the complexity of her emotions for him. She couldn't pinpoint how she was feeling.

She crouched down, ensuring he wouldn't catch her staring, but the longer she looked at him, the more she wondered what it would be like to be held by him. It was only a few weeks ago that she had her first romantic encounter with someone, and she knew nothing would ever be the same. Would it be different with him? As she watched him, there was a fluttering sensation deep in her stomach. She turned around, leaned against the wall, and put her head down until it almost touched her knees.

"Why are you making this so complicated, you loser?" she whispered. "You're a girl. He's a boy. This is how normal girls feel when they have a crush."

Emily heard a door slamming, so she quickly turned to look. She watched as a man walked up to Eric's driveway. He looked similar in age and was dressed in a baggy shirt and jeans. She unlatched the window, nudging it open to eavesdrop.

"Did you hear about the party tonight?" the man asked.

"Nah, what's up with it?" Eric asked.

"Remember Janet from high school? I guess her parents are out of town, and she's throwing a rager. Should be a good mix of chicks there."

"Janet Grant?"

"Yeah, that's her, I think. Big-ass house off Cedar."

"Sounds dope. I'll drop in. It'll be mainly high school girls?" Eric asked.

"Probably. But those are the best type," the guy laughed. "They can't handle their liquor, and they're an easy lay."

"Oh, dude. C'mon," Eric said with disgust.

The man laughed. "Dude, what happened to you, bro? You don't like getting laid anymore?"

Eric rolled his eyes. "Of course I do. But it sounds creepy as fuck when you say it like that. I'm not a pedo."

"Ha! You were in high school last year. No big deal, bro."

Emily jumped when her door swung open. "What the fuck are you doing?" her dad asked, reeking of booze.

"Nothing."

He walked close to her to see what she was looking at. "Why are you watching the neighbor?"

"I'm not."

He grabbed her arm, pulling her face to his. "You better not be whoring yourself around," he barked.

Trembling, Emily responded, "Dad. Of course not. I just heard talking out there. I was curious."

He stared at her without blinking, then squinted his eyes. "That better be all that's goin' on here," he said, as he dropped her arm.

"I swear!" she pleaded.

After a brief pause, he spoke. "I'm hungry. Make me some dinner." He stormed off before she could answer.

When she turned back to the window, both Eric and his friend were gone. Emily wished that her mother didn't spend so much time away from home. Emily had to make up for her absence. She was forced to do all the cooking and cleaning. Emily didn't want to do that anymore — she wanted to be a regular teenager, and that meant going to parties.

* * *

When Penelope, Christina, and Emily arrived at Janet's house, the party was in full swing. As they approached the house, "Ruff Ryders' Anthem" by DMX blared, and through the window, several people could be seen dancing.

"Good call, Em. This party is da bomb! How'd you hear about it?" Penelope asked.

"I didn't say I wanted to leave," Emily insisted.

"All right then, we will stay and drink all the shitty beer from the keg. What about tomorrow? You wanna go to the lake?" Christina asked.

"Oh, sure. Sounds fun," Emily responded, sipping her beer.

"Are you waiting for someone?" Penelope asked.

"No, why?"

"You keep looking around like you're waiting for someone."

"I'm just looking at everyone. Doesn't this remind you of the movie we saw a few weeks ago?"

"Which movie?" Christina asked.

"*Can't Hardly Wait*," Emily replied.

Penelope looked around. "Oh, shit! You're right!" She pointed to the kids smoking weed. "There are the stoner kids. Oh! The jocks and cheerleaders are in the kitchen."

"They're even picking on the nerdy kid!" Christina pointed out.

"Right? Teenagers are so predictable," Emily said.

"So, who is our Mike Dexter?" Penelope asked.

"That's a good question! And who is Amanda?" Christina asked.

Penelope scoffed. "Me, obviously!"

"There is no way you are Amanda!" Christina chuckled. "She was way too pure and friendly. Maybe one of the bitchy girlfriends, though."

Penelope rolled her eyes. "Well, actually, that's probably more my style, now that you point it out," she laughed.

Emily observed an awkward boy approaching with blonde hair and blue eyes. "Can I get you another drink?" he asked Penelope.

"No, I'm solid. Thanks," she responded, dismissing him.

Emily watched as Penelope and Christina giggled at the boy's failure. The guy looked back at them and shrugged.

"Yup, definitely one of the bitchy cheerleaders," Christina chuckled.

"I just have high standards, that's all," Penelope said.

"As if! Did you see who you made out with two weeks ago?! That guy was gross!" Christina laughed as she put her finger in her throat.

"I forgot about him," Emily laughed.

"It was the beer goggles. I could've sworn he was hotter," Penelope joked.

As Emily sat there, feeling out of place and awkward, she admired Penelope's charisma. She couldn't understand how someone could be so carefree. She glanced at Penelope — her platinum blonde hair thrown up in a purposeful mess, with the multi-colored butterfly clips scattered throughout. Her makeup was minimal; just mascara and bright red lipstick. Emily noticed how Penelope's black silk spaghetti-strap dress draped luxuriously against her skin — the elegance offset by her fishnet stockings and combat boots. She was elegant and edgy and absolutely beautiful — but Emily could never tell her that.

Emily's attention was diverted toward the door when she heard a commotion. She saw the crowd part, and suddenly, her eyes met Eric's. She felt relieved. The alcohol was loosening her resolve, allowing her to indulge in her fantasies. Eric's presence would ground her and remind her where her focus truly belonged.

He smiled at her and walked to the couch. "Emily!" He leaned down and hugged her. "You listened to me and left the house! It's about time!" He looked at the girls. "You need to drag her ass out more. She's too young to be cooped up at home all the time."

"It's not our fault," Penelope said. "She hates having fun."

Emily felt her cheeks get hot. "That's not it," she said. "No one hates having fun."

"Well, whatever it is, I'm happy you're here. You need a drink?" he asked Emily. "Any of you guys need a drink?"

Before Emily could respond, Penelope spoke. "Actually, I'll go with you." She stood up. "I could use a refill." She wrapped her arm around his, and they walked away.

She turned back. "At least this one doesn't need beer goggles," she said and winked.

Emily watched as they walked to the kitchen, Penelope's flirtation in high gear, which made her feel nauseous.

"Well, that's new," Christina said.

"What do you mean?"

"Penelope flirting with Eric. Does she know him?"

"Has she ever needed to know someone to flirt with them?" Emily said, annoyed.

Christina giggled. "You have a point there."

Emily watched them saunter into the kitchen, Penelope laughing and caressing him in an over-the-top way. Eric's hand gently brushed her bare shoulders as she leaned her body into his. How could this be happening?

Emily's jealousy brewed inside her, steadily increasing in intensity, like a pot of coffee percolating. Emily seethed with anger at every obnoxious giggle and embrace. She brought the red solo cup to her lips and chugged the remaining beer — twisting her face as the sour foam touched her throat.

"I've been meaning to talk to you—" Christina said.

"What the hell?" Emily whispered.

Christina looked toward the kitchen and saw what Emily was looking at. Penelope pressed herself against the wall in an intimate moment, entwining her arms around Eric's shoulders as they shared a deep, lingering kiss.

"Oh, wow! Get it, girl," Christina said.

"How can you say that? She's in the middle of a party."

"Look around," Christina said, pointing in various directions. "People are making out everywhere."

Emily scanned the room, and there were three couples in the living room kissing each other. "But with him?"

Christina tilted her head, her eyes widening. "He's single, right?"

"Yeah," Emily mumbled.

"So, what's the big deal?"

"I don't know. Just surprised, I guess."

Penelope's hands became frenzied on Eric's back as she dug her nails into his shirt. Emily couldn't describe what she was feeling. She wanted to know what it felt like to have those hands on her skin, those lips on her mouth, that body pressed against hers, and that passion without a care in the world. The real dilemma was not knowing who stirred her jealousy more — Eric or Penelope?

CHAPTER 12

Present
Christina

The blaring of a horn snaps me out of my thoughts. I look — steering wheel, windshield, restaurant. I listen — radio, engine, voices outside. I move — blinking my eyes, wiggling my fingers, tapping my feet. *You are safe.*

I try to build the courage to meet Ryan in the restaurant. My hands are gripping the steering wheel so tight that my knuckles are white. *So much about this is wrong. I came here to mourn his sister, not to reconnect with him. I am here to understand what happened to me, and that won't happen if I waste my time with him.*

"I can't do this," I say.

Putting the car in reverse, I look in the rearview mirror. I jump when I see Ryan. I slam on the brakes, and he puts his hands up in the universal surrender position, acknowledging that I almost hit him. I park my vehicle as he walks to the driver's side window.

I roll the window down. "You weren't thinking of splitting on me, were you?" he asks.

I smile with an uneasy grin. "Maybe."

His eyes meet mine. "Come on, CJ. I know the owner. I'll find us somewhere private in the back."

My cheeks flush. "CJ, wow. I haven't heard that since high school. It takes me back."

He smiles. "Good. That was the point. Come on."

We walk into the restaurant, and he waves to a man behind the bar counter. He points to a booth in the back, and the man gives him a thumbs up. He ushers me to our seats, having me sit first. I avert his gaze as I wait for the silence to be broken, uncomfortable and fidgety.

After a few moments, he speaks. "It's nice seeing you. I'll be honest. I looked up and saw you walking toward us, and I thought I was looking at a ghost. You haven't changed at all."

"It wouldn't have been right if I didn't come." I pause for a moment. "And don't flatter me. I'm in my forties now. Look at all these wrinkles!" I say, pointing to my forehead as I raise my eyebrows.

"It doesn't count if you have to force them." He smiles.

"Maybe one day I'll try some Botox or something, but I'm afraid I'll look eternally surprised," I say, raising my eyebrows and staring forward.

He laughs. "It's nice to see that you haven't lost your sense of humor over the years."

I purse my lips. "Oh, it's lost. I guess old times die hard. That's how it goes, right?"

He nods.

"So, what have you been up to all these years? Married? Kids?" I ask.

He smiles. "Ah. We've made it to the background-check part of the conversation."

I shrug. "I could talk about the weather if that's better," I chuckle.

"No, this is better. To be honest, life has had its difficulties, but it's been good. I'm divorced. I'm sure that is a total shock," he jokes.

"What?! That is unbelievable! I kinda pictured you as the settled-down type. You always had that hopeless romantic vibe to you," I say, with a soft smile.

"Hopeless romantic? Ha! Hardly. It is what it is, though. Unfortunately, I was married to a woman who ended up being a horrible human being."

"I'm sorry you had to find out after you were married."

"They can't all be keepers like you, right?"

I roll my shoulders forward, suddenly feeling a bit timid. "I see you're still full of flattery. Some things never change."

"Oh, lots of things have changed," he says, as he pushes his hair down to reveal his hairline. "Look at that receding hairline. I'm gonna be bald soon."

I laugh. "Copycat! I already showed my wrinkles! It's not a competition to see who let themselves go more, is it?"

He laughs. "Nah. You got me! Just tryin' to keep the mood relaxed," he says.

"Well, even with your receding hairline, you don't look too shabby yourself. You know, for an old man, of course."

"Ha! An old man and a father!" he says.

"You have a kid? Please tell me more! Any pictures?"

He pulls out his phone and starts swiping through photos. She is beautiful — soft brown curls, porcelain skin, a smile stretching ear to ear. It takes me a minute before I realize that in every photo, she is sitting, and then I notice the black handles protruding from her back. She is in a wheelchair.

"Maddie is wonderful. I love being a dad! It's the only thing I seem to get right."

"Sorry if I'm overstepping, but is she in a wheelchair?" I carefully inquire.

"Yeah. It's not the ideal situation, of course. She was born with cerebral palsy, a pretty severe case that requires extensive care."

"Cerebral palsy? I'm sorry; I'm not sure what that is."

He grins. "I'm guessing you don't have kids?"

I shake my head. "How could you tell?"

"Most people without kids have no idea what it is. It's not something you can prevent or test for, but most parents are aware to look for symptoms as their infant is developing. I mean, hell, I didn't even know what it was until she was born with it."

"I've never heard of it before. Do you mind explaining what it is?" I ask.

"Of course, and I appreciate your curiosity. It is a movement disorder caused by brain damage. There are different levels, like with any disability. It can cause muscle stiffness, poor coordination, involuntary tremors, and difficulties with precise movements. Some people can't speak, eat, or walk."

"Wow, that must be so hard," I say.

"Yeah, I'll admit. It was unexpected. Maddie appeared healthy in all the prenatal tests and scans. Then, when my wife was giving birth, the umbilical cord got wrapped around her neck, causing brain damage."

I put my hand over my mouth. "Jesus, Ryan. I can't even imagine what that was like."

He stares past me, focused on something I can't see. "One minute you're excited about having this baby in your life with all the future adventures, then the next you're just grateful she survived." His eyes focus on mine. "It's been such a life-changing experience. In a way, she's given me purpose. I know that's how it is with all kids, but I know she needs me, and it makes me want to be a better man. I don't know if that makes sense," he says with an awkward chuckle.

I tap my fingers on the table. "It completely makes sense! I'm glad she has a father like you, who cares so much about her," I say, pausing for a moment. "So, what about her mom? Is she still in the picture?"

"Hell no! Once she realized Maddie was disabled, she was withdrawn. Then, one day, she left us both in the middle of the night, and I never heard from her again."

My jaw opens. "Ryan, I'm so sorry. I don't have the words."

"Somehow, my life is more depressing than the funeral we were just at," he says, trying to lighten the mood.

"I didn't mean to pry. I'm so sorry," I say, frowning.

"Don't be. I mean, it's not an easy life, but I love my time with Maddie. I had to give up teaching, but now I'm a full-time writer, which is so much fun. Things work out the way they're supposed to in the end, you know?"

A cheerful young blonde walks toward us, and my heart beats faster. I slide closer to the wall, looking down at the table and focusing on my breathing. "Ryan, how are you? It's been a while. What can I get for y'all?"

"Joanna, thanks for breaking up the depressing talk we were having! I think just a couple of waters would be good. We have some catching up to do."

"Sure, no problem. Come and get me if you need anything," Joanna says, turning and walking back toward the bar.

"Joanna," I say, winking.

He blushes. "Nothing like that."

"Mmm-hmm. Apparently, you still got it," I say. "So, you were saying something about being a writer?"

"Oh, right. Obviously, I haven't written the next great American novel yet, but I'll get there eventually," he laughs. "For now, I ghostwrite, but I do some investigative journalism when something really fascinates me. Eventually, though, I'd love to get my manuscript published."

"Maybe you'll be the next Ernest Hemingway."

He laughs. "At this rate, I'm just trying to find an agent willing to give my queries a chance! It's a rough business."

"I bet!"

"Let's just say it's not for the faint-hearted. I've lost count of how many rejections I have at this point."

"That's where I'd struggle. I'd hate being told no all the time! I would get in my head and think I was the worst writer ever," I say.

"Don't worry; I do that, too. Imagine waiting for a response to work you took months or years to write, only to see the email, the excitement building, opening it, and having a generic response like 'This is a subjective industry, and just because it's not for me, doesn't mean another agent won't love it,' blah blah blah. It sucks, for sure."

"Ew. That sounds terrible. Definitely not for me!" I pause. "So, have you written a full-length novel?"

"Yeah, well, a manuscript. In the querying process as we speak."

I smile. "Is the querying process what you were just talking about with the rejections?"

"Exactly. So, right now I'm sending it to agents and publishing houses, looking for my big break! But it's just so competitive. We'll see what happens. It's out of my hands now."

"What's it about? I'd love to read it."

Joanna walks to us, placing two glasses of water on the table. "Let me know if you need anything," she says, turning and walking away.

He looks away and pauses. "Maybe someday. I don't think I'm ready for you to see it yet."

I sit there smiling. "What? Is Ryan Henderson shy all of a sudden? Who are you?" I say, pausing for a moment. "Either way, it looks like you really did well for yourself. I'm happy for you."

"So, your turn! What have you been up to?" he asks, taking a sip of his water.

I sigh. "What's there to tell? I'm still a freak!" I joke. "I'm a transcriptionist, since it's a job that I can work from home. I was never married. No kids. But I have a rottweiler named Thor, who is like my kid, so that about sums me up. I haven't done much over the years. Life just passed me by, I guess."

"You're not a freak! Do you have any pictures of your dog?"

"Of course! That's pretty much my entire photo library." I open my phone and start scrolling through pictures. Several of them are him sleeping or lying on his back with his feet in the air. I smile with each image as I give a brief explanation. It makes me yearn for my home and the puppy snuggles.

"I always thought rottweilers were aggressive, but this guy looks like a sweetheart," he says.

"He really is. They are the best dogs! So loyal! He's a big baby, too, but I love him."

We sit there looking at each other in silence. When we were teenagers, I would have bet everything I had that he and I would have ended up together. I never experienced happiness like that again, and sitting across from him now, I wonder what life would have been like if I had made different choices that summer.

If only I didn't go out that night.

He breaks the silence. "Well, I tried my best to avoid the elephant in the room, but here we are. I gotta ask. How did you know about Emily? I didn't know you guys kept in touch all these years. I mean, she never told me you guys were still friends."

"We had kept in touch in a general sense. Other than my family, she was the only person who had my address and new name. We'd write letters sometimes, or she'd send me random gifts that reminded her of me. But we never really hung out after I left."

"That's crazy. I had no idea. I wonder why she kept it a secret?"

"Because I asked her to. I didn't want anyone finding out where I was," I say.

"That makes sense, I guess. So, did you see it in the paper or something?" he asks, sipping his water.

"No. I had no idea. Her husband left a note on my doorstep," I say, tapping my fingers on my glass.

"Oh."

"Well, there was a little more to it than that."

He shifts in his seat, taking another sip of water. "What do you mean?"

Uneasiness overcomes me as my hands tremble. "She wanted him to leave me a note that she wrote for me if anything happened to her, basically suggesting that Penelope was still alive."

He chokes on his water. "Wow. Penelope? That must've been a slap to the face. Did she say why she thought she was still alive?"

"No, it was very vague. That's why I'm here. I don't know why she would even want me to look for her. Why now? It's been so long. I don't understand any of it."

Ryan leans back and clasps his hands on the table. "Well, what are you going to do?"

"I don't know what to do. I feel like it was Emily's dying wish to find Penelope. Maybe it's time I figure it all out, you know? It has never sat well with me. They never found out who did it," I say, with a new determination. "Or found her body," I whisper.

"Well, don't think the worst yet. Do you have a plan?" he asks.

"Not really. I mean, where do you even start?" I shrug my shoulders. "But now that I'm here, I'll figure it out."

There is a brief silence as he stares at me, studying me. "You don't want to go to the police?"

"And say what? 'My dead friend said my other missing friend isn't dead after all. Please re-open the case?'"

"Well, I wouldn't expect you to say it like that. But I guess you have a point. Are you sure you want to do this?"

I look at Ryan and then at the ceiling, studying the bright silver ductwork against the black paint. "I don't really have a choice. I shouldn't have waited this long to begin with," I say, refocusing on his eyes.

Ryan sighs. "All right. I'm in!" he says.

"Pardon me?"

"You can't do it alone. Every investigation needs a good partnership — a good duo. I'll be the Mulder to your Scully, the Booth to your Brennan, the Watson to your Sherlock—"

I interrupt him. "I get it."

"So, where do we start?"

I bite my lip. "I guess we go back to the white house in the woods. Metaphorically speaking, of course."

CHAPTER 13

Before
Penelope

THUMP. Penelope fell to the ground, knocking over the lamp on the way down.

She laid on the floor and giggled uncontrollably with her legs in the air.

Her door crashed open, rattling the closet doors. "What the fuck is going on in here?" her mother screamed, with her hands on her hips.

"Get out of my room!" Penelope yelled.

Her mother stormed toward her. "Are you *drunk*?" She lifted her by the collar of her shirt, sniffing her. "Of course you're drunk! Where did this happen?" She let Penelope fall to the floor as she towered over her.

With a shrug of her shoulders, Penelope giggled louder. Despite her intoxication, she knew that this was a dangerous game she was playing.

"I said, where did this happen?" her mom asked, voice elevated and irritated.

Penelope's laughter halted, and she remained on the floor, refusing to acknowledge her mother's presence.

"I'm not going to ask you again. Where were you at, Penelope?"

"I'll never tell," Penelope whispered, then started laughing more.

In a whirlwind of motion, her mother lunged toward her, gripping her hair and yanking her to the bed. Penelope cried out, her voice piercing through the air, grasping her mother's hand in a futile attempt to halt her relentless pulling.

"I will not have you run around acting like the local degenerate, doing who knows what, flashing your shit all over town!"

"I'm just doing what my mother taught me to do," Penelope cried.

SMACK. Her mother's hand stinging her face.

SMACK. SMACK. SMACK.

"It doesn't even hurt," Penelope taunted, with tears rolling down her cheeks.

"You are an abomination. Do you realize that? When I was your age, I was already Miss California Teen USA. I wasn't sneaking out, getting drunk, running around town like a whore."

Penelope hiccuped.

"Seriously, what is wrong with you? Do you want to be a loser for your entire life? Do you think I became the mayor of this town by whoring myself out? No. I worked my ass off to get here. But you just want to throw away all your opportunities."

Penelope stared at the ceiling, hiccuping once more.

"You will never get out of this place if you keep on acting this way. And I'm telling you right now, if you were an adult, I would've kicked you out of this house already."

"Don't make me laugh, mo-mmm. You'd n-never kick me out. It would look too bad for your preciousss reputation. You — you are no better than me, and that's what pisses you off,"

Penelope said, with slurred speech. "You h-hate me because I have a chance to get out of this hellhole of a town, and you're s-stuck here in this fucking hick's paradise," Penelope spits toward her mom.

Her mother's eyes narrowed. "I should have aborted you," she said with an unsettling calmness, before turning around and leaving.

The alcohol weakened her resistance to her mother's callousness. Emotions overwhelmed Penelope as she curled up on her side, muffling her cries into the comforting embrace of her pillow. She heaved as she took in large breaths, trying to calm herself down. *The only person who should be guaranteed to love you is your mother, but she couldn't even have that.* She tried to remember the good times, and wondered if there were any. Throughout her entire life, her mother carried an intense hatred toward her. But never once had she stooped so low, wishing that Penelope had never been born. At least, she never said it out loud.

She rolled onto her back, wiping the tears from her face. The happiness of the night vanished, leaving behind a sobering emptiness. Penelope soon realized that for as long as she remained in this house, her mother would resent her.

She heard the faint sound of a door opening, realizing it was coming from her computer. She walked over to see who was on AIM, and there he was: *sn95lover*. The tears cascaded down her cheeks as whatever tough exterior she had broke down entirely.

I miss you, sn95lover wrote.

> *I miss you too. I wish things didn't have to be this way.*

What do you mean?

> *I can't do this anymore.*

What do you mean? Us?

> *No, not us. This. This house. My mother. She's the fucking worst. I hate her.*

What happened now?

She wiped the tears from her cheeks and sniffled.

> *She slapped me and said she wished she aborted me. If that bitch died, I would fucking dance on her grave.*

Fuck, man. What do you want to do? Want me to come over?

Her fingers hovered over the keyboard before she had the courage to write what was on her mind.

> *I need to get rid of my mother.*

What do you mean, get rid of her?

> *Remember that night when we were at the lake? And we talked about how horrible she was, and we joked around about what should be done with this whole situation?*

Well, of course, I remember that night. It was the first time I got to see you naked! LOL!

> *I'm being serious.*

Yeah, what about it?

> *I want to do that. I can't do this anymore.*

Are you for real?

> *Yes, I am totally for real. I can't do this alone. I need your help, baby. I will literally kill myself if I have to deal with her for another minute.*

How about you sleep on it?

> *No, I've been putting it off for too long. I don't need to sleep on it.*

Don't bite my head off. I just wanted to make sure you really thought about it.

> *Trust me, I have. This is the only way.*

OK, babe. Give me a few days, and I'll figure it out.

> *I knew you'd come through for me.*

You know I'd do anything for you, babe.

> *That's exactly what I was hoping to hear. Gotta go. Talk later. Xoxo*

She closed down the computer and walked to her wall. Surrounding the mirror were years of pictures of her and her friends. Sniffling as her fingers hovered over each photograph, each memory transported her back to the day it was taken. There was no doubt in her mind that for the last couple of years, she had been a selfish friend. Emily and Christina had been patient, often defending Penelope when the rumors went wild. In fact, their reputations had suffered as she adapted to constant conflict with her mother. They deserved better than her. Penelope knew that if she went through with this plan, however, all their lives would change for ever.

CHAPTER 14

Present
Christina

I knew that coming back here would stir up the memories I had been trying to forget. I am overwhelmed with emotion as I lay here in this foreign bed, in this beautiful home. When I left town, I swore I would never come back, but life had other plans for me, I guess.

I reach for my phone and pull up my photos. I was feeling homesick, and I missed Thor. I began scrolling through dozens of pictures of him. His entire life was memorialized on my phone — sleeping on his back with his legs in the air, chasing toys, patiently waiting for his treats, his trips to the dog park.

The quiet is broken by the low, rhythmic *whoo-whoo* of an owl outside the window. I put my phone down and turn on my side, closing my eyes as I try to go to sleep.

A gentle tapping resonates throughout the house, startling me. *What is that?*

There is a brief lull, and then it begins again. Deep breath in, deep breath out.

"It's just the breeze or an animal," I whisper to myself. "No one is out there."

Tap. Tap. Tap. Tap.

I cover my ears with the extra pillow and shut my eyes.

I stare at the etching on the wall. I pull my hand up, using my thumbnail to dig into the plaster. My nails are so tender that pain shoots through my arm as I groan. As my fingernail tears into the rough texture, it makes a sharp, grating sound, leaving a jagged white line in its wake — day four.

I look — comforter, bedroom dresser, mounted television. I listen — gentle creaking of wood panels, ceiling fan, water dripping. I move — licking my lips, rolling my head, tapping my fingers. *You are safe. You will never be back at that place.*

Tap. Tap. Tap. Tap.

I reach for the pistol on the bedside table. I inhale and quietly search for the source of the tapping. My breath quickens as my muscles tense. In the dim moonlight seeping in through the windows, the barrel of the gun dips and jerks as my hands quiver.

Tap. Tap. Tap. Tap.

The noise gets louder, drawing me toward the back room of the house. As I get closer, the tapping stops. *Is there someone in there?*

I lower the gun, and it starts again.

Tap. Tap. Tap. Tap.

I hook the corner into the room, gun on target, but the room is empty.

"What the hell?"

I walk to the table and turn on the lamp, searching for something that may be hidden in the darkness, but my initial observation is confirmed.

Tap. Tap. Tap. Tap. I jump at the noise, spinning and facing the window.

I scream when I see two large, round, yellow eyes staring back at me. The owl startles at the noise and lifts from its perch, with its wings spread wide and steady as it glides into the air.

"Fuck me," I murmur. That is when I see it — the branch tapping the lower corner of the glass. "Are you kidding me right now? I got this scared over a damn tree branch?"

I shake my head as I walk back to my room, shutting the door behind me. I place the gun back on the table and lie down.

Ever since I got the note, I've been on edge. Being here has only made it worse. I am so tired of being scared all the time. I close my eyes, cover my head with the pillow, and try to get some sleep.

* * *

I meet Ryan at the same restaurant and booth from the night before. He sits there, looking inconspicuous in a black baseball cap and a hoodie. As I approach him, he smiles and stands to greet me. We exchange pleasantries, and I observe a stack of papers and folders on the table.

As we sit down, he notices my interest. "Sorry, I got a little ahead of myself last night and started some research. You want anything to eat or drink?"

I half-smile. "No, I'm not that hungry."

"Are you sure? We have a lot of investigating to do. It's going to be a long day!"

"I'll be honest. I don't really have an appetite," I pause. "But please, eat something!"

He waves at a waitress with brunette hair, and she walks toward us. "You ready to place an order?"

"Yes, please. I'd like a stack of pancakes with eggs and bacon. Oh, and an everything bagel with cream cheese on the side."

She looks at me. "What can I get for you, miss?"

"Nothing but coffee for me, thanks."

She smiles. "All right, I'll have that out for you shortly."

"Wow, you have quite the appetite," I say.

"Hey, no fat shaming!" Ryan jokes.

"I'm not fat shaming!" I chuckle.

"Sounds like fat shaming to me," he says, winking at me.

"I gotta be honest, Ryan. Seeing these papers is a lot to take in. I don't even know where to start. How do you find someone the police couldn't even track down, you know?"

"Well, you can't start an investigation being negative! We'll see where this leads, but I think this is where we should begin," he says, as he shuffles through the papers on the table. He pulls a photograph of the night I escaped, and I gasp. I am standing there with a blanket around me, bruised and malnourished. I looked like a walking corpse. Beside me was the officer who arrived first, escorted me to his car, and comforted me when they realized everyone was gone. He attempted to shield me from the flashing cameras as we entered the Tranquility Ridge Police Station.

I am overwhelmed by a deluge of emotions.

I'm speechless.

I close my eyes, and it all comes rushing back.

Officer Swanson has an arm wrapped around my shoulders as I try to cover my face with my raised hand — exposing the scrapes and bruises on my pale skin. There's so much noise — sirens and shouting. The flashing camera lights disorients me as I try to walk, blinding me as if I have looked directly into the sun. But somehow, in all the noise, Officer Swanson's voice calms me.

"You're going to be OK, kid. I promise we will find Penelope even if it's the last thing I do! I promise we will find the people responsible for doing this to you — and I have never broken a promise!"

I look — dozens of papers, Ryan's hands, photographs. I listen — door chime, chattering voices, music. I move — blinking my eyes, tapping my fingers, biting my lip. *You are safe. It's all over now.*

"CJ, you OK?"

I fight back tears. "Yes. I didn't realize how hard all of this would be. Look at me! I'm a mess," I say, sniffling, bringing a napkin to my nose.

He smiles. "You're not a mess. You've been through a terrible thing, CJ. I'd be more concerned if you weren't reacting this way," he pauses, pointing to a photograph. "This officer is the only one still around from then. He's retired, and everyone else has moved away or has died. I say we start with him, since he's local."

"He was the one that rescued me," I say. "I think that it's the perfect place to start."

The waitress walks over with a large tray of food and drinks, placing them around all the items already on the table. "Anything else I can get you two?"

I nod my head.

"No, I think we're good," Ryan says.

Ryan pushes the plate with the bagel over to me. "Everything bagel and cream cheese. Is it still your favorite breakfast food?"

"It is! How did you remember?" I say, surprised at the gesture.

"You ate it all the time. I know you're not hungry now, but just to be safe, I can't have my fellow detective's stomach growling during our investigation," he says, winking.

I take a bite of the bagel. "Mmm. Now that is good! I haven't had one in so long. Thank you, Ryan."

He sips his coffee. "All right, back to business. I have to ask. Do you know what happened? Were there ever any suspects? Did they ever follow up with you?"

I take a deep breath and begin tapping my fingers on my thighs. "You have so many questions already! I know no one believed me, but I couldn't help the police when I escaped. I was a terrible witness."

"Oh, come on. Don't be like that. I doubt you were terrible. You were traumatized. I'm sure they're used to it," he says, shuffling eggs into his mouth.

"No, I was. I didn't know how many suspects there were. They always had me blindfolded, and when I wasn't, I was so terrified to look that I kept my eyes shut. They even distorted their voices. I couldn't identify anyone. I don't know. Once the media stopped covering it, they didn't care anymore."

He sighs. "Well, if we're going to do this, we have to go all in. I'll be right by your side, but it won't be easy. But if at any time — and I mean any time — you want to quit, then we quit."

I bite my lower lip. "No, no quitting. It's time to uncover what really happened."

"I should've been there for you," he says.

"Ryan, there was no way you could've changed anything."

"It doesn't matter. I just didn't know what to say and didn't know if you wanted to be around me. I'm sorry I wasn't there for you."

"No need to apologize. We were so young. I wouldn't have known what to do, either," I say. "It's not something you learn in the boyfriend manual, right?"

He is silent for a moment. "Well, at least I can be here now when you need me! Let's go talk to the officer. I'm eager to get this investigation started! I want to see if my years of watching cop shows pays off," he says with a quiet laugh.

We finish our food in silence, ready to see where this will lead us. Ryan picks up all the material scattered on the table, throws some cash down, and I follow him to his car. Truthfully, while I escaped that night, I've felt imprisoned ever since. The scenes replay in my head daily, haunting my thoughts and leaving a lasting imprint on my soul. The fear of knowing they are still out there terrifies me. I think that's what my phobias stem from — the uncertainty of knowing anyone around me could be responsible for my abduction.

Ryan respects my contemplation as he drives us to Officer Swanson's house. I gaze out the window, taking in the sights of the town — it feels so familiar. The town is nestled amid the trees — small cabins dotting the landscape, with their roofs peeking through the dense foliage. We pass the brick and wood buildings of downtown, many adorned with vintage signs and classic Western facades. How can a place like this harbor such a terrible past?

I am lost in my thoughts as he turns into the driveway of a cabin-style tract house. The water pools on my palms as sweat trickles down my back. My heartbeat intensifies as I take deep breaths to calm down — deep breath in, deep breath out.

"It'll be OK," Ryan whispers. "I'm right here with you."

I look at him, forcing a smile.

Walking to the front door, I don't know what to expect. Will he provide the answers I am looking for? Or will he leave me asking more questions?

Ryan knocks on the door. I look — brown door, rocking chair, hanging plant. I listen — knocking, lawn mower, sprinklers. I move — curling my fingers, rolling my shoulders, tapping my foot. *You are safe. You are not in danger.*

The door opens, and he stands there. His raven-black hair is now a subtle salt-and-pepper, his crystal-blue eyes cradled in soft layers of excess skin, and a tan wool jacket and jeans replace his police uniform.

His mouth opens wide. "Well, I'll be damned. Is that you, Christina?" he asks. "You haven't changed a bit. Come over here." He crosses the threshold and wraps his arms around me. It is a fatherly embrace — warm and comforting.

He pulls back, looks at me, and smiles. "Look how beautiful you've grown up to be!"

I smile. "Officer Swanson, it is so good to see you."

"Oh, please. Call me Dan." He looks over at Ryan, peering intently. "I'm sorry, have we met before?"

"Not that I know of. I'm Ryan," he says, shaking Dan's hand.

Dan draws his lips into a thin line. "Well, please, come in," he says as we follow him inside.

He leads us into the living room with memorabilia of his career at Tranquility Ridge Police Department — awards, photographs, and news articles. I focus on the article with him shielding me from the cameras, surprised that he has it memorialized on his wall.

"Can I get you guys anything?" he asks.

"No, thanks," I say.

"So, what brings you here today? I am still shocked to see you, Christina."

I look over at Ryan. He begins, "Well, I don't know if you heard of the hit and run a couple of weeks ago—"

Dan interrupts, "Oh yes. Very sad. Such a young woman, and with a young daughter, too."

Ryan continues. "Well, that was my sister—"

"Oh, my! That is tragic. I'm sorry, son," Dan interrupts.

"I appreciate your condolences, sir. She was friends with Christina and Penelope. Prior to her passing, she thought Penelope was alive, and Christina wanted to look into it."

Dan looks at me sympathetically. "Ah, I see. I never forgave myself for breaking my promise to you, Christina. I told you I would find her, and never did."

"It wasn't your fault," I say.

Dan looks at his feet. "Back then, I was still new to the force. I was still a beat cop, not a detective or anything. But I can try to help as much as I can. I still remember so much about the case."

I shift in my chair with anticipation. "Anything helps. This is the first stepping stone. And trust me, I realize we're probably not going to find the answers we're looking for, but we have to try!"

Ryan hands the stack of papers to Dan, and I watch as he peruses and sorts through the documents. We sit there waiting to see if anything sparks his recollection. "That's all we have so far," Ryan says.

Dan shakes his head incredulously. "This is unbelievable. I remember this case just like it was yesterday. All these details have just stuck with me."

Ryan looks at him. "And?"

"And I wish I had more, but there's not much to tell you. First, you start with motive," he says, as Ryan hands me a notepad and pen to write. "The obvious motive had to do with the mayor. Everyone assumed Penelope was being kidnapped for ransom or some political bargaining tool, but nothing ever materialized. So it was a dead end."

"But if it was political, then why was I taken?" I ask.

"Collateral damage," Dan says. "You just happened to be there with her."

"Well, that's what every victim wants to hear," I say, rolling my eyes.

Ryan comforts me by rubbing my back with his hand; the touch startles me. Dan's eyes follow Ryan's hands.

"I know, it sucks, kid. The next focus was on the house. Who did it belong to? From what I recall, the detectives could never identify who owned the property. I'll be honest. I lived in Tranquility Ridge my whole life and never saw it before, but that happens in places like these, you know. I'm sure there are a lot of homes and shacks that people have no clue about," Dan says.

"What about DNA? Fingerprints?" Ryan asks.

Dan shuffles through the papers. "From what I recall, it was still in its infancy back then. It's not what it is now. With fingerprints, they will only be in the system with a prior arrest, and the same will be true with DNA. There were no matches. Another dead end," Dan says, handing the papers back to Ryan. "It wasn't high-profile enough for the FBI to respond, so it was just TRPD, because it was our jurisdiction."

"Even with it being the mayor's daughter?" I ask.

"Maybe if it had been a big city like Los Angeles or New York, but ultimately, jurisdictional responsibility remained with the TRPD. They had no reason to believe it was part of something larger like human trafficking or you guys being taken across state lines, so they weren't interested," Dan says.

"Fuckin' FBI," Ryan says, shaking his head with disapproval.

"I know, it was brought up, and from my understanding, the calls were made, but they just had bigger cases to focus on."

I shake my head. "Unbelievable."

"What about," Ryan pauses, "sex offenders?"

Dan looks at me as if asking for my permission to answer. "Well, that was another point of interest. Megan's Law was still new, but from what I can remember, this wasn't sexually driven," Dan says, carefully choosing his words.

Ryan looks at me. "Oh — I just assumed, you know, 'cause that's usually why people are kidnapped, right?"

I look — Ryan's blue eyes, oversized living room window, coffee table. I listen — clock ticking, paper shuffling, beating heart. I move — biting my lip, fidgeting with my hands, bouncing my leg. *You are safe.*

"They didn't do any of that to me, thankfully." I pause. "I don't know the real motive, but it seemed like they just wanted to humiliate me and torture me."

Ryan's jaw drops, and his eyes widen in disbelief. "Jesus. Well, I'm relieved you weren't sexually assaulted, but damn. I had no idea they tortured you. I'm so—"

I interrupt him. "No need to get into it. Next clue."

Dan's eyes are filled with grief, reflecting the pain that weighs heavily on his heart. "As far as suspects are concerned, there wasn't much to work from. I remember you said you were supposed to meet some boys at a bonfire, and when you showed up, no one was there. Is that right?"

"It was just your regular high school party. We assumed we were in the wrong place. Next thing you know, we're being attacked and thrown in a truck," I say.

"Do you remember where you heard about the party?" Ryan asks.

"Emily or Penelope had said one of their friends or neighbors had told them about it," I say.

Ryan looks at Dan. "Any other leads?"

"Not really. There was just this kid in your class who was obsessed with Penelope. Everyone said he was pretty dark. He was into that emotional rock music, kind of goth. Once again, it never panned out," says Dan.

"Do you remember his name?" Ryan says, looking at me.

"Oh, shit. What was his name? That's going to bother me. I think it's Bobby something," I say.

"Bobby Duke," Dan says. "He's a vet now. His practice is on the main street through town."

"Didn't peg the goth kid to be an animal lover," I say. "Talk about a lifestyle 180."

"He's a pretty upstanding citizen. You'd be surprised what growing up will do," Dan says.

"Maybe he's overcompensating for being a kidnapper," Ryan says, half-joking.

Dan shifts in his chair, crossing his legs. "I doubt it. Never had run-ins with the police. We all go through our weird phases as kids," Dan says. "I'm sure you have some skeletons in your closet too."

"That's true about the weird phases," I add. "At one point in time, I wanted to be a vampire slayer," I say, trying to lighten the mood. "That obviously didn't come with a good retirement plan."

Dan and Ryan chuckle, and we all sit there in silence. "I wish I could answer more for you, but it's a small town, and sometimes things have a way of disappearing, if you know what I mean."

I feel defeated. "Is there anyone else we should talk to? What about the other officers on the case?"

"Most have moved or are dead now. I don't think they'd have much more to tell you," Dan says.

"Do you have any of their contact info? Just in case," I ask.

"Of course," he says, scrolling through his phone and writing some numbers down. "Here are the few I have. I don't know if they are still good, but I'm sure you kids can track them down if you need to."

"I can't thank you enough, Dan. Thank you for letting us barge into your home — which is absolutely beautiful, by the way," I say.

Dan smiles as we stand up, and he ushers us to the door. "If I can help with anything, please let me know."

He gives me another hug, lingering in my embrace. There's something in the way he holds me that makes it clear he hasn't told me everything I need to know.

CHAPTER 15

Before
Christina

It had been a week since I last saw Pen and Em, and this summer hadn't been what I was expecting.

I couldn't help but wonder if this was the natural progression of friendships. We were developing different versions of ourselves. Somehow, I felt like I was the glue holding everyone together, and it was getting exhausting. Was I trying too hard to keep this ship from sinking? And who was really to blame for the fractures in our friendships?

I think the root cause of the issues with our friendships had to do with Penelope's turmoil with her mom. Ever since they started fighting all the time, she was becoming one of those mean girls — attention-seeking, condescending, and selfish. She was becoming someone I didn't recognize at all, and it made being her friend difficult. Deep inside, I was hoping it was just a passing phase, but how long could I deny it had become an integral part of her identity?

And Emily had been so weird the last few months. She had always been the most reserved in our group, but something was off, especially whenever she was around Pen. Seeing how she reacted to Eric and Pen kissing at the party was so uncharacteristic. I knew Emily was keeping a secret from me, but what could be so bad that she felt like she couldn't tell me?

"Christina!" I heard my mom yell from down the hall. "Telephone!"

I hurried toward her and grabbed the phone. "Hello?"

"Hey, it's Em."

"I was just thinking about you. What's up?"

"Pen called and said we should go to the lake today. Have you heard from her yet?"

"Nope. Did you want to go?" I said, as I walked over to the couch and plopped down.

"To be honest, I was surprised she even called," Emily said.

"Maybe she feels bad for the other night?"

"About the party? I don't even care. I had just had a little too much to drink," she lied.

"Oh, good! It just seemed like you were a little jealous. I thought you had a thing for Eric, maybe."

"No. It's not that. It's complicated," Emily said.

"It can't be that complicated. I'm here if you wanna talk about it."

"I know. And maybe I will, but not now."

"Is that complication why you haven't wanted to chill with us all week?" I asked, kicking my feet in the air.

"I don't know. I guess. But I've been lazy too," she paused. "So, you want to go to the lake?"

"Yeah, sure. Just know I'm here to talk whenever you're ready."

"I know. I appreciate it."

"Who else is going? Just Pen?" I ask.

"Nah, I'm sure the usuals."

"OK, cool. Yeah, let's go. That sounds fun."

"Awesome!" she said. "I'll call Pen back and let her know."

"Cool! See ya soon!"

I hung up right as my mom walked into the room. "Lake today?"

"Yeah, I think so. Wait! How did you know about the lake?"

My mom smiled. "I'm your mother. I know everything."

"Were you eavesdropping?" I asked.

"Always. It's my job as your mom to know what you're doing at all times."

I rolled my eyes. "As if, mom!"

"Can you bring your sister?" she asks.

"Mom! Come on!"

"It wasn't an actual question."

"Fine. Whatever."

She hugged me and kissed my forehead. "Don't 'whatever' me. Someday I won't be around, and it'll just be you two girls to lean on each other. You need to be thankful for that. I would have loved to have a sister growing up."

"That's because you didn't have one," I said.

She kissed my forehead again. "If you say so, honey."

* * *

The water sparkled in the sunlight. I sat there listening to the chatter of people around me. And for the first time this summer, things felt normal. Penelope and Emily were laughing together. Maybe we could save our school vacation after all.

"I'm bored," Nicole said.

"What do you want me to do about it?" I asked. "You're such a pain in the ass sometimes."

"I don't know why you even brought me," she responded.

"Because mom made me!" I said, throwing my hands in the air.

Nicole grunted in disappointment. "It's so hot out here."

I rolled my eyes. "That's what the lake is for!"

"I don't want to get wet."

Before I could respond, she got up and walked away. Then I heard a deep voice from behind me. "Hey, ladies."

I turned, blinded by the sunlight. After a few moments, my eyes adjusted to recognize Ryan and his friend.

"Do you guys know Brandon?" Ryan asked.

"Kinda. I think your brother goes to school with us," I said as I waved.

"You're cute. Sit next to me," Penelope said to Brandon as she patted the spot next to her. Emily and I exchanged an eye-roll.

Ryan sat down between Emily and me. "Good call on coming to the lake. It's crowded here today!" I felt his pinky gently wrap around mine, hidden from view in the sand, giving me butterflies.

"Don't you have your own friends to hang out with?" Emily pouted, throwing a gum wrapper at Ryan.

"Yes, I do. But I'd rather annoy you instead," Ryan replied. "That's brother code." He threw the wrapper back at Emily.

I looked at Penelope — her arms wrapped around Brandon and giggling. I guess she was over Eric already and on to the next guy.

"I didn't realize you knew each other," Emily said to Penelope.

"Oh, we don't. But I plan on changing that," she said, running her fingers through Brandon's messy hair.

Emily's face distorted, her eyebrows dipped as her lips pursed together. I could sense her lingering distress, so I swiftly diverted the conversation. "So, did you hear about Mr. Ridgerson?" I asked.

"Bro, I can't believe he got caught," Brandon said.

"No, what happened?" Emily asked, eagerly leaning in to hear better.

Before I could respond, Ryan answered. "He got caught with some seventeen-year-old chick."

"No fucking way!" Penelope exclaimed. "Mr. Ridgerson? He's such a nerd!"

"Who did he get caught with?" Emily exclaimed, licking her Blow Pop.

"No clue. The name is under wraps 'cause she's a kid. But I heard his wife followed him to some skeezy motel on the I-80 just out of town. She was so pissed she called the police on him," Ryan said. "Didn't even give him a chance to explain."

"A chance to explain?" I shout. "Explain what? How do you have a reason for being with a high school student in a motel?"

Penelope cackles. "What a loser! How did I not hear about this?" she said.

"I heard they are keeping it lowkey 'cause they don't want parents suing the school," I said. "I think he's looking at serious time. He already got canned."

Penelope laughed. "I fuckin' love it. What a loser. I always hated his classes."

"So, he's gonna go to jail?" Emily asked.

"Fuck yeah he is," Brandon chimes in. "Now he's gonna be someone's bitch in prison."

Everyone laughed in unison.

After a brief silence, Emily asked, "So, what's the plan for tonight?"

Ryan and I already had plans, so I had to figure out how to get out of it. "Honestly, I'm going to be so tired from the sun today, I think I'll just stay home," I said.

"Do you have a boyfriend or something?" Penelope asked, catching me off guard.

I laughed as I felt my cheeks blush. "Oh, yeah! I definitely have a secret boyfriend! Like I could even keep a secret that big from you guys," I said, digging my feet into the sand.

"Well, we have noticed that you have been staying home more than usual," Emily added.

I scoffed. "That's calling the kettle black, Em. We've had to beg you all summer to hang out with us!" I responded. "I mean, it's obvious you're the one keeping something from us."

Emily's face turned red. "Stop it. I don't have a secret."

"Then what was all that talk about being confused—" I said.

"Shut up, Christina!" Emily barked.

"Whoa, Em! I've never heard you yell. This must be something juicy—" Penelope said.

Before I could say anything, Emily jumped up. "Thanks a lot, Chris!" she said, storming away.

Ryan pulled his hand from mine, crossing his arms over his knees. "What was that about?"

"I have no clue," I said, as I watched Emily walk away.

Penelope turned to face me. "Obviously she told you something."

"She didn't, though. She won't tell me what's been bothering her. She just kept saying she was confused and that it was complicated. Like, what does that even mean?"

Penelope pulled her hand to her neck and began rubbing it as her face tensed. "She didn't say what was causing it?"

"No, I swear! It was just a joke. She was picking on me, so I thought I'd do the same—"

Ryan stood up. "I don't know what's up, but I'll talk to her. Maybe she felt like you guys were being bullies or something," he said and chased after her.

"I didn't mean to cause a fight," I mumbled.

"Hey, guys," a soft-spoken voice said to my right. I looked up, and it was Jeremy, Brandon's younger brother, who I knew from school. He was the complete antithesis of Brandon, with contrasting personalities and traits. Brandon exuded the All-American varsity football player look with his well-built physique, groomed hair, and sharp jawline. While Jeremy paled in comparison, more diminutive in stature. Brandon stood over six feet, making him much taller than Jeremy, who stood at around 5'9". There was something about his shyness and introversion that gave off an air of mystery, as if he was always watching and listening, privy to everyone's secrets.

"Bro, what are you doing here?" Brandon asked.

"Everyone is here today. Thought I'd stop by too."

"I'm not your babysitter," Brandon said, annoyed. "Get your own friends."

Jeremy's face turned red, embarrassed by his brother's comment.

"You can join us," I said.

He sat down, and Brandon stood up. "Fuck this. I'm leaving," he said, walking toward Ryan and Emily.

"I guess I'll go too," he said. "Sorry for crashing."

I put my hand on his knee before he could stand up. "No, it's OK. Stay with us. We'd love your company."

His cheeks flushed as he looked at the lake. "OK, thanks."

"So, Jeremy," Penelope started. "What's the deal with your brother?"

He looked at her, confused. "What do you mean? Like, why is he such an asshole?"

She scoffed. "No, his status! Single? Dating? I'm not looking for anything serious."

I watched as he looked uncomfortable and hesitant to respond. "I don't know. We don't really talk about that stuff."

"What? Really?" Penelope said.

"Yeah. As you can tell, we don't really get along," Jeremy said, grabbing a fistful of sand and throwing it.

I chimed in. "I doubt he wants to spend his time talking about his brother. Am I right?"

He smiled. "You wouldn't be the first girl that tried to find out if he had a girlfriend. I'm used to it."

Jeremy's eyes met mine. There was a kindness to them. It would be difficult living in your brother's shadow — desperately searching for the spotlight.

"What about you? Do you have a girlfriend?" I asked.

"Me?" he said as his voice cracked. "No, no girlfriend."

"Why not?" I asked.

"Just no one I'm interested in. There are a lot of shallow girls in this town," he said matter-of-factly. "Not you guys, of course," he quickly added.

We giggled. "Thanks for the exclusion," I said.

Penelope and Jeremy talked for a little bit as I maintained my focus on Emily and Ryan in the distance. Eventually, she walked off with him and Brandon in tow, never coming back to hang out with us. Something was going on with her that she didn't want Penelope to know about, and I was determined to figure out what her secret was.

CHAPTER 16

Present
Christina

I stare out the passenger-side window, feeling defeated. *What am I doing here?* I look — black asphalt, gravel shoulder, tree bark. I listen — passing cars, coins rattling, whistling wind. I move — licking my lips, balling my fists, tapping my feet. *You are safe. You are not going back to that place.*

"Christina?" Ryan asks, bringing me back from my trance. I look at him. "I'm sorry. What did you ask?"

"That was a lot to digest. Did you want to talk about it?"

"No. I'm fine. It was a long time ago. I wanted to understand it. I knew it wouldn't be easy and that he probably wouldn't be able to provide all the answers anyway."

Ryan scoffs. "He's just the first step. We take what he gives us, and we build off that! Don't get discouraged yet."

"Oh, I'm not at all. Trust me."

"Good. Just making sure, CJ." He looks toward me and smiles.

Before I can respond, he pulls into the driveway of a residence. "I thought we were going to meet up with Bobby Duke?" I ask.

"We are," he says as he parks the car. "It's just a little pit stop. I have to check in on Maddie."

"Oh, of course. Take your time."

"Please, come in. I'd love for you to meet her. If you're up to it, of course."

I follow Ryan up the custom ramp built for his home. He opens the door, and I follow him into the living room, where I see an older woman in scrubs tending to a little girl about seven or eight years old in a wheelchair.

"Hey, Brenda," Ryan says.

"Wasn't expecting you so early, sir."

"Just stopping by to see my favorite girl!" he says, as I watch Maddie display an infectious smile. He walks closer to her and kisses her head. "How's she doing today?"

"She's doing well. She's been eating most of her food and taking part in her learning activities," Brenda responds.

Ryan looks at me. "Brenda, this is a long-lost friend, CJ. I'm helping her with a project." She nods and smiles at me. "And this is Maddie. The only woman in my life that matters," he says with a smile.

"Very pleased to meet you, Brenda," I say, then turn toward Ryan's daughter. "Pleasure to meet you as well, Maddie." She smiles in my direction.

I stand there watching him as he interacts with his daughter. He runs his fingers through her hair, causing her to look up at him with admiration. He leans down and kisses her forehead, then kneels beside her.

"Are you being a good girl?" Ryan asks.

"Yeah!" Maddie says, raising her arms.

"Is Brenda teaching you lots of cool facts today?"

"Yeah, Daddy!" she giggles.

"Are you almost ready for naptime?"

She shakes her head. "No naptime, Daddy!"

He grins. "Maybe just a little nap?"

She shakes her head again, and he stands up, kissing the top of her head. It was a side of Ryan I had never seen before.

There is a gentleness to him now, vulnerable yet strong and determined.

His gaze meets mine, and I feel like I am spying on a private moment not meant for me.

"I love you, baby," he says to Maddie.

"Love too," she says, struggling to complete the sentence.

"All right, Brenda, if she has an episode or if anything changes, let me know. I'm guessing we'll be out for a few hours," he says.

"No problem, sir," she responds.

"Try to have her nap soon. I don't want her to be overstimulated."

"Of course, Mr. Henderson. I'll make sure she's down within the hour," Brenda says.

"It was nice to meet you," I tell her.

"Nice to meet you, ma'am," she says.

We exit the home, and we walk to his car. "She is lovely," I say.

He smiles. "Maddie is my world. I am so fortunate that she doesn't have one of the cases that requires that she live in the hospital. That was my biggest concern when we learned about her condition."

"I imagine it gets hard, being a single dad with her disability?"

"Of course. I mean, I lost her mother over it. But I see nothing but pure love when I look at that little girl. There is nothing, and I mean nothing, I wouldn't do to protect her, and I mean that. It's been Maddie and me against the world ever since the day she was born."

* * *

We pull into the vet's office parking lot, unsure how to approach this. Neither of us has a background in investigative work. We are following a lead that went nowhere twenty-five years ago, but we have to start somewhere.

When we entered the vet's office, I didn't know what to expect. Inside, the lobby is full of smelly dogs and loud noises. My attention is immediately drawn to a woman sitting with a rottweiler puppy in her lap. He couldn't be more than a few months old — probably getting his last set of mandatory vaccine shots. It makes me think of Thor and how much I miss him. I remember how cute he was at that puppy phase. He was so clumsy, with the cutest high-pitched growl. The sooner I get done with this investigation, the quicker I'll be back at home with him.

We walk toward a woman in blue scrubs sitting at the front desk. "Hello, how can I help you?" she asks.

Ryan takes the lead as I try to control my nerves. "Yes, is there any way we can talk to Dr Duke? We are old friends of his."

She looks at Ryan and then at me with curiosity. "Sure, right this way."

Ryan looks at me and shrugs, surprised it is that easy. We follow the assistant down the hall. She knocks on the doctor's door. "Dr Duke, these are two friends of yours. Do you have time for them?"

He looks up from his desk. "Sure, let them in."

We walk in and sit down on a couch in his office. The room is small, but big enough to fit a desk, loveseat, and filing cabinet.

As I take a seat, I study Bobby Duke. There's a slight recollection of the man before me, but the image is out of focus. "We are old friends, you say?" he asks.

"Well, acquaintances is more accurate," Ryan responds. "My name is Ryan Henderson. We went to high school together."

Bobby leans back in his chair. "So, what brings you in today, Ryan Henderson?"

Ryan looks at me. "Do you know who this is?"

Bobby looks at me. "No. Should I?"

"This is Christina Johnson."

Bobby looks shocked. "Wow! The girl who was kidnapped? No shit, huh? You disappeared after high school," he says, leaning forward with his hands folded on his desk. "I don't blame you, though. Obviously."

I half-smile. "We believe the police looked into you as a suspect back then," Ryan says.

Bobby laughs. "Is that what this is about?"

"Just trying to figure out what happened back then," Ryan says.

"Holy shit, man. That was over twenty years ago, and if it were me, they would've arrested me," Bobby says.

"We know that," I say. "You don't need to get defensive. We're just trying to follow some leads."

"Isn't that what the police do?" Bobby asks.

"Of course, but that didn't seem to work out back then, so we're branching out on our own," Ryan says.

"Gotcha. Please enlighten me on how I'm getting dragged into this again?"

"We know you're innocent," I say, trying to break the tension. "But I'm just wondering if you remember anything that could help us. Apparently, you were one of the few suspects, and once they realized it wasn't you, they had no more leads, and the case went cold."

Bobby laughs. "I'm not surprised Tranquility Ridge's finest botched this investigation. One of the few suspects? I was the *only* suspect, which is comical," he pauses. "So, why do you think you can solve it if they couldn't?"

"Technology has changed. She deserves to know what happened to her and why," Ryan says.

Bobby's eyes softened with sympathy as his shoulders slumped. "The whole thing was messed up; there's no doubt about it. I feel for you. I really do. But I got accused of kidnapping you guys just because I was a little goth and had a crush on Penelope. That wasn't right either, was it?"

"I'm not saying it was—"

Ryan interrupts me, "But whatever you can tell us to lead us in the right direction will help exonerate you, because your name is the only one that has ever been linked to the case."

"I see what you did there," Bobby says, raising his hand and pointing at Ryan.

"Well?" Ryan asks.

Bobby sighs. "Everything about that entire kidnapping was strange. I always thought it was because Penelope's mom was the mayor. I think that's what everyone thought."

"Seriously, anything you can remember, or even what cops said during their interview, could help us out now," I say.

"I'll tell you what I told them: I don't know anything," he says, crossing his arms over his body.

"Please," I say, my eyes pleading with his as I fold my hands in front of my heart.

"Fine, there was one person who seemed a little too interested in what was happening with the case. I was a kid then, and never thought about it twice, but when I looked back, it was suspicious."

I shifted in my seat. "Really? Who?"

"It was the guidance counselor. He kept calling my house to see how I was doing since we were out of school for the summer. But he wasn't asking the normal questions about how I was coping. It was as if he was trying to determine the status of the investigation. Like what the cops knew, any other suspects . . . does that make sense? Kinda like what you two are doing now," he chuckles. "Never really sat well with me."

"Did you ever tell the police?" Ryan asks.

"No. By the time I put two and two together, they had moved on, and I wasn't being looked at anymore. Now, it seems wrong, but I was a kid. I was just happy they were off my back." He looks at me. "I'm sorry that I never said anything. I don't know if it would have changed things."

My eyes meet his. "Do you think they ever considered him as a potential suspect?"

"Never heard anything. Case died out after they stopped looking at me," Bobby says, "at least that's how it seemed at the time."

"OK. Well, thank you for telling us now. It's a lead. It helps. Is there anything else you can think of? Any other suspects, or anything that may have stood out?" I ask.

He shook his head. "Not really."

"Do you remember what the police asked during their interviews?" Ryan asks.

He raises his hand to his chin. "It was very stereotypical. They had their whole good cop, bad cop routine. The only thing that I found weird was when I walked out of the interrogation room, the door next to mine opened, and the mayor was there. So, if they had that two-way mirror, I think she was watching."

Ryan looks at me. "The mayor? That seems strange that they would let one of the victims' parents watch an interrogation. Do you know if your mom got to listen?"

"Hell no. She would've told me," I say.

"I don't know. It all seemed very sketchy," Bobby says.

"Well, if you think of anything else, please let us know. This really has been so helpful!" I say.

He smiles. "Of course. And, for the record, it's a terrible thing you had to go through. I'm sorry they never caught the bastards responsible."

I purse my lips together. "I appreciate it."

Ryan and I walk out of the vet's office. "So, what's up with the guidance counselor? Does he still work at the school?"

He faces me and chuckles. "Not even close."

"So, what does he do?"

He hesitates. "He's a reverend now."

"A reverend?" I ask. "You think he's trying to atone for his sins?"

"Maybe he has the burden of kidnapping two girls weighing heavily on his conscience, and he's trying to make amends."

CHAPTER 17

Before
Emily

Emily was awakened by the thunderous rumbling of an engine outside her window.

She got up and peered outside, watching as Eric sat in his car, Snoop Dogg blasting from the speakers.

As she observed him, a wave of jealousy washed over her, her mind replaying the image of Penelope's hands gripping his biceps, her lips pressed against his. She wasn't sure why she felt this way — her uncertainty grew with each passing day. Was it because of Penelope kissing the only boy Emily ever had feelings for, or was she jealous that Eric was also into Penelope?

"Of course they'd be into each other," she fumed. "When will I ever catch a break?"

She brought her right hand to her mouth as she began chewing on one of her nails. "How is this my life right now?" she mumbled.

Things had been off for a while now — well, ever since that particular weekend. Christina had been busy, and Pen had been fuming about something her mom had done. Emily had gone to her house like she had dozens of times before, but everything had changed that night. Pen had grabbed some vodka from the cabinet, and with every sip, the barriers dissipated.

Emily recalled with every sip of alcohol, Pen inched closer to her on the couch, and their inhibitions evaporated. While how it happened was choppy in her mind, Emily said something that made Penelope laugh, and the next thing she remembered was Penelope's lips on hers. There was an urgency as Penelope's lips lingered, and her tongue swirled intensely with Emily's. Penelope's hands traveled over her body — time stood still. Emily was lost in the heat and intimacy of the powerful embrace — something she had never shared with anyone before.

Not long after, Penelope's mom came home, Ryan picked up Emily, and they never talked about it again. But Emily couldn't stop thinking about it. She had always dreamed about her first kiss being filled with passion, but had hoped it would be Eric — definitely not Pen. Emily longed for that feeling again, but with every passing day, it seemed like it meant nothing to Penelope. Did she even remember what happened between them or had the night been a blur?

How did life get so complicated? Was Penelope using Emily, just like she had been doing with all the boys? Was Emily a joke to her? Why would she risk their friendship?

To be fair, Penelope wasn't always a terrible friend. If she had been, then Emily would have made new friends a long time ago. Penelope had a reputation for her thoughtfulness in the past, always striving to make others feel special and important in their interactions. The memories of nights spent watching scary movies flooded back to Emily, and she couldn't help but smile at how Penelope comforted them whenever they got scared. Emily realized she had this desire to be protected — being drawn to the two people who had guarded her from the family turmoil and bullies.

Emily couldn't pinpoint when Penelope's character shifted. She had always been known for her kindness and empathy, but then she surprised everyone one summer with an altered personality. Emily and Christina always assumed that she would grow out of that bitchy phase, so they remained patient. They justified it as a manifestation of typical teenage rebellion and convinced themselves she would work it out of her system. But she transformed into one of those catty girls somewhere along the way — becoming petty, critical, and driven by self-interest.

So why did Emily desire her friendship so much? Why was she trying so hard to make it work? Friendships ended all the time. Maybe had Emily dedicated more time and attention to her own needs and desires to begin with, she wouldn't be in this quandary.

Emily was scared. She'd been in Tranquility Ridge her entire life and never met someone who was gay or bisexual. Emily had heard about those relationships in the city and had seen things about it on TV, but this was a small town. People were closed-minded and resistant to change. She could only imagine the beating her dad would give her if he found out, and who knew what the mayor would do to her?

"Stop it, idiot!" Emily said. "You don't even know what you want. I bet if you kiss a boy, it'll be just as amazing." Emily grabbed her pillow and screamed into it. "This isn't fair! Why, Pen?" she cried once more.

She heard the phone ringing down the hall, so she jumped off the bed and walked down to answer. "Hello?"

"Em, it's Christina," she said.

"What's up?" Emily said, still angry about the lake.

"I'm so sorry. I didn't mean to embarrass you the other day with what I said."

Emily scoffed. "It was fucked up."

"I didn't mean anything by it. I swear. I know you've wanted to tell me something, but I didn't think it was a secret."

She sneered. "Of course it was a secret!" Emily bit another one of her nails.

"I'll do anything to make it up to you."

Emily paused. "Just forget it," she said, leaning against the wall.

"Come on, Em. I don't want to ruin the summer. I don't want to feel like we're all fighting."

"Wait. What do you mean we're *all* fighting?" Emily asked, standing more erect against the wall.

"I didn't—"

"Did Pen say something?" Emily asked, biting her fingernail.

"You know Pen. She always has her comments."

Emily felt her stomach ache with anticipation. "Like what comments?"

"Oh, come on, Em. Please don't make me the middle person. It's just an expression."

"Tell me what she said, Christina," she demanded.

Christina groaned. "She said that if you didn't want her making out with people because you liked them, you had to stop being so secretive. How was she supposed to know you had a thing for him?"

"I wasn't being secretive! I don't like him. He's just my neighbor, and I don't want her fucking it up."

"Ah," Christina paused. "OK. I'm sorry I brought it up. You don't like him. Got it."

Emily balled her fist. "I'm not picking a fight. I'm just tellin' you how it is."

"All right, all right. I'll drop it."

"Good!" Emily exclaimed.

"You know, we only have two more years before we go off to college. It would be nice if we didn't waste our entire summer fighting with each other over boys that won't matter down the road."

Emily sighed, gently hitting the wall with her fist. "You're right. I'm sorry." She had been so focused on her romantic interests that she didn't stop to think about how they had a short time left together. It was doubtful they would end up going to the same college or living in the same city, even though that's what they always planned to do.

"I just hate being stuck in the middle. That's all I'm saying," Christina added.

"No, you're right. I was being immature," Emily said.

"That's not what I was saying. I want us to have a good summer. Is that too much to ask?"

There was a long pause. "Me too. I'm sorry. I'll be better," Emily replied.

"I think she's acting out because she's been fighting with her mom. I know she'll never tell us, but ever since her mom became mayor, she's been a total C-word to Pen."

"That bad?" Emily asked.

"Yeah. That bad."

"Thanks for telling me. I'll try not to take whatever she says personally from now on."

In the backyard, Emily overheard arguing. "I gotta go. I think Ryan is getting into it with my dad."

"Oh, shit. OK. Call me later!"

"I will," she said and hung up.

Emily walked to her room and looked through the window. Tension filled the air as her dad and Ryan engaged in another explosive shouting match. In shock, she watched as her dad forced Ryan to the ground, his voice booming with angry curses as he stood over him. With a sudden burst of energy, Ryan leaped up and shoved him, sending him stumbling backward and catching him off balance.

Caught off guard, her dad turned and walked away until he was out of sight. Emily ran outside to check on him.

"Damn, Ryan. You OK?" she asked.

"Yeah, I'm fine," he responded as he paced.

"What pissed him off this time?"

"Who the fuck knows? He's a douchebag," he barked.

"I'm sorry."

Before he could answer, Eric walked over. "Bro, I saw what happened. You good?"

"Yeah, I'm good. That fucker needs to die already," Ryan said.

"It's not that much longer, you know. You guys will leave the house soon, and you won't ever have to see him again. What does your mom say?" Eric asked.

"She's so messed up from the emotional abuse, she just keeps her mouth shut whenever she is here, which lately hasn't been often," Emily said.

Eric threw one arm around Emily's shoulders. "It'll get better. I promise."

Emily gazed up in his direction, making eye contact with him, and it was at that moment she realized things were shaping up to be even more convoluted than she thought. Emily needed to determine her true feelings, and there was only one way to accomplish that.

CHAPTER 18

Present
Christina

"Did you hear what I said?" Ryan asks.

"No, sorry. Can you repeat that?" I say, looking at him.

"That's pretty exciting. We made more progress during our first interrogation than the police, right?"

I smile. "I guess watching all those true crime documentaries paid off," I chuckle. "Or they weren't very interested in solving the crime to begin with."

"Well, let's not jump to conclusions yet," he pauses. "A guidance counselor seems predictable and clichéd. Don't they always look at the inner circle first? The family, the significant others, the friends, then the teachers? I'm surprised they wouldn't have started there."

"I'd imagine so. But who knows? Maybe they didn't have a reason to look into those people," I say as I shrug my shoulders.

There was a benefit to Ryan having remained in Tranquility Ridge. He knew this town well. Before that summer, I never thought I would leave this place either. I loved it here. It was the way the summer breeze would smell of fresh pine as we lay by the lake. And how magical the winter landscape was transformed with the trees adorned in a heavy coat of snow. It was my home — until someone robbed me of that.

I understand why Bobby has been a suspect in our kidnapping. He was the outcast, the weird kid that kept to himself. His black spiked hair, eyeliner, and piercings stood out. He would walk around wearing T-shirts with his favorite metal bands and didn't have a care in the world, which we didn't see much in a small town. Sure, in a big city, no one would've given him a second look, but not in a place like this. He was the polar opposite of Penelope, yet he had this attraction to her that everyone could spot from a mile away. That was Penelope, though; everyone was drawn to her like a moth to a flame.

I couldn't remember the guidance counselor's name until Ryan reminded me — Mr. Charles Stanley. Ryan insisted he was always around: tall, with blonde hair, black wayfarer-style glasses, and he always wore brown suits. I racked my brain, but that man never popped up on my radar, making him more peculiar. If this man was so fascinated by our case, why can't I remember him?

Ryan parked in front of a small white chapel. "Do we really have time for a confession right now?" I say jokingly.

"Well, you wanted to interrogate a reverend," he responds.

I chuckle. "To be honest, I can't tell you the last time I stepped into a church," I say as I look toward the building.

"Oh, don't worry. It's not that bad. No one will tell," he says. "It's not like you'll be struck down by lightning."

I sigh. "We go where the investigation leads us. Lord, forgive us!"

"Exactly!" he says. "If the police would've done their jobs right in the first place, we wouldn't be in this predicament."

Apprehensively, I follow Ryan into the chapel. I take deep breaths to control my anxiety. *You are not in danger*, I remind myself. The large room is empty but warm. There are large stained-glass windows in honor of various figures from the Bible. *Do not fear; this is a safe place.*

I glance toward the front of the church and spot a large crucifix. My eyes fixate on Jesus' hands — the nails bore the raw, agonizing evidence of suffering and sacrifice. Sweat trickles down my back as my heart pounds. I close my eyes and inhale.

The chair feels cold and unforgiving against my skin as I strain to hum songs, but the familiar tunes seem to slip away, leaving me with a sinking feeling of despair. Since I set foot in this place, a heaviness has settled upon me, as if my innocence has been stolen.

I feel the vibration on the floor as they walk toward the room. The air shifts when they enter — scents of sweat, aftershave, and cigarette smoke come with them.

"Do you want water?" the distorted voice asks.

"Yes. Yes, please," I say.

"Okay, this is a test. I am going to remove your blindfold. If you open your eyes, you will never get water again. Do you understand?"

I sigh. I am so thirsty. "Yes."

Someone slightly lifts my blindfold from behind me, and I follow the directions. I open my mouth, waiting for the hydration, but nothing comes. Instead, I feel a blast of liquid shooting between my eyes. I try to raise my hands to wipe it, forgetting that I am still strapped to the chair. My eyes slightly open, but I am blinded; the burning sensation stings my entire face, making breathing almost impossible. Tears stream uncontrollably down my cheeks, but only intensify the pain as I am in a haze of panic.

Suddenly, I can't breathe, and the pain is too much to bear.

My eyes shoot open as I feel Ryan's hands on my shoulders. I look — Ryan, stained glass, pews. I listen — waterfall, organ music, Ryan's muted voice. I move — pursing my lips, touching my fingers, tapping my feet. *You are safe. You are never going back to that place.*

"CJ, are you all right?" Ryan asks, moving his hands from my shoulders down to my hands.

"Yeah . . . um. Sorry. I'm fine."

"You zoned out, almost catatonic, for a minute. I was about to yell for help."

Ryan and I exchange a suspicious glance. "No one is saying she's dead, Reverend."

"Oh, my apologies. You're right. It's been so long that it's easy to assume. I don't know how gossiping about a missing woman is beneficial," Reverend Stanley says, crossing his hands on the desk.

"But it might help us find her," Ryan says.

"Well, going back to free therapy, I remember running into a student one day on the street. She was so upset, and I could see it. So, I sat next to her, and she was practically in tears about Penelope kissing some boy at a party."

"How close was that to our kidnapping?" I ask.

"A few weeks before. I could tell she didn't really want to tell me, but once she started, she couldn't stop. She thought Penelope was doing it on purpose to make her jealous, I guess," Reverend Stanley says. "But the girl said that it wasn't even like that, and it was much more complicated than a crush."

"By any chance, do you recall who it was that told you that?"

"Not really. It just stuck in my mind because the kidnapping was relatively close to the outburst."

"Damn, that could have been a good lead," I say.

"What about Bobby Duke? You remember him?" Ryan asks, re-directing the interrogation.

"How could I forget? He was one of the first suspects, right?" Reverend Stanley says.

"We talked to him too. He said you were very interested in the case," Ryan says.

"Of course I was! I wanted to get to the bottom of it, you know? Once I heard they released him, I wanted to make sure he was handling everything reasonably well. Then I figured I'd ask him more questions."

"Did the police ever come and talk to you?" I ask.

"No, never. I was surprised, actually. I would've thought they would want more info on the students. But they never asked me anything."

We sit there in silence momentarily. "Is there anything else you can think of to help us?" Ryan asks.

"Not now, but I'll really think hard on it and pray, and hopefully I can find some answers for you." He smiles. "And please, come join us for service one day. There's a lot of calm that comes with prayer. It might help guide you during this journey."

"I — I'll think about it," I stutter.

Ryan and I smile and show ourselves out of the chapel. "Did you catch that?" I ask.

"You mean the Freudian slip of calling her dead instead of missing? I sure did," Ryan says.

"Wait!" a boisterous voice yells from behind.

I turn around and see Reverend Stanley. "I remember something." He jogs down the stairs. "There was one kid that I never trusted during that time. Not that I suspected him of this, but he was just off to me. While he was Mr. All-American teenager to everyone else, I got strange vibes around him. Maybe just a sixth sense."

"Who?" I ask.

"Brandon," he says. "Brandon McCormack."

I look at Ryan. "Brandon McCormack? Why does that sound familiar?"

"He was one of my buddies in high school."

"Seriously?"

He bites his cheek. "Yeah. He's also the chief of police now."

CHAPTER 19

Before
Penelope

Penelope felt the comforting embrace of Eric's arms around her.

She turned to face him as he gently tucked a loose strand of hair behind her ear. "You are so hot," he said, kissing the tip of her nose.

She felt her stomach tighten. "Thank you."

He pulled her closer, kissing her forehead. "You know you're hot, don't you?"

"Obviously," she said, grinning.

As he tightened his arms around her, she found solace by tucking her head into the crook of his shoulder. She could feel his heart pounding against her chest, a comforting rhythm that made all her problems disappear. Whenever she allowed herself to be vulnerable, the concern about this romance always weighed on her mind. The deeper their connection grew, the more fearful she became — she didn't want someone to have control over her. It was the main reason she kept her options open — flirting and kissing others to remind her that if he left her, she'd be just fine. There was a level of comfort that came with having people on the back burner if you needed them.

She couldn't remember how her life became intertwined with Eric's, but for months, they had been sneaking around, hiding their affair from everyone. Initially, it made it more fun, but then she realized it also allowed her to limit her commitment and maintain her independence.

While she fought the traditional concepts of commitment, Penelope liked that her relationship with Eric was different. Maybe it was his maturity, but it just felt real when they were together. She couldn't ignore that he was offering her something she had never had before — a chance at a future.

What she appreciated the most was that he believed she could do much more than Tranquility Ridge — their partnership brought out the best in them both, igniting their potential. With him by her side, Penelope felt like she could take on the world, especially her mother. However, even with that potential, she still kept him at arm's length.

She knew her mother would never approve of their biracial relationship, and that excited her. Although her mother didn't openly express racist beliefs, she held reservations about intermingling bloodlines. She dreamed of having grandchildren with blonde hair and blue eyes, and she firmly opposed the idea of Penelope dating an African American man. Penelope knew this would destroy her.

As his fingers moved to the back of her neck, she experienced a tingling sensation that spread down her spine. Their eyes met, and at that moment, he leaned in and softly brushed his lips against hers. As her hand traveled up his back, she could feel the heat radiating from his skin and the goosebumps forming in its wake. Her heart raced in response.

Suddenly, the moment was broken by a slamming car door. It made Penelope jump and grab her phone. "Shit! I lost track of time. My mom is home! Hurry!"

They both ran to the window, which Penelope opened hastily. He leaned in and kissed her, then jumped out.

with my brother all the time," she said, annoyed. "I hate living in a small town!"

"Isn't that your neighbor he's following?" Pen asked, already knowing it was.

"Yeah, that's him," Emily said quietly.

Penelope was excited that Eric was here, but also ashamed that he would see her with the welt on her face. She worried he would notice it and feel responsible for being at the house.

She watched him from afar as he stood with the newly arrived group. He would casually glance in her direction, monitoring what she was doing. She listened to the girls' gossip, but she felt like she was a million miles away.

"I'm gonna go say hi to my brother," Emily said.

"I thought you were pissed he was here?" Christina asked.

"I am, but I should still say hi."

As she walked away, Christina said, "She doesn't want to say hi to Ryan. I bet she wants to be close to Eric."

"Yeah, I'm sure," Penelope smirked.

"I wonder why she doesn't just own up to it? We'd never judge her," Christina said.

Penelope watched her closely as she strolled over to the group. Eric threw his arms around Emily, and as he pulled back to talk to her, his eyes focused on Emily's. Penelope took a long drag of her cigarette as she watched them, suddenly, for the first time, feeling a tinge of jealousy.

"Maybe she's just embarrassed 'cause he doesn't want her," Penelope said.

"We don't know that! Maybe he does! That would be good for her!" Christina said.

Penelope knew Eric didn't have feelings for Emily, but there was something about the way he looked at her. Now that Emily's feelings were on full display, Penelope didn't want to risk losing Eric either.

"It's so obvious he's not diggin' her," Penelope said.

Christina looks over at the group. "I don't know. I think he's kinda flirting with her."

Penelope felt her blood boiling. She knew he wasn't trying to make her jealous, and he was only acting that way because she asked him to keep everything a secret. As she observed Emily's overt flirtation — giggling and casually touching his arms — Penelope didn't want to play this game anymore. She realized she couldn't put it off any longer — it was time to put her plan in motion.

CHAPTER 20

Present
Christina

I gaze out the passenger-side window as we wind through the narrow road. The trees stretch high overhead, their branches filtering the sunlight.

He's the chief of police now.

My breath labored. I look — Ryan driving, steering wheel, windshield. I listen — air blowing in the vents, the radio, passing cars. I move — lick my lips, tap my fingers, wiggle my toes. *You are safe. There is nothing to be afraid of.*

I break the silence. "So, let me get this straight. The only person the reverend ever got a bad feeling about was one of your friends, who is now the chief of police."

Ryan chuckles. "Crazy, right?"

"Wait. Why is that so crazy? That he's the chief, or a suspect?"

He looks at me in disbelief. "You don't honestly think Brandon had something to do with it, do you?"

"I mean, is it so far-fetched?" I ask.

He pulls over on the dirt shoulder. "Well, he's a cop, so that's a pretty big one-eighty in lifestyle choices."

"But I thought we would go wherever the evidence led us?"

"You don't think I would have realized if one of my best friends was a kidnapper?"

I look away and then back at him. "I mean, I don't know. But just 'cause he's a cop doesn't mean he's not a bad guy," I say.

"Oh, please don't tell me you are one of those cop haters?"

I scoff. "No, not at all! I'm just saying maybe he wasn't a good kid."

"Well, you were there. Was it him?" he says, catching me by surprise.

"That's not fair!" I cross my arms and look out the window.

"I don't think we should be wasting time on investigating a cop, is all I'm saying," he insists.

"Why are you getting so defensive?" I ask.

"I'm not! But I think it is a waste of time."

I throw my hands in the air. "You don't have to be here! I came here to do this on my own. You invited yourself to help, without me asking!" I say, my voice rising.

He tilts his head. "You know what? You're right. I invited myself. It's not like I don't have other stuff to be doing."

"So, why don't you drop me off and I'll continue this on my own."

He grips the steering wheel, causing his knuckles to turn white. "I forgot how much of a pain in the ass you can be sometimes, CJ," he says, grinding his teeth.

"Me? A pain in the ass?" I say, pointing to myself. "I'm sorry that my kidnapping is such an inconvenience in your life."

"Oh, fuck. That's not what I meant, and you know that!" he yells.

My emotions rise, and I choke back tears. "I just want to find my friend. I should've never left her. It's my fault she was never found. I should've stayed with her and fought back, but I ran, like a coward. I'm the reason she never got home."

He shifts his body, facing me. "Shit, CJ. Is that what you think? It's not your fault," he says. "You had an opportunity, and you took it. How did you know they'd be gone when you got back?"

"I should've *known*, is the problem. It's not like I was gonna run outside and someone would be there to save us. I should've known it would take hours."

"No one thinks about stuff like that. You were trying to survive. Anyone would've done the same."

"No, they would've stayed and helped her. How do you leave someone behind as they are fighting someone? There were two of us! We outnumbered him. I — I didn't know what to do," I say, burying my head in my palms.

He reaches for my hand and takes it in his grasp. "I'm sorry, CJ. I was being an ass. It kills me you've spent your whole life blaming yourself. Had you not escaped, they could've killed you. You took your best chance."

"Yeah, at Penelope's expense."

"Christina, stop blaming yourself. You're doing the right thing. You're trying to find out who did this. And you're right. I am your partner in this, and a lead is a lead. After all, it might be good that he knows we're looking for Penelope and trying to solve this. Maybe he can try to help us."

"Thanks."

He releases my hand and looks at his watch. "It will all work out, and we'll sort this out. But we have to call it a night tonight. My baby girl needs me back home."

"Of course. I totally get it."

"I will call Brandon and set up a meeting for us tomorrow. Does that work?"

"Of course. Family always comes first. Always," I say. Ryan's eyes meet mine with intensity. *Please don't look at me like that. We can't do this. Not now. Never.*

* * *

Ryan drops me off at my car, and I sit there, deciding where I should go from here. There is something I need to do, but I am having trouble finding the courage to do it.

Before I can change my mind, I put my car in drive. I can't put it off any longer.

As I navigate the roads of Tranquility Ridge, I view this place through a new lens. Growing up, these streets offered me comfort and a sense of familiarity. But now danger lurks in every corner. Driving past the businesses, I wonder if my captors are in there, living their lives as if nothing ever happened. Do they fear being caught someday, or has it been so long that I am just a distant memory? I wonder if somewhere, hidden in this town, there are more people missing, being held captive in the basement of one of these businesses or homes? The ghosts of trauma remain, and all I can see is the evil that is this place.

I arrive at the house at the end of Pine Tree Lane, and it hasn't changed since I last saw it. I spent so many nights here, laughing with the girls, living our best teenage lives possible. Every inch of the yard I see Penelope in the various stages of her youth — praying that she emerges from the door as an adult.

As I walk up the driveway, my hands tremble. *Deep breath in. Deep breath out.*

I lift my hand to knock but hesitate. What am I doing here? *Just breathe.*

I realize I can't do it and turn to walk back down the path.

"Can I help you?" a voice says from behind me.

I turn, and it is Bonnie Solace. She is a skeleton of the woman she used to be. Her hair is gray and disheveled, glasses adorn her makeup-free face, and she is wearing baggy sweatpants and slippers.

"Mrs. Solace," I say, walking closer. "It's me, Christina Johnson."

Her mouth drops as she covers it with her hand. "Christina Johnson? My God. What brings you here after all this time?"

"I — well, I was out here for Emily's funeral and thought I'd see how you're doing."

"Well, I'll be damned. Please, come in," she says, moving out of the doorway.

I smile and walk inside. I've been in here a thousand times before, but now the once magazine-photoshoot-ready home is filled with boxes and clutter. "Are you moving?" I ask.

"Eventually," she laughs awkwardly. "Not at this time, though. I guess I've become somewhat of a hoarder in my old age. I don't get a lot of visitors these days."

Unsure of how to respond, I smile and follow her into the living room and sit on the same couch that had always been there. The moment my body contacts the sofa, there is a pungent smell of animal urine, and I realize the fabric is torn and shredded by cat claws.

"So, do you have any animals?"

"Yeah. A few cats are running around here somewhere in all this mess. They are shy, though, so the minute they hear a stranger, they hide out until whoever is here leaves."

"That's a shame. I love cats. I would've loved to meet them."

"Maybe you'll get lucky and they'll come out of hiding," she says as we sit in silence for a moment. "Can I get you something? A glass of water or milk?"

"Oh no, I'm good. I just thought I'd see how you were. I haven't really heard anything since I left town."

"Well, life didn't turn out how I planned after my Penelope was taken," she says.

"I'm so sorry to hear that," I say.

"After that happened, I only served one term as mayor, and then my political career was pretty much over," she says with disdain, staring out of the window.

"I'm surprised. I thought this town loved you. If I remember correctly, you were pretty good at keeping your campaign promises, which is an anomaly for a politician," I say, trying to lighten the mood.

She laughs. "I tried! Apparently, never finding your daughter somehow makes you an inept leader."

"Oh, I'm sure that wasn't the reason," I say.

"Are you saying I wasn't re-elected because of things I did in office?"

I cross my legs as I stiffen in my chair. "No, not at all. I'm sorry; I didn't mean it that way. It just came out wrong," I say, wishing I could escape this unsettling exchange.

"I'm just messing with you. I'm sure there were other reasons. It's easier to blame it on that rather than my ineptitude."

I could feel myself losing control of this conversation, heading in a direction I didn't want to follow. "So, about that — I mean, Penelope. Did the police ever follow up with you or the case? I never heard anything once I left town."

She cackles. "Hell no. They got you back, and that was good enough for them. Complete incompetence."

"How come they never called in anyone else? Like the FBI?" I ask, un-crossing my legs.

"Do you think the FBI cares about one incorrigible teenager?" she says.

I fold my hands on my lap. "But she was the daughter of the mayor."

She snickers. "The mayor of a small hick town in the middle of nowhere! They don't care about people like us."

"I don't think that's true," I say, getting more uncomfortable.

"Oh, the optimism. Gotta love it," she says, getting up and walking to the liquor cabinet. She removes a whiskey decanter and pours herself some. "Want one?"

"No, thanks. I'm more of a wine drinker."

"Your loss," she says, shooting the alcohol and pouring herself more.

"I — I'm sorry. I don't know what to say," I tell her as she comes back and sits down.

"Say nothing. Life goes on. I'm sure she's dead."

"How can you say that?" I ask, shocked.

"She's been gone for over twenty years. I'm sure she's buried somewhere in these mountains by now."

"How can you be so cold about it?"

Bonnie sneers. "Cold? She ruined my life! Look at this shithole I live in. My career was ruined 'cause of that brat. Truth is, if you two hadn't been out doing who knows what, I'd be a senator by now. She destroyed everything," she says, shooting the remaining whiskey.

Her true personality revealed. This must be what Penelope endured every day. Bonnie Solace had done a great job acting the part of the loving, concerned, and distraught mother. I had seen the footage of her crying on the news, begging for her daughter's return, no questions asked. *"All I want is my beautiful baby girl home. She is my life — my best friend! Please, bring her home. We will reward you greatly,"* she would plead on the nightly news. It was all for show. But it all makes sense why Penelope had changed so much that year. Her mother was a horrible and selfish human being, and no one knew it but poor Penelope.

"I'm sorry for just showing up like this. I don't know what brought me here. I just felt like I should see how you were doing, I guess," I say.

"Still stuck in this piece-of-shit hellhole. That should say enough about how my life is going."

I stand up. "I'm sorry; I'll go. I didn't mean to upset you."

"I'm not upset; just tellin' ya how it is. You should've gotten away from her, too. Maybe your life would've turned up better."

"I'll show myself to the door," I mutter.

"Don't let it hit you on the way out," she yells as I walk away.

* * *

Back in the cabin, the quietness envelops me, and I can't stop thinking about how cruel Penelope's mom was about everything. I'd known Penelope was struggling with her mom, but to witness firsthand how callous she could be, even after all these years, I can only imagine what Penelope had been going through behind closed doors.

My phone vibrates, and I look at the screen. *Mom finally copped out. Her cancer is back*, Nicole wrote.

"Fuck. Poor Mom," I say.

How's she taking it?

Better than I thought she would. She seems really optimistic.

> *Did she say what stage?*

I bite my lower lip.

No, that's what worries me.

> *Shit. I'm out of town, but I should be back in a few days. I can come out there.*

Out of town? You? Where?

> *I don't know if you remember Emily, but she passed away. I came to T.R. for the funeral.*

Geez, Christina. You're back there? I wish you would've told me. I could've come with you.

I sigh.

> *I'm fine. Just keep me updated on Mom, please. I'll be home as soon as possible.*

Nicole replies with her thumbs-up emoji, and I put my phone down. I was worried about my mom, but I knew I had to focus on getting the answers I was looking for. The faster I track Penelope down, if she's still alive, the quicker I can get back to my family.

I reflect on the day and everything I have learned thus far in our investigation. Now more than ever, I realize that the TRPD investigation was a complete failure, lacking any substance. It was surprising to see how little attention the disappearance of the mayor's daughter received, given the significance of the event. But after speaking with Bonnie, I wonder if she even wanted to find Penelope in the first place.

Looking back, I do recall that the TRPD was interested in Penelope's ex-boyfriends. I tried to convince them she had always been known for her carefree and independent nature, but they didn't believe me. She had a deep aversion to settling down with just one guy, preferring to keep her options open and live life on her terms. In hindsight, I find it strange that I couldn't remember the name of a single ex-boyfriend. Sure, there were people she had flings with, but nothing serious. Was she really that independent, or had she just been keeping that part of her life concealed from us? And if so, then why?

The entire ordeal was so overwhelming that I don't even remember how they homed in on Bobby as the primary person of interest. I never singled him out, and I know Emily wouldn't have pointed to him, so it came as a shock when they revealed he could be involved somehow. All I could see was that he was a kid, and how could a kid execute something like that? It doesn't seem logical.

But then Bobby pointing the finger at the guidance counselor seemed off too. Why would anyone at our high school want to kidnap us? And the enormous elephant in the room was that if Penelope were still alive, they would still have her. Wouldn't they? There was no way that the vet or the reverend I talked to today was holding her captive. I am no detective, but I couldn't fathom that being the case.

Sitting at the table, I look around at this place. What am I doing here? My mind races with uncertainty as I grapple with the daunting challenge of solving a kidnapping and uncovering the whereabouts of someone who had vanished such a long time ago. It was a long journey of therapy before I could finally step outside my house and feel comfortable being around strangers. Now, I am back in the town, where the memories of my past haunt every corner, and the possibility of encountering one of my tormentors is real. What will I do when I find the people responsible? Will I magically be healed?

I doubt it. Knowing my luck, it'll just make everything substantially worse. I'll probably end up dead this time.

My thoughts are disrupted when, off to the left, a light-activated motion sensor springs into action. *It's just an animal, right?* I stand up and walk toward the window. A different sensor draws my attention closer to the front door, and I feel my body tense as I shut my eyes.

I stare at the etches in the wall — my nails are covered in blood and dirt. Nine lines for the nine nights I've been in here. I haven't seen Penelope yet. I've only heard her piercing scream from down the hall, leaving me terrified. How long are they going to keep us locked in here?

Thump. Thump. Thump.

A tear rolls down my cheek. One of them is coming.

As the door swings open, they swiftly lift me, carrying me away like a feather in the wind, destined for sacrifice.

Returning to the torture room, I can't escape the musty smell of dampness and fear that hangs in the air. My strength wanes as I battle the effects of dehydration and malnourishment. I can't recall the last time I ate, and they gave me just enough water for a day to ensure I didn't die.

The lingering pain in my eyes reminds me of the intense spray that was used on them the night before. Please, whatever they have planned, don't let it be that bad. I don't know how much longer I can take this.

The door opens. It's time. They approach me, and I feel one person on my right and my left removing my restraints. Please take me back to my room.

I feel my knees buckle, but they stand me back up.

Without warning, an immense force slams into my thighs, sending waves of pain through my body, like the impact of a baseball bat. They let me fall to the ground, and I don't know what is happening. Again, I'm struck with the same amount of force, so to protect myself, I curl up in the fetal position.

Again. Again. Again.

BANG. BANG. BANG. I jump when there are three loud knocks at the front door, bringing me back to reality. I look — fireplace, couch, door. I listen — heart racing, fridge humming, clock ticking. I move — eyes blinking, fists balling, feet tapping. *You are safe. Do not fear the person at the door.*

I walk toward the door and peer through the glass. The porch is empty.

I'm not crazy. There were three distinct knocks. I run to my purse and remove the pistol. I inhale as I slowly walk toward the lights.

Cautiously, I open the door. Without stepping out, I lean over and look in both directions.

The porch is empty. But as I close the door, something white catches my eye.

It is a piece of paper with three words:

LEAVE TOWN NOW

CHAPTER 21

Before
Christina

The air felt crisp and refreshing as a cool breeze wafted from the lake, caressing my skin. The black sky provided a perfect backdrop for the stars, which twinkled like diamonds catching a ray of sunshine.

Ryan and I lay in the back of his truck. He'd filled it with bedroom comforters and pillows and parked it at our favorite spot by the lake.

KC and JoJo's "All My Life" played on the speakers. I looked at Ryan and he smiled. I leaned over and kissed him.

"I'll never regret taking that wrong turn," he said.

His fingers intertwined with mine, and I turned and smiled at him. "I agree. While running around in secret has been exhausting, it has also been a lot of fun."

He leaned in and kissed my cheek. "We don't have to run around in secret, you know? We could tell her. I'm sure she wouldn't mind."

I sighed. "Of course she would mind. There are two rules with girlfriends: no ex-boyfriends and no brothers."

He laughed. "Is that so?"

"Duh!" I said, striking his chest playfully.

He placed his right hand on my cheek. "I love you, CJ."

"I love you, too!" I kissed his lips once more. His fingers glided through the strands of my hair. He never took his eyes off mine.

"Do you think it will always feel like this?" I asked.

"What do you mean?"

"This feeling — the romance, the excitement. It seems like when you get old, people stop looking at each other the way you're looking at me right now."

He smiled. "I don't think it's because they get old. I think it's because they don't love each other the way we do."

"Then why do they stay together?"

"Adult obligations, probably. Marriage, house, and kids. Don't want to pay child support and alimony," he chuckled.

I gently slapped his arm. "Stop it! They don't stay together just to avoid alimony!"

"I bet a lot of them do!"

"I wonder what it would've been like if my mom and dad were still together," I said.

"You never talk about your dad."

Running my fingers along his chest, I said, "I don't know much about him. Mom just says it was for the best and leaves it at that."

"I mean, it's not so great having parents stay together. You're better off. My dad is the biggest dick on the planet. My mom should leave him. To be honest, I think she already has someone on the side," he said.

"No way! Really?"

"Yeah. I don't give a fuck what she does. It keeps her away from him. Pretty soon, I won't have to deal with his bullshit, either."

I kissed his cheek and rested my head on his chest. "Do you think parents can screw us up?"

"Fuck yeah, they can!"

"So, what does that say about us? My mom's a single parent. Your parents fight all the time. Your dad is a raging asshole — does that mean we're destined to be like them?" I asked.

"I don't know. Sometimes, I think we can't escape it. Like it's bad genes or something," he said, his eyes fixed on the sky.

"Wait. You think you have bad genes? You're nothing like your dad." I grasped his hand.

"Sometimes I think I'm more like him than I'd care to admit."

"Babe, seriously. You're not your dad — far from it."

"There's so much you don't know about me, CJ."

"So, tell me, then! I want to know everything."

"Maybe someday. Just not right now."

"Promise me you'll never stop looking at me like this," I said.

"I promise," he said, kissing my nose.

As our mouths connected, I could feel the softness of his lips against mine. I pressed harder into him, feeling a surge of passion as I shifted my weight on top of him. I straddled his hips, leaning forward and smiling. "I don't want to wait any longer."

"Wait for what? Telling Emily?"

I felt my cheeks flush as my heart beat faster. "No. Wait for this," I said, as I bent down to kiss him while my hands found his shirt and lifted the cloth.

"Wait, are you sure?" he asked, stopping my hands from lifting his shirt any higher.

"I've never been more sure of anything in my life," I said.

His hands released mine, and I removed his shirt over his head, exposing his bare chest and chiseled abs. As my lips brushed against his neck, I felt the subtle rise and fall of his torso beneath my touch. Locking his eyes, I unfastened his pants. He held my face in his hands, lifting me to meet his mouth in a lingering kiss. In a flurry of movement, his hands removed my shirt, unhooking my bra. The night air chilled my body.

He pulled away, looking at my exposed body. "You are absolutely perfect." He shifted his body, laying me down as he hovered over me, and I felt so vulnerable. "Are you sure?"

I nodded, suddenly overcome with shyness.

He leaned down and whispered in my ear, "Are you ready?"

"Yes," I whispered back.

Even though I was nervous, I was excited that I was about to become a woman.

* * *

"I love you," he whispered, waking me up.

We lay there, wrapped in blankets in the bed of his truck, my head resting on his chest. "I love you more," I whispered back.

He kissed my forehead as he rubbed my back with his fingers. The sun was cresting on the mountains, casting a warm glow of orange and pink on the rugged terrain. I felt different this morning. I wasn't a kid anymore.

It was the perfect moment. For the first time in my life, I felt things couldn't get any better.

* * *

After breakfast, he brought me home. We pulled up to the driveway, and from the looks of the house, no one was there.

"Did you want to come inside?" I asked.

His hand caressed my cheek. "I wish I could, baby, but I have to get back home so I can get to work."

He leaned in, his lips meeting mine. The world spun with emotion.

"What the actual fuck?" a sharp voice said next to my window.

I pulled away from him, quickly turning to see who was there.

Emily.

How could I have been so reckless?

How did I let Emily find out this way?

I jumped out of the truck as she turned to walk away. I grabbed her arm, hearing Ryan close behind me. "Emily, what are you doing here? It's so early!"

"I can't believe you!" she screamed.

"Emily, please! Please! Let me explain!" I said, my eyes pleading with hers.

She ripped my arm from her grasp. "Explain what? You fucking slut!"

"Whoa! Come on, Em. She's your best friend!" Ryan defended me.

"You have a lot of nerve!" she screamed, pushing his chest.

"Please! Stop fighting! Let me explain," I begged.

"Explain what? That you've been messing around with my brother behind my back? What is there to explain?" She turned to walk again.

I ran to block her from leaving. "Please, Emily! I was going to tell you!"

She stopped in her tracks. "You were going to tell me? How long has this been going on?"

Shit.

"A while," I said.

"A while? How long is a while?"

"I don't remember exactly—" Ryan started.

"Shut up!" she barked. "How long, Christina?"

I looked at Ryan and then back at her. "Maybe a year."

"A year? A whole year? Jesus. You are a fucking piece of work! You've been accusing me of not telling you my secret, and you're fucking my brother," she yelled, walking away from me.

Tears streamed down my face. "I'm sorry! I wanted to tell you. I just didn't know how. You're my best friend!"

"Obviously not!" Emily barked.

I continued walking after her. "Please, please! I'll do anything."

She stopped and looked at me. Her eyes swelled with tears. "It was bad enough that Penelope is hooking up with my only real guy friend. But you, Christina? Hooking up with my brother is a whole new low."

"We're not hooking up. I love her," Ryan stated.

She laughed maniacally. "You love each other?"

"Yes," I whispered.

"Fuck you," she said to Ryan. "Fuck you, Christina, and fuck Penelope, too! I hate all of you! I never want to see any of you again," she screamed.

As she walked away, the world felt like it was exploding around me like a nuclear bomb. What had I done?

CHAPTER 22

Present
Christina

I hardly slept after finding the note left on my door. How could I? I knew Tranquility Ridge was a small town, and news of my presence spread like wildfire. There is only one reason someone would want me gone — the person responsible for my kidnapping is still here. I feel an anxiety attack brewing. I shut my eyes and inhale.

They're coming. Like hyenas racing toward their prey, the cackling echoes throughout the halls. I am blindfolded and strapped into a chair. I am back in the torture room — where they drag me to humiliate me. I keep reminding myself that I am fortunate, that it could be a lot worse than what I have endured thus far.

The wind tickles my face as they enter the room. My breath becomes rapid and shallow as my heartbeat intensifies. I clasp the chair's arms with my hands. The floors creak as they all surround me.

A shiver runs down my spine as I feel a leather glove graze my face. The laughing continues.

Something is happening — they whisper to each other.

In an instant, a surge of electricity courses through my body, rendering me motionless and helpless. The restraints hold my extremities captive as they attempt to lock out, reacting to the current, leaving me feeling trapped and powerless.

Make it stop! Please! Fear grips me as I try to scream, but my voice is paralyzed. I can't endure this much longer.

Finally, it stops as they laugh.

"Should I do it again?" the deep voice says.

"Yes! Again!"

Suddenly, a sharp, crackling noise erupts once more, causing me to jump in the seat. He holds it close to my ear, drowning out all the other noises.

"Please," I beg. "I'll do whatever you want."

He turns it off, and there is a pause.

"Wrong answer," he whispers in my ear, before driving the device into my torso once more.

I look — ceiling fan, window, sunrise. I listen — whirling fan, crickets, humming electricity. I move — lick my lips, clasp my hands, roll my feet. *You are safe. You are not in danger. You are far from that place.*

* * *

I arrive at the restaurant before Ryan and bring the note.

I sit at the same table, my fingers drumming against the wood in a rapid, uneven rhythm as I await his arrival, my mind buzzing with a whirlwind of theories. My eyes shoot from one direction to the next, scanning the area. I feel like someone is watching me.

I look up as Ryan saunters toward me — exuding confidence with every stride. I have mixed feelings about everything now. The surrounding air is heavy with danger, making me believe that everyone around me was privy to my return, and is waiting to expose me. My usual anxiety has been heightened, and I'm feeling even more on edge. My senses are on high alert as every sound around me seems to be a warning.

I can't breathe.

"I hope you got some sleep," he says.

I exhale. *Calm down.* "Actually, none," I say as I slide the paper across the table.

"What's this?" he asks, opening it. "Where did you get this?"

"Someone left it on the door of my rental last night. While I was there."

"You have to be shitting me! Did you see who it was? Why didn't you call me?" he asks as he puts the note on the table.

"I didn't want to bug you, and I have no clue. I didn't hear a car or anything. I'm like a mile off the road, too," I say, grabbing the note and placing it in my pocket.

He scratches his beard. "How did they know you were there? How did you rent this place?"

"Airbnb," I say.

"Okay. That will be next on our agenda after meeting with Brandon. We can track down the owner."

His reaction helped calm me. He didn't seem worried, and his solution was reasonable. It made sense — find the owner, ask questions, and discover who knows I'm here. The anxiety was washing away like sand in the waves, and my breath was slowly returning to normal.

"Ryan, I don't know how to ask this."

"I think we've known each other too long to be shy. I mean, I have seen you naked before," he says, with a flirtatious smile.

I nearly choke as I spew out my water in a splattering burst in his direction. "Ryan!"

"What?"

"That was so long ago," I say as my cheeks redden.

"Still seen you naked! You can't take that back!" He winks. "So, what did you want to ask?"

I sip my water. "Why do you think Emily thought Penelope was alive? Why do you think she would have still been looking for her in the first place?" I ask.

He relaxes his posture. "That's the million-dollar question, isn't it?"

I bite my lip. "She never brought it up? Talked to you about it?"

He sips his coffee. "No. I didn't know she even cared after all these years. Not in a mean way, obviously."

"No, I get what you mean."

"She took it hard, CJ, those few weeks when you girls were missing. She was helping with the search parties every night — we all were. The whole town. How come you stopped looking?"

That was a question I wasn't expecting. I felt like he had punched me right in my stomach, and I was breathless. I hadn't stopped looking, but this was the guilt I felt for leaving. I promised I would come back and save her. I searched for years the best I could. I followed the news when they had their anniversary stories. I would read the theories the trolls wrote on the internet about what happened. Eventually, I had to let it go. I had to accept that she was dead. If I wanted any hope of living the rest of my life, I had to face the reality that Penelope had died the night I ran out of that house in the woods.

I don't answer Ryan's question. I shrug, and we eat the rest of our meal in silence.

As Ryan drives toward the police station, I start feeling nauseous. I haven't been inside since that fateful summer, and immediately, I feel like I'm seventeen again, wishing I could escape this place.

Ryan turns into the driveway, and I'm surprised at how much the building hasn't changed. The wooden planks are weathered, and remnants of the brown paint and green trim remain. A simple wooden sign hangs above the door with *TRPD* engraved.

We enter the room, and to my surprise, a sense of calm washes over me, replacing my usual overwhelming anxiety. It feels safe here.

Ryan waves to everyone as they engage in pleasantries. No one inquires why we are there; he just asks where "the big guy" is, and everyone points toward a back office.

We walk into a large room with giant windows covered with white blinds. Behind a desk is a man with dark brown hair, a mustache, and wearing a tan uniform. He stands up and smiles when he sees Ryan.

"Ryan, my man! Your message was so cryptic. What brings you in today?"

They shake hands. "Brandon, this is Christina Johnson from high school. She came to town for my sister's funeral."

Chief McCormack looks at me, smiles, and then back at Ryan. "Aww, man. I'm sorry I couldn't come to that. We are so short-staffed." He looks back at me. "Some fuckin' tourists got themselves lost in the woods, so we had a whole damn search party lookin' for them that day."

"Of course they got lost. Did you find them, at least?" Ryan asked.

"Yeah. They thought they could rely on their phone's GPS. In the woods! Gotta love city folk."

Ryan shook his head.

"Anyway, please have a seat," he says as he sits down. "What brings you two in here today? High school reunion? Or official police business?"

I look at Ryan, pleading for him to take the lead. "Unfortunately, nothing pleasant."

"Well, that's no fun," Chief McCormack says. "Talk to me."

"So, when Christina was kidnapped, another girl, Penelope, was also kidnapped. Do you remember that?" Ryan says.

He nods, so Ryan continues, "Christina escaped, but Penelope didn't. My sister, Emily, believed Penelope was still alive," Ryan pauses.

Chief McCormack leans back in his chair and folds his hands on his lap. "No shit, huh. That's wild."

Ryan continues. "Christina has come back to town to see if she can figure out what happened back then."

He squints at us. "Are you asking me to re-open the cold case? You realize this is a tiny department. We only have thirty officers, including myself."

"No, we understand how time-consuming it would be to re-open it. But what if we could look at the case files?" Ryan asks.

"To be honest, when that happened, the department was even smaller. Maybe ten cops, and I doubt it's the type of police work you're used to seeing on TV."

"It would help put me at ease," I say. "I hate knowing the monsters are still out there."

Chief McCormack scratches his head. "I don't know, Ryan. It's been over twenty years. I don't even know where to find that stuff." He pauses. "There was a big fire years ago and we lost a ton of old files. I don't even know what we still have on the case." He looks at me. "And I shouldn't be letting civilians look over the files, you know? It can jeopardize the integrity of the investigation."

"I get that. But, at this point, what investigation? You don't even know if you have the evidence anymore. We won't tell anyone. It's just important to us," Ryan says. "You can go through it before you give it to us, too. If there's anything we can't see, take it out—"

I interrupt: "It's important to me. I have to know. If there's a chance she's still out there, I need to find her. I want to move on with my life."

His eyes meet mine in a sympathetic gaze. "Rachel!" he yells. "Can you come in here, please?"

A young woman comes running in. "Yes, sir?"

"Do you know where we keep all the old files?"

"I'm guessing in the storage somewhere," she says.

"See if you can get one of the other girls to help you. We're looking for an old kidnapping case from 1998."

"Kidnapping case from 1998. Got it," she says. "Anything else?"

"Yes, some black coffee would be great."

She walks out, and he looks back at us. "I can't guarantee anything, but I'll see what we can do for you."

"I appreciate it," I say. "I don't know what we're looking for, but I'm sure it will remind me of something."

He leans forward and crosses his arms over his desk. "So, is it true you couldn't identify the guys who took you? At least that's what I remember the news saying."

"I—"

Ryan interrupts me. "You don't have to answer that if you don't want to."

"No, it's OK. If he will help us, he needs to know, right?" I look toward the chief. "I was blindfolded the entire time. There were rules. They wouldn't give me water or food if I looked at them."

"You didn't recognize their voices?" Chief McCormack asks.

"No. It was distorted. It reminded me of the movie *Scream*."

"No shit. Interesting. You think they were horror fans or something?" he asks.

"That, or they are just psychopaths," I say.

He takes a brief pause. "Why do you think they kidnapped you?" the chief asks.

"That's the root of the mystery. Back then, the cops thought it was because Penelope's mom was the mayor, that I was just collateral damage. But it seemed personal once they heard that I was tortured, so they didn't think it was the mayor thing anymore."

"Hmm. Fascinating stuff," the chief says. "Well, I will let you know when we find those files. Is there anything else I can help you with?"

"Not now. Whatever you can find out would really help," Ryan says.

"Of course. Hey, how's Maddie doing, by the way?"

"Oh, she's so good. Here, look at how big she's getting!" Ryan pulls out his cell phone and starts scrolling through pictures.

"You weren't kidding! She's huge!" Chief McCormack says.

"What about you? How's the family?"

"Oh, they're great. Jonathan just started T-ball, and Jennifer is in her second year of ballet!" He grabs some photos off his desk to show Ryan.

"Let's barbecue soon! Have a few beers," Ryan says.

"Great call. Let me know what works for you!"

"Well, thanks a lot again, Brandon," Ryan says as he stands up.

Brandon shakes his hand and then mine, and we walk out of his office. I'm relieved that he's willing to track down the files, but there's a persistent, dull ache forming in my stomach. It's an uncomfortable weight sitting heavy and unsettled that makes me feel like I am missing something.

We walk to Ryan's car and don't speak until we get inside. "So, what do you think?" I ask.

"What do you mean?"

"Well, Reverend Stanley says he could have been a suspect."

He scoffs. "He seemed more than willing to help us now. Does that sound like a suspect?"

"He could be trying to make it seem like he's being helpful to throw us off."

He drives out of the parking lot. "I think that's a stretch."

"I didn't realize you guys were still such good friends. Makes sense why you were so offended," I say.

"I wasn't offended. I just wanted to use our time wisely."

"So, what do we do now? We're kind of stuck until we get those files. Right?"

"Not necessarily. You say you had followed some podcasts over the years and anniversary stuff. Anything worth checking out online?" he asks, stopping at a red light and looking at me.

"There was this one pretty interesting YouTube channel. I think it was someone local."

"Local? What makes you think they were local?" he asks. The light turns green, and he continues to drive.

"Oh, you know. There are things only Tranquility Ridge people would know."

That piques his interest. "Like what?"

"Oh, little references to where the kids used to sneak out to when they ditched class, the door that was always broken at Jameson's ice cream shop, little things like that," I say.

"I'm surprised people here haven't heard about it," he says.

"I don't think it was like a mainstream thing. I came across some videos on Instagram. Short little videos with links to the website. That's why I never really followed through with it."

He shook his head in agreement. "Maybe we should check it out. It might lead us in the right direction. What's the worst that can happen?"

I shrug. "We can uncover who has Penelope, and they can come after me and try to finish what they started?"

CHAPTER 23

Before
Emily

Knock. Knock. Knock.

"Go away!" Emily screamed.

Her door opened, revealing just a sliver of the hallway. "Please, you can't be mad at me forever," a deep voice said through the crack.

She turned away from the door, covering her head with her blankets.

He walked in and sat on her bed. "Emily, this isn't like you. Why are you acting this way?"

"You know why!" she barked.

"Why is it so bad that we're together?" Ryan asked.

"Because she's my friend! Why did you choose her out of all the girls in this stupid town?"

"The same reason you chose her! She's amazing." He paused. "I love her, man."

She turned and faced him. "You love her now? But what will happen when that's over, huh? She won't want to be around anymore. She'll hate me because I'll remind her of you. Did you ever think about that?" Emily begins biting her fingernails one by one.

Ryan looked down at his hands as he cracked his knuckles. "I think I want it to be a lifetime thing, you know?"

She scoffed. "Forever?! Are you kidding me? You're barely eighteen! This will not last forever."

"How could you say that?"

"Because I know you! You're a player. This is just something to keep you occupied until the next best thing. You watch!" Emily's voice cracked.

"It wasn't supposed to happen. I had no intention of it happening. But I don't regret it, because I know I'll never feel this way about anyone again."

"Oh, save the bullshit."

He stood up. "You can be mad at me all you want. Just don't be mad at her. She fought it for a long time because your friendship meant more to her."

"I don't want to hear it!" Emily screamed.

"Imagine if you were into someone, and you knew your friends would disapprove, and you felt like it had to be a secret. How would you feel being torn that way? Now put yourself in Christina's shoes — you're making her choose between someone she loves and her best friends."

"If she were really my friend, she would've never started messing around with you in the first place!" Emily threw a pillow at him, but he dodged it.

"C'mon, you know that's not fair. If it helps, it wasn't planned at all. It was just an accident. She's not like other girls in this town. She makes me happy."

"Must be nice to get what you want. Not all of us have that opportunity!" she screamed.

His shoulders slouched. "I know you don't get it, and I don't expect you to. But someday, you're gonna like someone that your friends might not approve of, and you'll be stuck between a rock and a hard place, too."

"Get out!" Emily yelled. "I don't want to talk about it! You don't know anything about me!"

"And whose fault is that? You hide away in here all the time and keep to yourself. How is it my responsibility to know what is going on in your life?"

"I'm done talking to you. Leave. NOW!"

He went to speak but turned around and left instead.

Emily rolled around in her bed, still fuming from the recent events. How could Christina do this to her? How could she even be attracted to her brother? He was rude, immature, and condescending. Emily tried to recall how many times she told the group about all of Ryan's indiscretions, yet Christina still allowed herself to be one of them? What was wrong with her?

Emily grabbed a pillow, placed it over her head, and screamed. Ryan's words continued to echo through her mind because she knew how Christina felt. Emily recognized the predicament she was in and how she was a hypocrite. Her friends would never understand how she felt and what she was going through.

Why did her life have to be so complicated?

Why was everything going so wrong? All she wanted was to have a great summer with her friends. While she loved both Christina and Penelope as you would any of your best friends, she kept feeling this pull to Penelope ever since that drunken encounter. Was it just the kiss making her torn, or was it something deeper than that?

Penelope embodied everything that Emily desired — uninhibited confidence, humor, and beauty. Even though she had lost some of her sparkle, Emily saw through that facade. She wanted to bring out the old Penelope — the same girl who protected her from bullies, made her laugh until she was in tears, and was there through every bad incident she had in her life.

Grabbing the pillow even tighter, she screamed once more. Why couldn't she feel normal? It shouldn't be this convoluted. Emily had been trying to talk to Christina for weeks about it. She needed guidance, but Christina was too busy running around behind her back with her brother. Now, there was a chance that Ryan would ruin that friendship, and she would never have the courage to tell Penelope — or Eric for that matter — how she really felt about them. She didn't want to be alone anymore, but now that Penelope had set her eyes on Eric, both of the people she desired were out of her reach, and the growing despair made it difficult to breathe.

* * *

CRASH. The sudden noise jolted Emily awake as she realized it was coming from the kitchen.

She sprang out of her bed and raced toward the disturbing noises to investigate.

As she turned from the hallway into the opening, she felt a wave of anxiety wash over her, seeing her mother cowering on the floor, sobbing and covering her face, as her dad towered over her.

"Stop!" Emily screamed, running and jumping on his back.

"Get off me!" he yelled as he struggled to free himself from her.

"Emily, no!" her mother yelled.

"Ryan!" Emily yelled. "Help!" she screamed, feeling like she would be thrown off her father's back at any moment.

"Stop it! You're going to get hurt!" her mom pleaded.

Emily threw her arm around her dad's neck, doing her best to choke him out. Her mom jumped up and joined in, to protect her daughter.

He squirmed, his body writhing to dislodge Emily as she maintained her firm grip on his neck. With every movement, her body launched from side to side. Her legs were wrapped around his torso as she pulled her right arm with her left hand to cut off the airway. When his attempt at bucking her off was unsuccessful, he scratched at her arms, causing the fresh wounds to sting as his sweat dripped into them. A few moments later, his knees buckled, and he fell to the ground unconscious.

"Emily! What did you do?" her mom yelled, falling to her knees to check on him.

Emily popped up. "I — I don't know. I was just trying to make him stop," she gasped.

Her mom checked for a pulse. "I don't feel anything!" she screamed.

"What do you mean?" Emily asked, panicked. "It was just a chokehold."

"Ryan!" her mom screamed. "Ryan! Come in here." There was no response.

"Where is Ryan?" Emily cried.

Her mom's eyes met hers, tears cascading down her cheeks. "Emily! I can't find a pulse! You killed him!"

Emily dropped to the ground, feeling for confirmation. "He can't be dead!" Frantically, she checked his wrists before his neck. "No! He has a pulse! I can feel it."

Her mom tilted her head, then sighed in relief. "You're right! He's breathing. Thank God!" Her mother sighed, putting her hand to her heart.

Emily stood up, staring at her dad's unconscious body. "I — I'm sorry! I didn't mean it. I was just trying to help you."

"I don't need your help! Get out of here before he wakes up," she said, standing up and pointing at the door. "Your dad will kill you if you're here when he wakes up."

Without hesitation, Emily turned and ran out the door.

* * *

A rumbling engine approached Emily as she walked along the abandoned road. "Emily, you OK?"

She looked and saw Eric. "No. I'm not OK." A tear rolled down her cheek.

He pulled to the side and got out of the Mustang. "What happened?"

"I don't want to talk about it."

He walked closer. "Are you all right? Did he hurt you?"

Emily sniffled. "No. He was attacking my mom. I tried to stop it."

"Oh, shit. Is she OK?" he asked, putting his hands on her shoulders.

"Yeah. It was just bad."

He wrapped his arms around her, and Emily gave into his embrace. "I wish there was something I could do," he whispered.

There was something he could do, though, Emily thought. The entire summer was flashing through her brain. Emily desired a connection — something to distract her from the flurry of thoughts clouding her mind. Maybe, just maybe, Eric could provide the comfort she sought. Perhaps just one moment of intimacy could help solve her dilemma and prove that her feelings were misdirected.

She looked up at him as he ran his fingers through her hair. Their eyes locked in a captivating moment of connection. Here was her chance.

She leaned in; her lips met his with a soft, unhurried touch. As she held his face in her hands, their lips brushed against each other, and their tongues entwined in a passionate kiss. Anticipation coursed through her as she pressed her body against his, feeling her heart flutter with excitement.

He pushed her away. "I'm sorry. I can't."

"Wait, what?" Her heart shattered. "Why?"

"I . . . uh . . . I'm seeing someone."

Rage boiled inside her. "Who?"

"It's not important."

She crossed her arms in front of her. "It's Penelope, isn't it?"

He hesitated. "No, no. It's not her."

"Please! Please don't lie to me. I can't handle any more lies!"

"I'm not lying," he said in a low voice.

"Then what is it? Am I not pretty enough?"

"Emily, come on. It's not like that," he said, putting his hand on her shoulder.

She brought her hand to her mouth, biting a nail. "Then what is it? 'Cause you are always protecting me. That has to mean something."

Eric sighed. "I just can't do this. You're like my little sister."

She felt the bile rising in her throat. Having been an introvert her entire life, kissing Eric was uncharacteristic and took incredible courage. How could he be so careless and hurtful?

"Your little sister? Are you kidding me?"

He tried to grab her shoulder again but she swatted his hand away. "C'mon, Em. Don't be like that."

She turned and sprinted away, concealing her tears from his sight. One by one, her friendships were falling apart, and suddenly, she felt a wrath that she had never experienced before.

CHAPTER 24

Present
Christina

My stomach churns with a knot of apprehension as I sit down, the YouTube video about my life poised to unveil secrets I'm not ready to face. While Ryan and I had history, he is a stranger now. Did I want him to know everything that took place in that house? He'd gone above and beyond since I came back, and I wondered if it was his compassion, or a need to see Emily's work through to the end. I always hated the pitying glances, the whispers, and the way people stare at me after they realize what happened. I can't bear the thought of his sorrowful eyes doing the same.

"So, what's the name of the show?" he asks.

"Hold on, let me check Instagram. I saved some videos," I say, scrolling through my phone. "Found it. Looks like it's called *Terror in Tranquility Ridge*."

"*Terror in Tranquility Ridge*? That sounds like a cheesy horror movie," Ryan jests.

I smile. "Well, I guess it kinda is."

"To be honest, it explains the uptick in tourism over the last few years. I'm sure the anniversary has something to do with it. A lot of sickos out there," Ryan says.

I sigh. "That's a real thing? Terror tourism? That's so weird."

He points at me. "Terror tourism! That's a great way to describe it. In a way, you're like our local celebrity."

I chuckle. "Add that to my resume! Local town celebrity for being tortured as a teenager! I can sign autographs on my *People Magazine* cover."

He purses his lips. "Well, it's not like there's a tour or anything, but people have asked about it."

"I'll make sure to give you an autograph before I leave town, if you ever need to pawn it for something," I say with a grin.

Ryan smiles as he scrolls through his phone and opens YouTube. "All right, you ready to watch this?" he asks as he continues to scroll. "Wow, I wish I would have known about this yesterday. I think it would have saved us some time."

"What do you mean?" I ask.

"Did you ever look at the titles of the episodes?"

"No, 'cause I just saw a few videos on social media. I never pulled up the entire show."

"I thought you said you thought it was a local?" he asks.

"Well, from what I saw on the clips. It wasn't much. It's weird listening to someone talk about your life. I don't think I'll ever get used to it," I say.

"Well, come here and look."

I leaned closer to him and read them out loud. "*Episode 1: The Girls. Episode 2: The Kidnapping. Episode 3: The Escape. Episode 4: What Happened to Penelope? Episode 5: The Suspects. Episode 6: The Cover-up. Episode 7: Will There Ever Be Justice? Episode 8: The Conclusion.*"

We lock eyes. "The cover-up?" we say in unison.

"I am so stupid! Why did I not look at this before?"

"Because it's social media bullshit," he says without hesitation.

"But if Penelope is out there and there were answers this whole time, I'll never forgive myself." I feel nauseous. *Remain calm.*

"We don't know anything yet. Don't get excited. We have to watch it first."

I fill up our glasses with wine. "OK, I'm ready. Let's see what this YouTuber thinks he knows about that summer."

* * *

A cold shiver runs down my spine as the stranger's voice, so calm and detached, dissects the deepest wounds of my past. In this era of artificial intelligence and unlimited access to resources, it's incredible how accurate the host's depictions are. The fear and horror are presented with such accuracy that it feels like this person has a direct line into my subconscious, their words mirroring my deepest fears.

Somehow, the host captured the essence of that summer — the innocence, the possibilities, the naivete. We weren't bad kids; we were trying to grow up too fast. We thought we were untouchable, that bad things didn't happen to people like us.

Despite the warnings, no one ever believes something like this would happen to them. There is no lesson here about how to prevent becoming a victim. Just like us that summer, most teenagers will act impulsively and recklessly, and they'll come out of it unscathed. The statistics were rare; less than one percent of children were kidnapped each year, so I never imagined it would ever happen to me.

We were your typical teenagers who wanted so badly to be adults. We lied about what we were doing and where we were going. I can't recall how many times I said I was sleeping over at one of the girls' houses, only for us to be out all night partying at an abandoned house or business. We were irresponsible at that age. Of all the girls and all the small towns, why did the two of us have to become a statistic?

Until now, the videos had revealed nothing we didn't already know — it was my life story, after all. While the details were accurate, the story had been embellished for a more exciting narrative. He painted me as a gentle soul, extending a helping hand to those who were mistreated. It was a sweet depiction, while not entirely factual. To make it seem as if I was some outspoken savior of my fellow tormented teens was a gross exaggeration.

I appreciated this man. He did something that most people hadn't done yet, at least from what I had read and listened to. He respected my privacy and gave me my dignity. While most articles attempted to dive into what happened during those few weeks in captivity and every disgusting detail of what was done to me, that didn't seem to be his purpose. He wasn't trying to get viewers through gratuitous violence, which was a sure way to make a quick buck. There was something more to it. Listeners already knew the crime had happened. He wanted to understand who did it and why. The host was trying to get justice for me.

"I'm thinking this guy has a crush on you, CJ," Ryan says.

I laugh. "Hardly."

"He speaks so highly of you, like he's a friend of yours."

"He uses a pseudonym and is clouded in secrecy. I couldn't find him if I tried," I say.

"Do you want to find him?"

I look at Ryan. "Do I sense jealousy, Mr. Henderson?"

"Me?" he says, placing his hands on his chest. "Jealous? Never," he adds, shaking his head.

I laugh. "Of course I want to meet him. I'd love to pick his brain and find out how he knows so much about that summer."

"You think he's involved?" he asks, his tone becoming serious.

"I don't know. I guess we'll have to keep watching to find out."

It had been hours since we started watching the videos. Ryan looks at me. "This whole thing is just crazy. How have you dealt with this your whole life?"

I chuckle. "Not very well, as you could tell."

He places his hand on top of mine, and I feel my cheeks flush. "I don't blame you for keeping to yourself. Knowing people have made a living off you has to be weird, right?"

"I guess. I don't know. I'm happy I changed my name. I wouldn't have survived the attention and the strangers showing up at my house."

"I bet you could've had some book deals, though!"

I smile. "My mom got a few offers. But if you had to relive that every day, you wouldn't want to capitalize on it either. I mean, I've done fine for myself, though."

"That's good to hear. Maybe I'll take your story and use it as motivation for my future bestselling novel!" Ryan chuckles.

"Hey, if we solve this thing, it'll be something worth writing about!" I half-smile.

He grins. "I'm going to take you up on that offer someday."

I smile and point at his phone, suggesting break time is over. It is time to learn if there was something more sinister to why the case was never solved.

The video pans to a shadowy figure tucked away from sight, with a microphone illuminated. To his left are giant photographs of the crime scene. The music fades, and a deep voice narrates. "Welcome back, everyone, to *Terror in Tranquility Ridge*. So, we've reached the episode you've been waiting for. Now, let's recap. Christina has returned, Penelope is still missing, and the investigation is pure shit. Even though there is nationwide media attention brewing, it doesn't seem to motivate TRPD or the FBI, for that matter. Who doesn't love two missing white girls? Am I right?

"Anyway, back to the point. The vultures flew in, spreading false news about the town. Yet somehow, the FBI never got involved, and the crime was left to be investigated by a few town police officers, who were way out of their league, running around with their heads chopped off. It seems fishy to me already, but I digress.

"According to the files, the only suspect they had at the time was some goth kid from the girls' high school, Bobby Duke. Once Christina returned, that was enough to satisfy the news for a couple of days. Then, a few weeks later, the Widowmaker started making the rounds nearby, and the reporters left to chase the breaking story. Not much longer after that the investigation seemed to die there.

"So, this pisses me off. The media leaves, and that's it? TRPD just closed up shop and pretended like it never happened? I understand that the Widowmaker serial killer was running rampant in Northern California, and all hands on deck were requested to help track him down, but didn't these girls deserve justice? Penelope was just a kid. How do you stop looking for her?

"So, if you ask me, it all seems strange, considering Penelope was the mayor's daughter. In Episode 1, I would have thought that since Tranquility Ridge had such a small police department in 1998, they would have called in outside resources to help with the search. But they never did. That leads me to a very curious, albeit controversial theory.

"It was brought to my attention that one of Penelope's classmates had a dad in TRPD. Additionally, it was no secret that Penelope was known for her indiscretions around town, which, for any rising politician, is a total nightmare. Who wants a kid running around that can dissuade voters from supporting your campaign? So, hear me out, because I think this is where being in a small town pays off.

"What if, when Christina returned, they let the investigation fizzle out because they were killing two birds with one stone? Penelope was a political liability; a cop's son was involved, and the cops didn't want anyone to know, so they let the whole thing disappear under the guise of sending resources to help track down the Widowmaker. It may sound like a stretch, but trust me, our next guest has some pretty solid theories on the cops being involved in a cover-up."

"To help me dive into that, I have my special guest—"

The video goes black when Ryan's phone rings.

"Hello?" His face distorts with concern. "Coming right now." He hangs up. "Hey, I have to go. Maddie is sick."

"Of course. Do what you have to do."

Before I can say anything else, he is gone. I sit there, taking in everything I just watched. Have I been wrong about this entire thing? Was this some kind of cover-up?

* * *

I drive down my childhood street. Somehow, it still makes me feel small. It hasn't changed much since I've last been on this block. The sidewalks were showing their wear — cracks and bulges from the roots of the oversized trees. The same trees are towering above the road, with a canopy of lush green leaves, providing abundant shade. Memories rush back to me as I pass the neighbor's house that always had a lemonade stand in the summer, which was adjacent to the white picket fence I crashed my bike into when I was six. Every foot of this block had memories.

But I left this town and moved to a large city to get lost in the noise. I didn't want to know my neighbors anymore. I didn't want to have neighborhood block parties or get invited to barbecues. I wanted to stay in my house and be left alone. Anyone could be a predator, and I didn't want to risk being in danger again.

I couldn't bear to stay after that summer, so I did everything I could to flee the place and the people who had caused me so much anguish. This town, with its quaint houses and slow pace of life, was a world apart from the vibrant, hectic city where I had settled down. This was small-town America. Everyone knew everyone. Tranquility Ridge was a place where people felt safe enough to leave their doors unlocked, a place untouched by the darkness that lurked in the outside world. White picket fences lined almost every yard, and the sight of American flags waving in the breeze was a common one. But as I drove down the street, something came to mind: this was also one of those towns where everyone knew your secrets, and my abductors could be hidden beyond any of these doors.

There it is. I park in front of my old house, and it looks similar to when I lived there — a time capsule unfazed by the changing seasons and years that had passed. It's one-story with a wrap-around porch, painted white with a dark gray trim. The only reason my mom and I could have ever afforded to live there was because her parents gifted it to us when they moved out of state.

Looking back, I didn't have a terrible life. I spent most of my time alone with my sister because my mom worked nights to support us. But the time we spent together was good. She was a wonderful mom. She did what she had to do, and I never forgave myself for putting myself in a situation that caused her to almost lose me. No parent should have to endure what she did while I was missing.

As I watch the house, the garage door opens, and a family of four loads up and drives off. I wait, watching the windows to see any movement inside the house. Nothing.

I open my door and look around, but no one is there. An occasional dog bark echoes through the empty corridor. Quietly, I exit my vehicle and walk to the side gate. Unlatching the gate, I walk to the backyard, looking for signs of a dog. The coast seems to be clear.

It is still there.

Near the back fence is a giant cedar tree. Walking toward it, I feel like I am being transported to my childhood. Memories rush back to me from slip-and-slide parties to overnight campouts and gossiping on the trampoline. I touch the bark to feel the etching as I get to the tree.

Pen, Em, CJ, BFF.

Etched less than a month before my life changed forever. I could have never imagined what would happen in a few short weeks from that moment.

One vanished. One is dead. I am the last one standing to uncover the truth. So much for best friends forever.

CHAPTER 25

Before
Penelope

Penelope sat looking at the bruises on her face — her fury building inside as her entire body shook with rage.

It wouldn't be long before her mother used her resources to find out who sneaked out of the house, and she would ruin his life somehow. Penelope's mom was determined to sabotage any chance of Penelope finding happiness, because she was such a vindictive woman.

Penelope was terrified of what her mother would do. Would she set him up or have the police harass him? Would she get him fired or prevent him from getting future work? Politicians have vast resources to enact revenge, and her mother was someone who was known to retaliate. Penelope's heart raced as an overwhelming dread of her mom's potential consumed her.

The sound of a door opening pinged, and she walked to her computer.

I think we have to tell her, sn95lover wrote.

Tell who.

Emily tried to kiss me today.

Penelope felt sick.

She did? Why would she try to do that?

Yeah, she got in a huge fight with her parents. I think it was just a fluke to get her mind off things, but I told her I was seeing someone.

Penelope couldn't pinpoint what she was feeling. She realized she had been careless the last few years, often using people in a twisted game of satisfaction. It didn't matter who they were — boys and girls were subjected to her manipulation. Even Emily fell victim to her prowess, and it was something she's regretted since it happened. The memory of that night with Emily, the whispered words and stolen kisses, now felt like a menacing shadow, casting a chill over Penelope's every interaction with her.

Because deep down, Penelope knew Emily was a good girl. She was innocent, kind-hearted, and reserved. But that's what made it fun to taint that, too. Emily was so pure that it was intoxicating to get her to be bad with Penelope — bringing her down to her level. Now Emily had secrets, too.

However, Penelope wondered if that was what motivated this sudden burst of courage. It was out of character and seemed like payback somehow. Was Emily trying to steal Eric from her now that she'd seen them together at the party? Penelope wasn't the jealous type. Yet she felt the anger rising in her stomach. She grabbed the textbook on the table and threw it at the mirror, shattering it into dozens of pieces.

That bitch.

She exhaled, gathered her composure, and went back to the keyboard.

Did she know who?

She asked if it was you, and I said no, but she was so angry. I've never seen her so upset, if I'm keepin' it real.

Penelope seethed with jealousy, because now it felt personal.

Fuck. This is the last thing I need right now. Let's get the plan in motion.

Now? But what about your friends? I thought you wanted to at least wait until after summer.

Penelope gazed at the shards of the broken mirror.

I know what I said, but mom's probably gonna fuck with you now that she saw you here. Is that what you want?

Well, no. It's just a big deal. I don't want to rush it.

I'm ready now. I don't want to wait anymore.

Is this cuz of Emily? I didn't mean to cause a catfight.

Penelope balled her fists. If she waited much longer, something might prevent him from making this happen. She needed him, and she couldn't risk Emily screwing everything up.

No, it's not. I wanted to do this for so long. I'm ready to get it over with.

I mean, I talked to my boys. They are down. But if we do this, there's no turning back.

With her fingers hovering over the keyboard, she could feel the weight of the decision she was about to make. She turned to the window; her bruise stared back at her in the glass.

Yes. Let's do it. She deserves what's coming. Fuck her.

All right, babe, I'll make it happen. When do you want to do this?

As soon as possible.

OK. I'll talk to them. I think we can do it before the weekend if you're down for that.

Thank God. Good riddance to that bitch.

I gotta go. A lot of work to do. We'll talk later.

Talk soon.

Penelope walked to her bed and sprawled out. Her stomach was in knots as her thoughts spiraled.

"It'll be fine," Penelope whispered to herself. "It'll all work out. I'm doing the right thing."

Her door burst open. "How many times do I have to tell you to put the dishes away?" her mother yelled.

"I guess one more time," she responded sarcastically.

Her mother rushed her, slapping her on her bruise, causing Penelope to shudder. "You are not pretty enough to have such a bitchy attitude. You will go nowhere in this life."

"I'll for sure get out of Tranquility Ridge, unlike you!" she retorted.

Her mom slapped her again. "I will not tolerate that tone."

"Or what? You'll keep slapping me?" she chuckled.

Her mother raised her hand but paused, looking at the broken mirror on the ground. "What is that?"

"Do your eyes not work?" Penelope quipped.

She grabbed Penelope, throwing her onto the ground, the shards slicing into her hands. "Clean every piece of this up, now. If you don't, I promise this will be a cakewalk compared to what's coming for you."

Her mother stormed out of her room before Penelope could respond.

"If you only knew what was coming for you," Penelope whispered to herself as a tear landed on her blood-stained hands.

CHAPTER 26

Present
Christina

There is this feeling of determination as I walk back to my car. I knew finding out what happened to Penelope wouldn't change my life or make up for that summer, nor would it relieve me of the guilt I'd felt all these years for leaving her behind. But it would be a step in the right direction.

Approaching my car, I noticed something wedged under the windshield wiper, a small, unexpected detail that made me stop in my tracks. The hairs on the back of my neck stand on end, and I feel a prickle of fear as my eyes dart back and forth searching for any threat. Is someone following me?

I continue to scan the area for danger. The street is eerily empty with a heavy silence, punctuated only by the nervous whisper of leaves — each rustle making my skin crawl.

I pull the paper from under the wipers.

Don't make me tell you again. Leave town. Now. This is my last warning.

I jump in my car and quickly drive away. I look — white fence, mailbox, trees. I listen — my heart pounding, running engine, music. I move — blink my eyes, tap my fingers on the steering wheel, roll my shoulders. *You are safe.*

I take a deep breath. *No, I am not safe anymore. Stop lying to yourself.*

* * *

I sit in my parked car on the busiest street in Tranquility Ridge, which wasn't saying much. The presence of other people around me makes me feel safer somehow. As I sit there idling, with the windows up and the doors locked, a sense of restlessness washes over me, leaving me unsure of my next move. Do I follow through and keep looking for Penelope, or do I leave town? Why am I subjecting myself to danger if it's not guaranteed that she is still out there?

I don't know what to do.

I stare at my phone, wondering if I should call Ryan. No, his daughter is sick. I don't want to be a burden. I startle when the phone vibrates in my hand.

Your baby is doing good, the text from my neighbor Mary read. *I'm having so much fun with him here.*

I write back but pause when another text comes through with a photo of Thor laying on his back, his feet high in the air, and his tongue hanging out. "God, I miss him."

> *Hopefully, I won't be gone much longer. I hope he's being a good boy!*

Oh, he's been an angel. He's obsessed with blueberries! It's cute.

> *Haha. He loves anything he can eat. He'll eat grass and act like it's the best treat ever.*

I'll send you some more pictures later. Just wanted to check in, so you knew he was in good hands.

I smile, now eager to get home to him.

I appreciate it! Thank you for taking such good care of him while I'm gone!

Anytime!

My heart aches to be back home with Thor, far from this place. What did I think I would accomplish by coming back here? I should leave and forget about all of this.

Tap. Tap. Tap. I jump and notice an officer standing beside my window with a flashlight in his hand.

I roll the window down. "Yes, sir?" I ask as he puts the flashlight in his back pocket.

"Christina?" he asks.

"Yes, that's me."

He smiles. "I thought so. Not sure if you remember me. We were a year apart in high school. Jeremy McCormack."

A flood of memories comes back to me — the parties, the times at the lake, with his brother always talking down to him and embarrassing him. He was always a quiet kid who lived in his brother's shadow. "Jeremy!" I say. "Wait, is it okay to call you Jeremy?"

He chuckles. "Of course!"

I get out of the car and hug him. "You look great. The uniform suits you!"

"Thank you! You look great, too. You haven't changed a bit," he says.

"Thank you! I just saw your brother yesterday. I didn't realize you both worked there!" I say, dropping my arms.

"That's actually what this is about," he says. "I was looking for you."

"Really?" I say as I lean against the car door.

He motioned to follow him back to his police car. "My brother said you were looking into your kidnapping. The girls scoured through storage, and they found some boxes," he says as he opens the trunk and continues. "Brandon tried calling Ryan, but no one answered, and he didn't have your number. So, it being such a small town, I thought I'd cruise around and see if I could find you. And luck has it, here you are."

My eyes widen as my mouth stretches into a broad smile. "They found the files! You have to be kidding me! That's great news!" I say as I put my hand on his shoulder.

"Yeah, there's not much, which is disappointing. Brandon wanted me to go through it with you to ensure that if something substantial, it doesn't get contaminated. Chain of custody is a big deal for prosecution."

"Are you sure you want me here when you do this? Doesn't this violate policy or something?" I ask.

He laughs. "We're a small agency. We don't have the resources for cold cases. I'm sure he told you that. Hell, we hardly have crime. But at least we can go through this together and give you some closure."

Closure. It's like he saw into my soul, because that is what I've been searching for since the summer of '98. "You don't realize how good that sounds. Are you available to look over it now?" I ask.

"There's only a couple of us working today, so if a radio call gets assigned to me, I'll have to leave, but for now, I have some time," he says.

"Where should we go?" I ask as my eyes search for something that'll work.

"I know it's a little clichéd, but that spot across the street has the best coffee and donuts I've ever tasted."

I smile. "Of course, a cop would know about donuts!"

"Don't hate. We all love donuts. I just get paid while I eat them," he says with a large grin.

I chuckle and follow him into a pastry shop across the street. It was like walking into a fairytale. The air was fragrant with vanilla, spice, and freshly brewed coffee. Floral plants hung from the ceiling, and the walls were multiple shades of pink. Inside, the giant glass displays were filled with donuts, pastries, and cupcakes.

"Officer McCormack. Welcome. Would you like the usual?" the middle-aged woman says from behind the counter.

"Yes, please," he says, then looks at me. "What would you like, Christina?"

"Uh, you tell me. Everything looks amazing," I say, peering into the display.

"We have a first-timer here! Why don't you give her something special," he says, winking at the woman.

"I know what you need! Any food allergies?" she asks.

"No, nothing like that," I respond.

"OK, hon, coming right up. Take a seat wherever you'd like," she says with a kind smile.

He walks to a large table in the back corner and puts the box down. He pulls another table adjacent to it. "There. One for food. One for work," he says, smiling.

I sit down, transfixed by the boxes before me, contemplating what may be inside. I could be moments away from knowing what theories and suspects were being considered back then. My hands trembled with nervousness.

"Before we start, why don't you tell me what you remember? Let's treat this like a proper investigation," Jeremy says.

"Uh. All right," I say. "Like all the details?" I mumble, feeling shy.

"Whatever you can remember. I realize it's been over twenty years, but you'd be surprised how fresh eyes on an investigation can really make a difference. Think about the house. The suspects. Anything that stands out. That way, when we see what's in the box, it's fresh in your mind. If we go in blindly, we might miss something important." His eyes glimmered with a quiet understanding.

"It's hard. I remember everything, but none of it is useful," I say.

"What do you mean?" he asks.

"Every single day, there is some memory that is triggered. Sometimes, it was the way I felt — pain, despair, loneliness, desperation, and self-loathing." I pause, looking down at the table. "Sometimes, it was the actual acts — restraint, neglect, starvation, emotional and physical torture," I continue.

He looks at me, processing what I'm saying. "Terrible things happen to good people. We do what we can to get justice for people like you. I am sorry that hasn't happened for you yet. Please take your time. I'm here to help you in any way that I can."

"No need to apologize. It's not your fault. It's not like you had anything to do with it," I say as the woman brings our order to our table.

"Officer McCormack, here's your usual: black coffee with the Nutella and banana donut. For you, my dear, a vanilla latte with a red velvet cheesecake cronut. Let me know if you need anything else," she says and walks away.

"Wow. These look so good. You weren't kidding," I say.

"Like you pointed out, I'm a professional!" he laughs. "Take your time, though. It will be a sugar overload."

"Ha! This thing looks like it can give me diabetes!" I joke.

"At least it will be worth it," he says, smiling.

I sip my latte as he pulls out a notepad and his pen. I close my eyes and try to remember every minute detail I didn't remember as a kid. This is my opportunity to get it right.

"Do you know Officer Swanson?" I ask. "He's retired now."

"Of course I do. He's a legend," he exclaims.

"Really? I had no idea. How?"

"Oh, too many capers to name. Rescued some kids. Also got in a shootout with the Widowmaker when they tracked him down."

I sip my coffee. "A shootout? I never heard anything about it."

He takes a bite of his donut. "Yeah, it was crazy. The guy would've escaped if Swanson hadn't risked his life to capture him. So brave!"

"Wow! That's amazing. I wish I had known before I saw him yesterday."

"I'm sure he doesn't like to talk about that stuff. Cops are usually private about those things," he says, sipping his coffee. "So, what about him?"

"Well, what I was going to say is that when I saw him yesterday, I couldn't think of anything that I hadn't already shared with the police. So, I don't know how any of this can be helpful."

He puts his pen down on the notepad. "I pride myself on being one of the best damn cops in Northern California. I can't say the same for the people who worked here before me. I'd rather do my investigation, ask the right questions, to ensure we're doing everything we can to solve this."

"I hear you," I pause, taking a bite of my donut. "Holy shit, that's good!" I say with a full mouth.

"I told you! Best donuts in California!"

I pause for a moment. "Jeremy, I don't know why they chose me. At first, I thought it was a joke. I guess I prayed it was some kind of prank. You know how teenagers are. But it didn't take long to realize it was real. At first, I thought maybe it had something to do with Penelope, but then it felt like I did something — like it was payback."

"Why payback?"

"It got . . . personal."

"Can you elaborate for me, please?" he asks as he writes notes.

I falter. "I'm tryin' to find the right words." I pause as I tap my fingers on the table. "Fuck it; I might as well not beat around the bush. It started with minor stuff and escalated to trying to drown me. Pretty fucking personal, if I say so myself. What did they think I was? A fuckin' terrorist?"

He stares at me with wide eyes. "Jesus Christ, you gotta be kidding me. How do they even learn that stuff?"

"That's my point. It got intense," I say, sipping my latte.

"You never could tell who they were?"

"I swear I'm not lying or trying to protect them," I say.

"I'm not insinuating that at all. Trust me."

"I never saw them, and they used some device to disguise their voices. Remember how they did that in the movie *Scream*? It sounded like that."

"That makes me think you knew them," he says, writing notes.

"I always thought I might have, because I overheard them talking in another room one time. They were fighting about me. One of them had a familiar voice, but I couldn't place it. I was so delirious at that point, I could've been imagining it."

"You never saw them? Do you know how many there were?"

I sip my latte. "I was forced to wear a blindfold whenever they came into my room. They threatened not to feed me if I ever looked, and I was a scared little kid. Of course, I obeyed them. I was trying to survive. When it started, there were multiple people, maybe three or four. But toward the end, it sounded like just one person. That's why I think something happened, and it shifted. Like the other guys didn't want to be part of it anymore."

"Damn, Christina. I don't have the words," he says. "I just don't understand how something like that doesn't get solved."

"It's ruined my life, Jeremy. I've been stuck in this purgatory." My voice is trembling.

"I bet. But I'm here now. We'll figure it all out. What else stands out? Close your eyes and try to focus on being in that place again."

"I don't know. I guess what I was saying about them not getting along at the end. One guy said they were taking things too far. It sounded like they were fighting each other."

"Do you remember what happened leading up to the conversation?"

"Not specifically. I had already been there for a couple of weeks," I say.

"I wonder why the other person didn't try harder to stop it?" he says as he looks through his paperwork.

"I really have no clue. I hate myself for not being able to remember more information. Like, how did I spend weeks there and have nothing to give to the authorities?" I say, burying my head in my hands.

As I place my hand on the table, he puts his hand on top of mine. "You can't blame yourself. Like you said, you were a kid. I can't even imagine what you went through. No one can be prepared for that."

I smile as my eyes meet his. "I just wish I could help more now. Like, I feel like I'm just failing. The answers are here; I know it. But I just can't seem to make it all make sense."

He offers a warm smile and then sips his coffee. "Hey, how about this? Let's take a step back. Regroup. We'll start going through the box, see what is in here, revisit possible suspects' motives, and break it down further. How does that sound?"

"It sounds good, I guess. Anything to help me find her, if she's still out there."

Taking a bite of his donut, he washes it down with coffee. "Do you really think she's still out there?"

I relax my posture. "God, I hope so. Well, I do, and I don't — if that makes sense. I do, because that means she's still alive, and I wasn't the reason she's dead. But I don't, because what if she's been in captivity this whole time? I can't even imagine—"

He reaches for my hand once more as I choke up. "Please, Christina. Don't think that way. You can't think that way."

"If you ran off and left your friend behind, would you be able to forgive yourself?" I ask.

After a brief silence, he takes his hand off mine and reaches for the box. "No. Probably not, but it's human instinct. You acted how any person in your situation would act," he says. "All right, let's see what investigations used to look like back in the day."

I expected it to be different — more strategic, clear-cut notes and theories. I assumed there would be several evidence boxes and envelopes, carefully preserved, waiting to be examined when the time was right. That's not what fills this box, though. All that's inside is a notepad, photographs, and a couple of evidence bags. How was this all that existed? There had to be more.

"That's all they could find?" I ask, disappointed. "How am I supposed to make a chart on the wall with a string like they do in the movies with no material to work with?"

He chuckles. "I wish that's how it really worked. It would make investigations a lot more fun! But don't be discouraged. This is all we have for now. It doesn't mean that's all that exists, though. You know what I mean?" He organizes the items into piles on the table, grabbing the notebook first. "The girls are still going through storage, so this may be just one of many boxes. It's possibly just a jump-off point. Don't lose hope yet."

I watch him read through the notes scribbled on the paper. I wonder what the theories were and how far their investigation went. Would fresh eyes on this investigation be what we needed to find her?

After a few minutes, he sighs.

"That doesn't sound promising," I say.

He purses his lips and taps his pen on the notebook as he leans back in his chair, contemplating before responding. "Something isn't sitting right with me here."

"What do you mean?"

"I remember that summer pretty vividly. I remember the searches and the media. Even I was out there searching for you. You couldn't turn a corner without seeing a poster or a news van. They even had a citywide curfew. I'd never seen anything like it before."

"OK, and?" I ask.

"And then it just stopped. I'm looking at the notes. They had a few notes about what you said the night you came, but then nothing."

Confused, I respond. "So what are you saying?"

"Looking at these notes, it seems like once they found you, they never tried to find Penelope."

CHAPTER 27

Before
Christina

I woke up wishing that it had all been a dream.

It had been a few days since Emily showed up at my house, catching Ryan and me together. I still saw the way her eyes narrowed into a sharp, focused glare, with her jaw clenched and her nostrils flared. Emily was one of the sweetest people I had ever known, and this was the first time I saw her display such anger and disappointment. Knowing I caused that pain was one of the worst feelings I'd ever had.

I tried to apologize, but she refused to talk to me. Ryan reassured me she would come to appreciate the positive aspects of our relationship eventually. But right now, it didn't feel like it would happen. I should have never let things get to this point. Boys come and go, but friendships are forever. I was selfish and didn't realize how much keeping that secret would hurt her.

I looked toward the door when I heard a light knock. "Christina, baby. Can I come in?" my mom asked.

"Yeah," I responded.

She smiled, closed the door behind her, and sat on my bed. "How are you feeling today?"

"Like I'm the world's biggest bitch," I mumbled.

She ran her fingers through my hair. "Oh, honey. It'll get better. It was just a fight."

My eyes swelled with tears. "But it wasn't, though. She said she never wanted to see me again."

She smiled. "She's a sixteen-year-old girl. She's going to say things she doesn't mean."

I sat up. "She hates me, Mom. You should have seen her face. It was like she caught me cheating with her boyfriend or something."

She put her arms around me, and I rested my head on her shoulder. "I'm sure by your birthday, she will come around."

"I totally forgot about my birthday!" I sighed, pulling my knees to my chest and resting my head. Somehow, that made everything worse.

She took my hands in hers, forcing me to look at her. "Well, let me ask you, sweetie. How important is Ryan to you?"

I sighed. "I love him — well, I think I love him."

She chuckled. "Do you think he's the man you will marry?"

I scoffed. "I'm sixteen, Mom!"

She grinned. "That's my point. Right now, it feels like the end of the world, but the boys you like in high school are far from what you'll need as a woman. He's a sweet boy and I'm grateful he's been so kind to you, but if it doesn't work out, you'll survive it. Somewhere out there is the man you will marry, but if it's not Ryan, your life will move on without him. I married my high school sweetheart, and look, he's nowhere to be found. I'm blessed that you came from that union, but it was never meant to last."

"I don't understand how this is supposed to make me feel better, Mom," I say, grabbing a pillow and wrapping my arms around it.

"I mean, high school love is rarely true love. Some people are fortunate to find their soulmates at your age, but it's unlikely. You're still learning who you are. Your interests will change, and what you want in a man will adapt. But friendships — those are things that can last a lifetime, at this age."

A tear rolled down my cheek. "I love them both, Mom."

"I know. It isn't easy. What do you want to do?"

"I want to be with Ryan, but she's one of my best friends. I don't want to lose her."

She wiped my tears. "So, what if you tell Ryan that maybe you guys slow things down until she's ready to accept your relationship?"

"What if he won't wait for me?"

"Then he's not your true love, honey."

She was right. I had to make a choice, and if he really loved me, he would let me right the wrongs with Emily.

* * *

I pulled the memory box from my closet and poured the contents on my bed. There were so many pictures of the three of us I couldn't remember what it was like without both by my side.

There were letters from each of them we had exchanged in class, ticket stubs, and various mementos picked up along the way. I grabbed a piece of paper, unfolded it, and started smiling. I had forgotten how many times the girls and I would play M.A.S.H. during class when we were younger. I saved this one, stowing it away in my treasure trove of memories. I somehow hoped it would manifest into my real future, which meant living in a mansion, married to Jonathan Taylor Thomas, with three kids, driving a Porsche.

Then I saw the Lip Smacker chapstick, and I crumbled. The same chapstick I wore during my first kiss with Ryan. I fell to the bed, turned on my side, brought my knees to my chest, and sobbed.

This is my fault for keeping secrets.

Had I told her sooner, I would have never allowed us to make love.

He will always be my first, and while it was perfect, the blowout is all that I'll ever remember about it.

In the box, I had dozens of memories of our friendships. There is only one to remind me of Ryan, even though we had been together a year. But there wasn't even a single photo of us.

I had to do the right thing because her friendship was worth it to me. No matter how much that broke my heart.

CHAPTER 28

Present
Christina

I am trying to process what Jeremy had just told me, but the memory of Penelope remains. "What do you mean, they never tried to find her?"

"I don't know how to make it any clearer than that. The investigation stopped. There isn't a single note, follow-up, or anything after the date you were found."

I look — box, notepad, photographs. I listen — music, chatting customers, mixers whirring. I move — eyes blinking, licking my lips, tapping my fingers. *You are safe.*

"Could it be in another box?"

"I hope so, 'cause if not, this is bad," he says, flipping through the notes.

"What do you think that means?" I ask.

"I think I don't want to say it out loud yet." He reaches for the photographs, looking at each one. His pen, scratching against the paper, fills the quiet room as he writes notes on the yellow steno pad. Curiosity consumes me as I wonder about the thoughts racing through his head.

I take a bite of my donut. Thoughts are rapidly firing through my brain of the police stopping their investigation, knowing a young girl was out there somewhere. They have a duty to protect and to serve; how can you give up because one person returned?

"It says here the property records show it belonged to Jason Edwards," he says.

"That's weird. Officer Swanson said they never could determine who the property belonged to."

"No, they knew. It's right here," he says, showing me the deed. "I wonder why they didn't disclose it."

"Wait. Did you say Edwards?" I pause. "No fucking way."

"You know him?"

"I'm pretty sure that was Penelope's dad, who left when she was a baby. She had her mom change her name to Solace when she learned about it," I say.

"Wait." He put his hands on the table. "That doesn't make sense. They checked the records. That would have been an easy follow-up. In this town, there's no way they wouldn't have connected one victim to the property."

"And the mayor!" I add.

"You're right. And the mayor. I don't like where this is going, Christina. I fuckin' hope this isn't what it seems."

"There was this YouTube show that suggested the mayor was involved. I just couldn't bring myself to believe Bonnie could do this. But now, I don't know what to believe. Her daughter went missing, and there's this old, abandoned property her ex used to own, but she didn't think she should check there when she was missing. It's not adding up," I say.

"Unless she didn't know about the property until after it was too late," he says. "They didn't know where you were until you came back. It could just be a coincidence."

"But don't they investigate family members first? Wouldn't that have been something easily found during the initial investigation? I think an absent father and a creepy abandoned house are huge red flags. Do you think he could have kidnapped us? Holy shit, what if it was her dad the whole time?"

"It's a possibility. We can run him for warrants and look up his rap sheet. It's a good starting point," he says, writing notes down.

"But looking at the bigger picture, why would he come back after being absent for Penelope's entire life and kidnap her?"

He taps his pen on the notebook. "Maybe the theories weren't too far off. What if he's a deadbeat, hears that his ex is the mayor, and kidnaps her daughter for ransom?"

"Do you think that's why the voices were distorted? Maybe he was scared that Penelope would recognize his voice?" I ask.

"You said he took off after she was born. Do you know if he had a relationship with her?"

"No clue. But it doesn't mean that she wasn't keeping secrets. She was so weird that year. Everyone was being weird. It's like our entire group was falling apart."

The waitress walks up to us, pours more coffee into Jeremy's cup, and says, "How's everything? Can I get you anything?"

"Oh, no thank you, we're doing just fine," Jeremy says.

She smiles. "All righty, let me know if I can get you anything," she says, turning and walking away.

He brings the pen to his lips, chewing on the tip. I blush when he catches me staring at his mouth. "It's not far-fetched. You were right; family is always the first to be investigated. It's worth looking further into."

I lean back in my chair. "Gotta follow every lead. Worst-case scenario it's not him, but at least it's worth a shot."

He smiles, but I watch his expression change as he looks down at the table. His eyes narrow, eyebrows raise, and his lips press into a thin line, slightly parted.

"What is it?" I ask.

He doesn't answer. He brings the photographs closer to his face — studying them.

"What. The. Fuck," he says. "Were these taken the night you escaped?" He turns them for me to see.

"Yes. Why?"

"I know you had said they tortured you. I want you to think back. Try to recall the tools or methods they used to do that. It's crucial. Just start at the beginning."

I close my eyes and try to drown out the noise. I exhale. "The first time, they forced me to drink alcohol to the point of passing out. Then it escalated from there. I remember they sprayed something in my eyes that burned, maybe pepper spray or something. Next, they were beating me repeatedly with something long and firm — some hard stick. Maybe a bat? I think after that was when they were shocking me repeatedly with something—"

He stops me. "Fuck. Fuck. Fuck. This is bad." He takes one photo and points to the bruising. "See that." I nod. "You know what that looks like to me?" I shrug. "It looks like someone beat you with a baton." He picks up another photograph. "See these little dot patterns everywhere? You know what that looks like?" I shook my head. "It sure looks like taser burns to me."

"I don't know what that means."

"I'm telling you that you were tortured with the tools police carry on them every day, Christina. We have a tremendous problem here. I think this goes way beyond the mayor."

CHAPTER 29

Before
Emily

It had been a few days since Emily's ill-fated kiss with Eric, and she couldn't help but feel like everything was slipping through her fingers, like fine grains of sand.

She didn't know why she had never been more forthcoming about her romantic history with her friends. There was a level of embarrassment that she was incapable of having a boyfriend, but the girls didn't know what she endured at home. Relationships were forbidden by her dad, and even though he was a worthless drunk, she didn't want to feel his wrath, either.

Emily assumed that's why she always liked Eric. She didn't have to pretend that she had a perfect life, because he already knew how terrible her living conditions were. His smile was always warm and genuine when they were together, and she felt a deep sense of trust with him.

The encounter with Penelope jolted Emily, and for the first time, she realized she might be attracted to girls. A spark ignited within her, the warmth of Penelope's kiss spreading through her like a wildfire, leaving her breathless and dizzy.

During that moment, with Penelope's radiant beauty and undeniable popularity, she was choosing Emily, a girl who had always been overlooked. It awakened emotions she didn't know she possessed, a thrilling mix of wonder and fear.

When she kissed Eric, she desperately hoped for a shared moment of connection, a spark of something real like she had with Penelope. For a brief instant, she thought it was happening, but his disgusted reaction ignited a torrent of emotions, making her acutely aware of her mistake. The awkwardness stung, leaving her feeling hurt and even more confused. The storm raged within her, and she knew she couldn't weather it alone; she desperately needed Christina's steady hand to help her through these troubled waters. Why did she have to find out about Christina's betrayal now?

The world seemed to be falling apart around her, and she couldn't understand how everything had gone so wrong in such a short amount of time. It was bad enough that she had feelings for two people who were probably dating each other, but seeing Christina and her brother together felt like someone had poured salt in her open wound. It was a nightmare that gripped her, leaving her feeling trapped and unable to escape.

It didn't seem fair. Her friends were liars, and her family life was no better. The exhaustion of pretending to be someone else was getting overwhelming. Her life had turned for the worse, and it felt like it would never get better. Emily's emotions were a jumbled mess, and she couldn't make sense of them. Her nails were short, bitten down to the quick, and she chewed on them systematically, each bite a quiet, rhythmic sound. Emily knew she couldn't be the only teenager on the planet going through something like this. So why did she feel so alone?

* * *

Metal falling to the pavement reverberated through Emily's room. She peered through the window and watched as Eric collected the items.

"How have I been so wrong about him?" Emily murmured. "I don't know anything about relationships, I guess."

He looked up and waved for her to come outside.

She hesitated, unsure if she should accept his invitation. She had crossed a line that couldn't be undone, and she didn't want to endure any more embarrassment. She shook her head from side to side, but Eric motioned for her to come out once again. Reluctantly, she complied.

He walked over and hugged her. She didn't want to let him go. "Hey, Eric," she said.

"How's everything going?"

"Eh. I've been better. Things have sizzled already for summer. I'm already looking forward to the fall semester."

"You want to go back to school? That's terrible," he said, smiling. "Things must be really bad."

"Yeah, I guess," Emily said, kicking rocks on the pavement.

"What's wrong?"

"You know what's wrong," she said, looking at her feet.

He placed his arm on her shoulder. "Emily, seriously, it's no biggie. Girls try to kiss me all the time," he jested, trying to lift the mood.

"I bet," she said.

"Oh, don't be like that. I won't tell anyone. It's our little secret."

Her eyes met his. "I guess."

"Don't let it ruin your summer. You'll be making out with other dudes in no time," he said.

"If you say so."

"I hate seeing you like this," he said, wrapping his arms around her in a giant hug. "You're better than this."

Emily sighed. "I don't want to talk about it anymore."

He pulled back. "Trust me. You'll get over this."

She half-smiled. "I know. I'm just being a dramatic teenage girl."

"Exactly. Now cheer up."

She smiled with a fake, exaggerated grin. "See, I'm over it."

"That's better!" he paused. "Not that I creep on your house or anything, but I haven't seen the girls around. You guys good?"

She sat down on the retaining wall separating their yards. *Of course, he was curious about where the girls were, specifically Penelope*, she thought to herself. "Nah. I mean, I don't know. Some things have popped up, and I'm not sure we're even friends anymore."

"What? How is that possible?"

She started fidgeting with her hands. "Let's just say you never know what your friends are doing behind your back."

"Wait, is this about what I said to you yesterday? I swear, I'm not messing around with Penelope. That thing at the party was just 'cause we were drunk."

She rolled her eyes. "No, that was just one of the many things."

"Don't be like that, Emily. You guys have been friends for a decade. Especially if you're fighting over boys."

"It's more than just boy stuff."

"Then what is it?"

"I don't want to talk about it." She crossed her arms.

"Emily, I've known you for as long as I can remember. They are your girls. I'm sure whatever it is, you can get past it."

She got up and started pacing. "I don't even know if they would want to see me. They have other priorities, it seems."

"You just have to give them a chance — make yourself a priority with them! How about this? A few buddies I know are having a bonfire tomorrow. It should be a good time. I'll be there. You guys should come."

An event where both Eric and Penelope could be there? Maybe this would be her chance to see if they really were together, now that she knows what to look for. "You think that would be cool?"

"Of course. The more people, the better."

"Where will it be?" she asked.

"The old, abandoned tow yard off Birch."

"OK, cool. What time?"

"Nine-ish," he said.

"All right. I'll see if they are up to it," she said, smiling.

"Well, I gotta take off, but I hope to see you there," Eric said.

As Emily returned to her room, she stood staring at the pictures on the wall. *What happened to those girls? They look so happy. I miss my friends.* The flames of anger toward Christina still flickered within her, yet she couldn't deny she missed her. There was so much history there; it was worth trying to fix things.

Emily's imagination ran wild. She had already embarrassed herself with Eric, but she didn't regret kissing him, because she didn't feel what she thought she would. Perhaps some clarification could come from attending the bonfire. Maybe it was time she showed her friends who she really was.

CHAPTER 30

Present
Christina

What did this have to do with the police?
"What are you trying to tell me?" I ask.

He sighs. "I'm saying I think that someone from the police department was involved, Christina."

"*What?* Why? How is that even possible?"

"We have to think this through." He turns the page on his notepad. "Penelope." He writes her name in the center and circles it. "This all has something to do with her, right?" He branches off and writes *Mayor* and circles it. He connects a line to *Jason Edwards / House* and circles it. "This is one piece of the puzzle." On the other side of the paper, he writes *PD* and circles it.

"When I was watching the YouTube series *Terror in Tranquility Ridge*, the narrator argued that there was a cover-up because the mayor thought Penelope was a liability, and *Oh, my God*!" I slammed my fists on the counter. "I'm so stupid! They accused one of the cop's sons of being involved! How could I forget that?!"

"Who is the narrator? Maybe we can meet up with him?" he says.

"There's no name attached, and he sits in the shadows during the show. I have no idea who it is," I say.

"Damn! That would have been a good lead. Did the host specify which officer? And why?" he says, taking his pen and preparing for notes.

"No, right as we were about to get to that part, Ryan had to take off. I haven't had the chance to finish watching," I say.

He draws a line below *PD*, writes *Cop's Son*, and circles it. He branches off that circle, writes *Access to PD Tools*, and circles it. Then he starts a new circle and writes *YouTube series*, branches off that circle with *Mysterious Host*, and circles it. "Christina, this is much more complicated than two girls going missing. I think we have an enormous scandal on our hands."

"What do we do?"

"Right now, don't say anything to anyone. This is a small town, and word travels fast. I don't think it's even safe to be talking about it in public anymore. If there's a chance our police department was involved in a cover-up, I can't go around making accusations until it's confirmed," he says. "Plus, I need to figure out which kid was involved. Most importantly, why? You understand?"

"Of course!"

He leans in closer to me. "I mean it. No one can know. Especially Ryan."

I hated the idea of keeping secrets. "But he's been helping me," I mumble.

"I get that, but he's close to everyone who works for TRPD. I don't want him slipping up and saying something," he says, leaning in even closer, he whispers, "This can be dangerous, Christina. We have to tread carefully. Got it?"

"Yes," I whisper.

"Good. Do you want to pull up the series? Let's see what theories they had."

"Sure, just a sec." I open YouTube on my phone. "OK, let's see if I can find where we left off."

Just like the previous episodes, the host is revealed as a silhouette sitting down with a microphone. The camera focuses on the pictures in the background and then zooms out to reveal two shaded figures across from one another. The host begins. "So, I have a special guest, but this guest has requested anonymity because of the seriousness of the allegations. We will call him Mr. X. Thank you for joining us today, Mr. X."

"It's my honor," Mr. X says.

I hit pause. "He sounds familiar. Right?"

"Which one?"

"The host. I can't place it," I say.

"I'll have to listen more," Jeremy says.

"Actually, he kinda sounds like you," I chuckle. "Do you know anyone who sounds like you?"

"I'd have to rack my brain, but if I do, I'm sure it'll come to me."

I hit play. "So, tell us, you think you know what really happened to the girls?"

"Without a doubt. It was a setup by the police and the mayor," Mr. X says. I shoot a glance at Jeremy.

"What proof do you have?"

"I was very close to someone investigating the crime. I can't say more than that, but trust me. This person said that when Christina led them back to the house, they immediately checked the records and realized it belonged to Penelope's deadbeat dad."

I mouthed *I told you* to Jeremy.

"No, shit! That would have been obvious, right? To make the connection," the host said.

"Yes. This person brought it up to the commanding officer, and it was dismissed as not being a connection."

"Why do you think that is?"

"My source told me that once they got eyes on Christina and saw her injuries, it changed the entire trajectory of the investigation. This same source said they saw the mayor in a closed-door session with the chief, and once the mayor left, he advised he'd be taking the lead on the investigation."

"Is that a common practice? The chief of police handling an investigation?"

"Absolutely not. Even in these small towns, the boss rarely gets involved in day-to-day operations."

"It was so high-profile. Wouldn't the chief want to be overseeing the investigation?" the host asked.

"By lead, he also meant the only person working on the case. He wasn't just overseeing it; he took over all investigative responsibility. He kept everything locked in his office and no one else was involved."

I cover my mouth with my hand in shock.

"Oh, shit. You're kidding, right? I'm smelling a cover-up," said the host.

"From my understanding, several people told the chief it didn't look good only to have a single investigator, but he refused to allow anyone else close to the case. And you know what happened after that?"

"It went cold."

"Exactly." Mr. X exclaimed. "Jackpot!"

"What about Penelope's dad? Did they ever find him?" the host asked.

"From my understanding, they could never track him down."

"Interesting," the host said. "Any theories?"

"I'd bet my entire salary the chief realized his cops were involved somehow, and they used the Widowmaker case to cover up their lack of investigating."

Beep. Beep. Beep. "Unit 1A2, prowler suspect at 175 Cedar Street. Respond code-three," a voice says over Jeremy's handheld radio.

I paused the video.

"1A2, Roger. Responding from 235 Pine Road," Jeremy says. "Fuck, I'm sorry, Christina. I gotta go." He gathers everything and places it in the box. "Please be careful. I will some pictures of someone and some notes. I think it's that girl you were kidnapped with."

"Wait. What? Penelope?"

"Yeah, I mean, it looks like her."

She told me to find her because she had seen her! "Do you mind if I come to see for myself?"

"That's why I was calling. I figured you should have it."

"I'll be right over!"

* * *

I look — pristine white couch, fluffy blue rug, toys scattered. I listen — children's music, voices, toys clinking. I move — tap my fingers on my thigh, bounce my knee, roll my ankles. *You are safe.*

My heart thumps as I wait for Thomas. Muted footsteps emerge from down the hall, and I feel my hands tremble in anticipation.

I look up as he enters, a brown shoe box in his hands. "It's not much, but I thought it wasn't right just throwing it away," he says.

I stand up as he hands the box to me. "Thank you, Thomas."

"I don't have any answers for you, but I hope it helps," he says with a friendly grin.

"What about you?" I ask. "I'm sure you've had your hands full. Is there anything I can help with while I'm out here?"

He puts his hands on his hips, looking toward his daughter in the other room. "It's been hard, no doubt. But luckily, we have an amazing support system. I'd be a lot worse if I didn't have our family, but they've been by my side the whole time."

"I'm so relieved," I say.

He smiles. "If I come across anything else, I'll let you know. I'm sure there's more around here."

"Well, let me know. I'd love to help any way I can."

After a few minutes of small talk, Priscilla started crying, so I let myself out. Quickly, I walk to my car and sit down. I stare at the box, unsure of what secrets are contained within.

The lid shakes in my nervous hand as I lift it. Lying on the top is a photograph.

I gasp, pulling my left hand to my mouth. *It can't be! Penelope is alive.*

Every essence of this woman embodies her — her confidence, posture, and overall features. This is Penelope Solace.

But how? How is she casually strolling down the street? This can't be the same woman who was held captive with me twenty-five years ago, can it? She looks like she doesn't have a care in the world. This woman seems healthy and thriving. This isn't someone who has been held against her will this entire time.

Where did you go that night, Penelope?
What happened to you?

My phone vibrates against my leg. It's a text from Ryan.

Sorry, I've been M.I.A. today. Daddy duties. Any luck on the investigation?

I hesitate in responding. My fingers hover over the letters as I decide what I should write.

It's been enlightening. But it's too much to text. When you're available, do you mind meeting me at the rental?

I watch the three dots as he types.

That bad? Maddie is doing better. I should be free later tonight. Maybe around six?

Perfect.

What do I tell him? Jeremy said to keep it between us. Can I trust Ryan?

* * *

I am pacing around the living room, biting my nails, when the doorbell rings. I walk over and let Ryan in.

"I'm really sorry about today," he says, placing his keys on the table.

"Please don't apologize! How's Maddie doing?"

"Much better. Her immune system is fragile, so it's always a code red if she shows symptoms. Luckily, she will be fine," he says, smiling.

I smile. "Wine?"

"Sure."

He sits down at the table as I pour wine into two glasses. "I'm not much of a drinker, but it has been a day!"

"I can't wait to hear what happened," Ryan says, twirling the wine in his glass.

"Well, the bad news is that I am no closer to knowing where Pen is."

He sips his wine, licking his lips. "And the good news?"

"I wouldn't call it good news," I say as I pull out some notes I had written.

He looks them over. "What am I looking at?"

"It turns out having fresh eyes is very helpful."

He looks up at me with a perplexed gaze. "Fresh eyes?"

"Oh, that's right. I didn't talk to you at all today. Officer McCormack brought me the box from the investigation," I say, sipping my wine.

"He did?" he asks, surprised. "How did that happen? I didn't know you guys knew each other."

"Yeah, all those times Brandon and you were mean to him and left him behind, we hung out with him. Sweet guy."

"Oh," he says, sipping his wine.

"Anyway, we went through those files today," I say.

"And?"

"It's bad," I say, gulping my wine. "I don't even know where to start."

He reaches across the table and places his hand on mine — my hand tensing. "You can tell me. I'm here to help."

Jeremy's words are repeating in my mind. *Don't tell anyone.* Ryan wouldn't betray me, would he? I remain unsure, wavering on the edge of my decision. I look into his deep blue eyes. I fell in love with the same ones as a teenager, but I'm not that girl anymore. Jeremy told me not to tell anyone about the police being involved, and I understand the magnitude of the situation. Maybe I'll just tell half-truths. I don't have to tell him everything. A little white lie never hurt anyone.

"It all had to do with Penelope. So, it turns out that once they found me, they just stopped looking for her," I say.

"Why do you think that? That doesn't make sense," he says, leaning his chin on his hand.

"Well, there are a few possibilities. But I think they used that serial killer as an excuse to stop the investigation. After all, everyone was scared to death with that guy going around murdering people."

"I totally forgot about that guy." Ryan says, leaning back and sipping from his glass.

"Yeah, me too. I was so caught up in my stuff that I didn't care about that at all. So, while Jeremy was going through the box, he found some notes from the investigation. They had a few scribbles with my interview that night, but nothing else."

"What do you mean?" Ryan asked.

"That they completely stopped investigating once I returned. And we learned from the YouTube series that the chief took over the entire investigation."

He rests his chin on his hand once more. "Even with all the media involved? Seems strange."

"Tell me about it," I say, sipping more wine.

"That's it? Nothing else stood out?"

I shrug. "Well, that was the only box they found so far, but they were still going to see if they could find another one in the storage. Don't get me wrong, it was disappointing, but it is fascinating, for sure."

"That can't be the only thing he found, though, right? What about evidence? Fingerprints? DNA? All that C.S.I. bullshit."

Not at all. It's pretty foolproof.

Nothing is ever foolproof.

Her knee bounced up and down.

You're right, but trust me, baby. We got this handled.

OK, I hope it all works out.

Are you having second thoughts?

No. I'm just ready to get this over with so I can move on with my life.

Are you worried?

I'd be crazy not to be worried. Are you?

What? Worried? A little, I guess. But like I told you, it's foolproof.

I trust you. I'm just psyching myself out, I guess.

She tapped her fingers on the keyboard.

Don't! Pretty soon, all our problems will be gone!

I appreciate you! I couldn't do this without you.

It's my pleasure, baby! It's gonna be bomb seeing how it all goes down.

Talk soon, xoxo, she wrote and then powered down the computer. As she walked back toward her bed, she heard ringing from down the hall.

"Hello?" Penelope asked, answering the phone.

"Pen? It's Emily."

"Hey," Penelope said.

"Sorry I've been so distant. Some shit has been going on at home," Emily said.

"It's cool. I get that."

Emily hesitated before speaking. "Um, I know things have been kinda weird. I think I just need to get something off my chest. But I wanna do it in person."

"Is it bad?" Penelope's chest tightened.

"No, not at all. But I think I'm doing myself a disservice by not telling Christina and you what's up with me. I think it would explain a lot."

Penelope grew concerned. "Are you in trouble?" She slid down the wall and sat on the floor.

"No, it's nothing like that. I just would rather talk in person, if that's cool?"

"You're being kinda cryptic," Penelope wrapped the telephone cord around her finger.

"I know. I don't mean to be. So, are you free later?" Emily asked.

"Yeah. I was planning on calling you guys to hang out anyway," Penelope said.

"I heard about a bonfire at the tow yard tonight. You wanna check it out?"

"Bonfire?" Penelope paused. "That sounds cool. Is Christina going?"

"I'm sure she will. I was planning on calling her next."

"Nice. I can't see her not joining us. Did you need a ride?" Penelope asked.

"No, I think I'll have Ryan drop me off."

"OK. What time?" Penelope inquired.

"Nine-ish."

"Sounds great, see you then!" Penelope said. "And Em, we've all been weird this summer, but we're your best friends. Nothing will change that."

"Promise?" Emily whispered.

"I promise. Whatever it is, we're here for you." Penelope stood up.

"That means a lot. Can't wait to see you guys later," Emily said, and then hung up.

Penelope couldn't help but feel uneasy as she walked back to her room because everything was going according to plan, making this entire thing real. Everything was falling into place. As she stood in the doorway, her eyes were drawn to the many posters covering the walls. Soon, everything would change.

CHAPTER 32

Present
Christina

I stare at the bottle lying in the sink, its fiery glow now extinguished.

How long can I ignore I am in danger? My eyes fixate on the threat written in black marker as my jaw and shoulders tense and my stomach churns with unease.

I look — glass bottle, sink, window. I listen — running water, fridge, Ryan's voice. I move — biting my lip, clicking my thumbs, tapping my feet. *You are safe. Maybe.*

Ryan walks back from outside. "Whoever threw it is gone."

"They must have turned off the sensors, too," I say. "Last time they left a note, the motion lights went off."

"I wonder who it is?" he asks as he looks at me. "Have you had any weird encounters with anyone?"

I shrugged my shoulders. "Honestly, I don't know." I return to the table and sit down, drinking more wine. "Everything has been weird since I came back here."

He joins me. "Can I ask you a question? I don't want you to be upset; it's just something that has been on my mind."

"Of course," I say.

"Is it worth it? All of this? If she's out there, what if she doesn't want to be found? Have you ever thought about that? Why go through all of this for someone who's a stranger to you now?"

I think about the picture I saw of her. The question was valid. Was I doing this for her, or was I doing this for myself? Finding Penelope wouldn't change anything that happened, nor would the closure change my life. Was I holding onto this fantasy that finding her would magically cure me somehow? It's not like I would walk through a door, see Pen standing there, and be transported back to the woods the night of the bonfire, with a second chance at my life.

Why was this so important to me?

"I wish I could explain it. I know damn well if I find her, she won't be the person she was when we were friends. You're right — she's a stranger. I know I'll never be healed. And I realize finding out what happened to her won't change that. But I feel like I owe it to Emily to finish what she started."

He sighs. "Can I be honest about something? From what I remember, you weren't a fan of her to begin with."

I roll my eyes. "I was a teenager. I was competitive, maybe a little jealous, too. She was really off that year. Don't you remember? Really secretive. It wasn't a good year. But I owe my life to her." My voice trembles. "The night I escaped, I gave up. I was broken, and I had lost all will to live. I don't think I would have survived much longer in there. I wouldn't be here today if it weren't for her. I owe my life to Penelope Solace. So, if you ask me why I am going through all of this, it's because she saved my life."

He smiles at me and places his hand on my shoulder. "I get that. So, we will keep looking for her. Threats and all." He reaches for his glass, accidentally knocking it on the table, spilling wine all over the notes. "Shit!" He jumps up, grabbing paper towels to clean it up before it ruined everything. "I'm so sorry, CJ!"

I helped him clean it up, and it's only a few papers that weren't important that were damaged. I take the soiled paper towels and throw them into the trash can.

"What's this?" he asks, lifting something from the table.

I turn and see him looking at the photo of the adult Penelope. *Shit.* "Oh, right. We got distracted by the Molotov cocktail thrown through the window. Um, your brother-in-law called today. Emily had that."

"Is this who I think it is?" he asks, bringing the photo closer to his face.

"Well, I hope it is. I can't be sure. But, if I were a gambler, I would bet my life savings that it is her."

"Jesus, CJ." His mouth is agape, and his eyes remain fixated on the photograph. "That looks exactly like her. Do you know where or when this was taken?"

"No clue. Still working on it."

His eyes meet mine as he puts his hand on my cheek. "Look at you. You might really find her after all."

My cheeks redden as I bite my lower lip. "I can't do it alone. There are still several obstacles ahead of me," I say as I point to the threat in the sink. "But I think we have a good chance."

"Does Jeremy know about this?" he asks.

"No, Thomas called me after I left. I didn't tell him yet."

"Do you plan on telling him?" he asks, bringing the wine to his lips, hovering above the glass.

"I probably should, right? Maybe they can trace where the picture was taken or something."

"It's worth a shot, for sure," he says. "Did you want me to call Brandon? Maybe he can get it expedited, or—"

"No!" I shout.

His shoulders slouch. "You don't want his help?"

Damn it. Wrong reaction, Christina! "It's not that, but I don't want to be a burden. It seems like he pawned it off to Jeremy, so why bother him?"

"I guess," he mutters.

We sit there in silence, unsure of where this juncture will lead.

Ryan breaks the uncomfortable quietness. "I know this may be counterproductive, but what if we took tonight off? We have spent every minute since you've been back focused on finding Penelope. What if we spent one night just enjoying each other's company? You know, catching up like friends do when there aren't missing people and funerals to attend."

"Oh," I say. That's the only sentence I could form at the moment. While the idea of relaxing seemed refreshing, I felt like we didn't have time to waste. "Well, what did you have in mind?"

He smiles. "We have wine. There's a couch over there — a fireplace. I'm sure it has Netflix or Amazon Prime. We can watch a movie or something."

He walks over to the couch as I uncork a fresh bottle of Cabernet Sauvignon. As I stand in the kitchen, I try to gather my nerves. Tremors run through my fingers, making it impossible to hold steady. It had been years since I had dated someone, and for good reason.

It's not that I didn't crave male companionship. Of course I did. I used to be an ordinary girl, longing for the day when I would find love, tie the knot, and have kids. But everything changed that summer. My fears are not irrational. I see the worst in people. Any person at any time can have a hidden agenda — can be a predator. Does anyone know another person's intentions? That summer erased my naivety. It robbed me of my innocence, leaving me jaded and skeptical of people's motives.

I didn't want Ryan to know this version of me. I wanted him to remember the carefree girl who dreamed of moving to Hollywood and becoming a movie star someday. Life was good that summer. Until it wasn't.

"So," I say as I sit down on the couch. "What are we watching?"

"I don't know," he says, still scrolling. "I can't find anything."

"It's been ten minutes."

"You know how it goes. You spend an hour finding something to watch, only to fall asleep fifteen minutes after you decide," he says, smiling.

I sipped from my glass. "So, are you happy you stayed here?" I ask.

He pauses scrolling. "I think things work out how they are supposed to in the end," he says. "Where is the restroom?"

I point behind me. "To the left."

I watch him as he walks down the hallway. I always hated that phrase, "*Things work out how they are supposed to.*" It has this connotation that there is this underlying, predetermined fate. That rationalization suggests that my kidnapping and torture were supposed to happen, that this was the life I deserved. Why me?

My thoughts are disrupted when he sits down next to me. "This is a nice rental. We still have to look into the property owner."

"I guess we'll add that to our to-do list tomorrow," I say, with an exaggerated wink.

He places his hand underneath my chin, raising my face to look at him. "Why did you leave?"

"Is that a serious question?"

"Yes," he says, his eyes staring into mine.

"Ryan, the only way I could attempt to have a normal life was to get away from here. They never caught who did it. I didn't want people looking for me whenever there was some anniversary special. People accused me of having something to do with it, for Christ's sake! Even though I escaped, I died in that house in the woods," I say as my voice cracks.

His eyes are sharp and focused. I know that look. His hand caresses my cheek, his fingers cold to the touch. "You didn't die in the woods, CJ. You were given a second chance at living. It was a miracle. I was out there every night searching for you. We all were. No one knew that place was out there. When I heard you were safe, I dropped to my knees and thanked God." He places his other hand on my cheek. "It's not like you were some girl no one loved. I was there. I could've helped you get past everything. Our lives could've been so different."

"I just couldn't face everyone. The sad glances and whispers were too much," I mumble. "And I was terrified! The kidnappers were still out there. They still *are* out there somewhere! They could be anywhere."

"I'm sorry it took so long to do this," he whispers.

He leans in, and his lips are on mine. It is an electrifying exchange of passion. His hands move to the nape of my neck, pulling me closer, and I can feel his heart pounding in his chest. He continues kissing me, his hands traveling down my back and below my shirt. The touch of his cold hands on my bare skin makes me shudder, and I tense at the sensation. It's been so long since someone touched me this way.

"We shouldn't—" I whisper.

"We both need this," he says, kissing my lips.

"But—"

His lips tickle my ear. "If you want me to stop, I will."

He looks at me, and I smile. I can't resist anymore and nod my approval. His lips move to my neck as his fingers unclasp my bra, moving slowly from my back to my chest. I touch his face, bringing his lips back to mine. His hands move down my abdomen, unbuttoning my pants as his hands explore me. I can't fight it any longer.

* * *

When I wake up, Ryan is gone.

I peer at the dresser and see a white piece of paper.

Sorry, I couldn't stay. Daddy duties once again. But thank you for last night. It was like no time had passed, and we were back in my truck by the lake, just kids being kids without the weight of the world on their shoulders. I missed what that felt like. Please don't let this be the last time this happens.

I sigh. "What are you doing, Christina?" I mumble. Frankly, I am relieved at waking up to a note, rather than a man, next to me this morning.

I reach over for my phone and see several texts and missed calls from Jeremy.

"What the fuck?" I say to myself. "Something is wrong." I sit erect and lean against the headboard, pulling my knees close to my chest.

I read through the texts.

Sorry to bother you so late, but it couldn't wait! I'm still looking into the cover-up, but the mayor definitely was involved.
Thursday 11:02 P.M.

I don't want to wake you up, but things are really spinning up. Talking to Brandon now. I think we're going to get a search warrant for her place.
Thursday 11:37 P.M.

Search warrant got approved. We're headed to her pad now. I'll keep you updated.
Friday 2:07 A.M.

Holy shit! It's worse than we thought, Christina!
Friday 3:07 A.M.

Dude, I can't believe it's been under our noses the entire time! I wish you were here to witness this in person!
Friday 4:00 A.M.

WE GOT HER! Cadaver dogs on scene. But we have enough for arrest. I'll call you soon! WE did it!
Friday 5:09 A.M.

I hate to do this via text. Remains were located. Can't confirm who they belong to, but the mayor has been transported to the station.
Friday 6:07 A.M.

Remains? I feel the bile rising in my throat, and I sprint to the bathroom. I thrust my head into the toilet bowl just as the vomit bursts from my mouth. I take a deep breath, saliva pooling against my tongue, waiting to see if there will be more. After a few moments, I wipe my mouth with toilet paper and flush the toilet, leaning against the wall for stability.

How could her mother do this to her? I can't believe Penelope is really dead. I knew it was a possibility, but I didn't want to believe it. Tears well up as my lips quiver, and I try to prevent myself from crying.

"I'm so sorry, Penelope. This is all my fault," I mumble. I stand up, rinse out my mouth, and go back to the bedroom. I reach for my phone and finish reading the texts.

> *Press conference planned for eleven today. Let me know if you want to be there. If not, we'll completely omit your involvement. But you did it! You solved it, Christina. I think we found Penelope.*
> Friday 7:19 A.M.

> *Call me when you're awake. I want to make sure you're OK. I know it's not the ending we wanted, but at least we know what happened now.*
> Friday 8:03 A.M.

I feel overcome with vertigo and sit down on the edge of the bed. That's it? Was it that easy? After all these years, the person I have been running from my whole life has been Bonnie Solace. How is that possible?

Nausea churned in my stomach, creeping up my throat as I was reminded of one significant detail. If the mayor was being arrested and they found remains on her property, then who the fuck was in those pictures that got Emily killed?

CHAPTER 33

Before
Christina

The lake glistened in the sunlight, reflecting the sparkling water on its surface. Even though there was a slight chill in the air, I could still feel beads of sweat forming and sliding down my back. A sickening churn in my gut and a deep sense of heartbreak consumed me.

I turned my head as I was alerted to tires crunching on the gravel road. *He's here.*

Ryan exuded a newfound aura of handsomeness as he stepped out of the car. It looked like he had just rolled out of bed, with his messy hair sticking out in all directions. His glasses couldn't hide the intensity of his gaze as he peered at me.

He sat beside me, wrapping his arm around my shoulders as he kissed my cheek. "I missed you."

I half-smiled. "Me too."

"I'm so happy you met me here today! I was thinking you were avoiding me 'cause of the blowout with my sister." I don't answer, so he continues, "'Cause I'm not just another notch on your belt, miss! You can't just hit it and leave," he joked as he kissed my cheek, causing me to tense up.

His eyes widened as his brows furrowed. "What's wrong?"

I turned to face him. "We need to talk."

"Uh-oh," he said. His shoulders dropped, and his arm fell from my shoulders.

"I've been thinking, and I can't do this anymore."

"Can't do what anymore?"

I hesitated. "Us."

He grabbed my hands. "What do you mean you can't do this anymore? You just slept with me a few days ago!"

"I know, but—"

"Please don't tell me this is because of Emily? She'll get used to it. I talked to her already, and she'll come around, baby," he said, grabbing my hands.

I pulled from his grasp. "It was wrong, what we were doing. She's my best friend. I can't do this to her. It's not right."

His voice rose: "How is it not right? You're allowed to have a boyfriend, CJ!"

"I know that, but I should've asked her permission, and I didn't."

"What the fuck? She doesn't control me, and she doesn't control you! You don't need permission from anyone!" He stood up and began pacing.

"I'm not saying that we need permission, but I owe it—"

He interrupted me. "You owe her nothing! Don't my feelings matter?" he asked as he stood in front of me, blocking out the sunlight and casting an eerie shadow on me.

"Maybe someday, but right now—" I pulled my legs in toward my chest.

"Please. I love you!" he begged.

"I love you too."

He fell to his knees, reaching for my hands once more. "Then why are you doing this?"

"Because I value her friendship and don't want to lose my best friend."

He started grinding his teeth, and his temples bulged. "So, what about me, then? I was right. My feelings don't mean shit to you!"

"Of course they do! But maybe we take a break, until she's okay with it?"

He threw my hands away from his. "You have to be kidding me!"

"Maybe we just cool down for a bit? It doesn't have to be forever," I say as I sniffled and tears started forming.

"Christina. I don't think you realize how much you mean to me," he said, looking off to the lake. "I — I don't know how to say this."

"Just tell me."

"Fuck, this is embarrassing. You were my first."

"First for what?"

He rolled his eyes. "The other night in my truck. I had never gone that far with a girl before. It meant something special to me. I was waiting for the right person — which was you."

"I wasn't aware of that," I said softly.

He cupped my cheeks with his hands. "So, please don't do this. I want you. I want only you! She will get past this, I promise."

I couldn't delay the tears any longer. "I have to do the right thing by her."

"Dammit, Christina! Do what is best for you! She wouldn't break up with someone for you."

"It's the only way I can forgive myself."

He stood up, peering down at me like I was a child. "Are you honestly telling me I can do nothing to prevent this?"

"There's absolutely nothing you can do to make me stay," I say, shattering my heart.

He balled his fists, and his demeanor shifted. Suddenly, he fell to the ground, striking the soft sand with his knuckles, displaying rage I had never seen before. "I can't fucking believe you! You guys deserve each other!"

He stood up and stormed toward the driver's door, kicking various items along the way before kicking the side of his truck, creating a giant dent. "Fuck!" he screamed, causing birds to fly from the trees.

He turned and faced me before getting in. "Don't you ever fucking try coming back to me. We're fucking done! You hear me? DONE!" he yelled. "You'll regret this someday, Christina. Fucking trust me!"

I jumped when he slammed the door shut, peeling off on the gravel back to the road. The dust settled to the ground just as I began to sob.

CHAPTER 34

Present
Christina

"Can you believe this?" Ryan asks.

"No, I can't," I say, looking at him. "It's too fast. It's weird."

"What do you mean? I thought you'd be happy."

I cross my arms in front of me. "I've been here for a couple of days. We ask a few people some questions. Go to the police department and have them look into it. And after twenty-five years of being a cold case, it gets solved almost immediately. I don't buy it."

Ryan places his hand on my lower back. "It's natural not to be trusting after what happened. They are the cops. They wouldn't lie to you about this. Let's listen to what they have to say."

My eyes meet Ryan's, and I try to give him a smile of agreement. I'm not an idiot. But I will play my part, acting like I am relieved it will all be over. I'm going to do what Jeremy asked me to do and give a brief speech, a bit of a show for the press. Despite my reservations, he insisted he wasn't done with his investigation into the *real corruption*. Jeremy said that we need to make whoever is involved think that we believe them. So, if that means facing my fears and sorting out this charade, I will do it.

My eyes rise to the clock ticking on the wall, and as the hand ticks closer to eleven, my heartbeat intensifies.

Tick. Tick. Tick.

The room's noise dissolves into a quiet hum as I fixate on the clock's rhythmic ticking — triggering the memory of the metallic clang of my teeth striking the floor during my captivity. I shut my eyes and take a deep breath.

The metal restraints on my wrists feel like sharp blades cutting through my bones with every slight movement.

There is a noticeable shift in the atmosphere here — I must have broken some unspoken rule and am facing the consequences. Today, I have been locked in the torture room since he woke me up. He stormed into the room in a frenzy, and his heavy breathing filled the air. With a forceful tug, he pulled me away from the cold, metal chains, with my hair gripped in his hand. Before I could comprehend my escape, he fastened me back to the dreaded chair. What did I do this time?

My muscles spasm, causing the aroma of urine to whiff up into my nostrils. The blindfold feels like sandpaper on my eyes as I sit and listen. Loud, thunderous footsteps reverberate in the corridor, heading in my direction.

The door slams open, startling me and causing me to jump.

Without warning, he yanks my mouth open. I feel a hard, metal tool forced inside, and I scream as he pulls on my molar — slipping from his grasp and striking the floor. The pain is so excruciating that I lose control of my bladder, and I feel a sudden warmth spreading between my thighs.

My eyes shoot open and I'm no longer in the torture room. I look — windows, podium, crowd. I listen — flashing cameras, chattering, cars. I move — blinking my eyes, licking my lips, tapping my foot. *You are not in danger. They found her.*

Tick. Tick. Tick.

It's time.

Chief Brandon McCormack looks the official part today. He's wearing a dress uniform — long sleeves, tie, and hat, with his police gear shined to perfection. He walks to the podium in front of the police station as the cameras flash, accompanied by a few of his officers, the District Attorney, and the current mayor.

"Good morning, everyone," he begins. "We have called you here today because it is important to recognize when justice has been served, regardless of how long it took for that to happen.

"While most of you know our quaint little town for its access to Lake Tahoe during the summer and the fantastic skiing during the winter, it has also been linked to a terrible kidnapping that took place back in 1998. If you recall, two girls, Penelope Solace and Christina Johnson, were abducted that summer, but only Christina could escape. Penelope, unfortunately, was never located.

"As is the story with many abductions across this nation, the media attention dies down, the leads stop coming in, and the cases go cold. Or something else noteworthy happens, which in our case was the involvement in the apprehension of the Widowmaker serial killer. The news neglects to revisit their previous stories, and everyone forgets about it and moves on. That happened here. I am ashamed to admit that we haven't kept investigating this case throughout the years, because if we had, there is a possibility that justice would have been served a long time ago.

"This is still an active investigation. However, early this morning a search warrant was conducted at former mayor Bonnie Solace's residence, the mother of Penelope Solace, who remains missing. Skeletal remains were located, and she has been arrested for the murder of her daughter, Penelope.

"I'd like to introduce Deputy District Attorney Maria Sanchez, who will answer questions regarding the charges."

He steps aside, and Maria stands in front of the podium. She looks professional, with a black pantsuit perfectly tailored to her petite frame. The red soles of her Christian Louboutin stiletto heels draw my attention, and I stare at them as she speaks.

"Hello. I'm Deputy District Attorney Maria Sanchez," she says. "As Chief McCormack stated, evidence was presented to the DA's office linking former mayor Solace to the kidnapping of her daughter. The judge signed a warrant, and when the warrant was executed at her residence, remains were located. There had been an attempt to burn the remains. However, those attempts were unsuccessful, and the sex and age of the deceased could be successfully ascertained. A forensic pathologist determined the remains were consistent with Penelope's sex and age, and the time of her disappearance. With great luck, while examining the surrounding soil for additional evidence, some teeth were found that allowed forensics to send them to a lab for DNA analysis.

"Because of that, along with additional evidence at the residence, former mayor Solace has been arrested and charged with the murder of Penelope Solace. She is being held without bail.

"I just want to reiterate what Chief McCormack said, because it is paramount to our criminal justice system. Time doesn't stop ticking. If you commit a crime, we will find you and prosecute you, especially in this town. I will not be answering questions at this time. Thank you."

She steps aside, and Chief McCormack walks back to the podium. "All right, now I'd like to call Christina Johnson to provide her statement."

Murmurs erupt among the crowd as heads swivel in a fury to get the first photograph.

"Christina," Brandon continues, "please join us."

I look — crowd of strangers, flashing, Ryan's eyes. I listen — murmurs, cameras clicking, beating heart. I move — licking my lips, tapping my fingers, taking deep breaths. *You are not in danger. They will not hurt you. They are just reporters. You've done this before.*

Slowly, I leave the concealment of the front of the station and walk to the podium. I feel like I am seventeen again, on the night I returned. I can feel my hands trembling and the sweat dripping down my back. I take a deep breath. I lock eyes with Jeremy as he stands beside his brother, and he winks.

As I pass him, he whispers, "You got this; just breathe."

I turn to the crowd, and I feel my knees buckle. Using the podium for support, I inhale and pull my statement from my pocket. I look into the crowd and see Officer Swanson sitting in the front row. He winks at me and gives me a thumbs up — helping quell my nerves.

I exhale and begin. "Hi, everyone," I say as my voice cracks. "My name is Christina Johnson, and I was the girl kidnapped here in 1998 with Penelope." The courtyard falls into a chilling silence as my voice echoes in the open air. Everyone hangs on to what I have to say.

"When I left here after that summer, I had no intention of returning. I was taken against my will and tortured for almost three weeks, and when I escaped, people started blaming me, like I had had something to do with it." A few gasps can be heard in the crowd. I continue, "I am sure most of you did your research about what happened, so I won't go into it, but I think it's important to know that things like this happen to girls every day, and they never get justice.

"I spent twenty-five years too scared to come back here. In fact, I spent most of that time locked in my house, completely afraid of strangers and unable to trust anyone because my captors were never apprehended. It took a note from a friend, who is now deceased, to motivate me to figure out what happened to us that summer and to find Penelope.

"I'm one of the lucky ones. I had people willing to help me. Officer Jeremy McCormack took the time to look into this, and with their limited resources at TRPD, helped solve a case that seemed unsolvable. The TRPD gave me a second chance at life.

"I want to thank them for giving me closure." I have a sudden burst of emotion, tears rolling down my cheeks. "This was not the resolution I wanted. I came here looking for Penelope, hoping to find her alive, but at least now I know what happened to her.

"And to her mother," I pause, biting my lip. "I realize now why you were so eager to kick me out of your home when I got back to town. I hope you rot in hell!"

I turn and walk away as the cameras flash and questions are shouted.

Jeremy wanted a show. I hope I gave them one.

CHAPTER 35

Before
Emily

After speaking with Penelope, Emily knew it was time to repair her friendship with Christina. While the level of betrayal she felt was like nothing she had ever experienced before, Emily needed Christina in her life, and had to be the bigger person.

She walked toward the phone just as Ryan entered the house, slamming the door behind him with such force that the walls cracked.

"Dude, everything cool?" she asked.

"Does it look like everything is cool?" he barked.

"No, that's what I am asking."

"Don't fucking talk to me right now," he said, rushing past her on the way to his room.

She followed him. "Seriously, what happened?"

"Get away from me. I don't want to see you right now."

Emily was accustomed to her brother's tantrums, but she had never seen him this upset before. "Ryan, talk to me."

"She fucking broke up with me because of you!" he said, slamming his door shut.

Emily stood there, shocked that Christina would do that. No one ever chose her. *She broke up with him?* Emily bit a fingernail.

The silence was replaced with Korn blasting from the speakers in his room. He never listened to that band unless he was struggling. The last time she could recall him listening to them was the first physical fight he had with their dad, resulting in a bloody nose that Ryan thought was broken.

Maybe Christina wasn't just another fling. Maybe he did like her after all. "What did I do?" Emily mumbled.

She opened his door, exposing a sliver of his room. He was lying on his bed face down, punching his fists into the mattress. The music blasted from the speakers — the bass booming, shaking the walls and rattling the windows. Emily placed a hand on his shoulder, causing him to flinch and look at her. He was crying.

"I'm so sorry—" Emily spoke gently.

"Get the FUCK outta my room, Emily! NOW!"

"I just want to help," she said.

"You can't help!" he yelled. "You ruined everything!"

"I didn't mean to. I just thought you were playing her."

"See, there you go, making fucking assumptions. How could you understand any of this? You've never even had a boyfriend! Don't make me say it again — GET OUT OF MY ROOM!" He buried his head into the pillow.

"I'm sorry, I—"

Before she could finish, he jumped up, grabbed her by the collar of her T-shirt, pushing her toward the door. "I said to get out of my fucking room, Emily!" he hollered, his nose almost touching hers. "I will not ask you again," he said, pushing her away, causing her to lose her balance.

She ran out of his room as tears flowed from her eyes. She knew what she had to do, and rushed to the phone to call Christina. Her hands trembled as she attempted to dial Christina's house. What did she do? Did she get this all wrong?

"Hello?" Christina's sister answered.

"Hey, Nicole, it's Emily. Can you get Christina for me?"

"Sure thing," she said. She yelled for Christina to come to the phone.

"Hello?" Christina said, sniffling.

"Hey, it's Em."

"Oh. Hey," she said, surprised.

"I just saw Ryan, and he seemed really upset. Is everything okay?" Emily chose her words carefully, trying to avoid making things worse.

"Yeah. It's fine. I don't know why he's upset."

"If it is because of me, I am really sorry. I know what I said was fucked up. I'm a totally shitty friend."

"No, you're not," Christina said, sniffling once more. "You had every right to be upset. I should've told you sooner. It just got away from us, I guess."

"No, it's my fault for not being a good friend. I showed up at your house because I've been wanting to talk to you about something, and I overreacted. I'm so sorry, Christina."

"It's fine. I'll get over it."

"Is there anything I can do to fix it?" Emily asked, biting her nails.

There was a hesitation in Christina's voice. "No, I'll be fine."

Emily realized that she had been wrong about everything. Was it so bad that they were together? Would she have been this upset if Christina had just told her rather than finding out the way she had? This happens when people keep secrets, and Emily was no better. How would Christina feel knowing that Emily and Penelope had a romantic exchange? Emily wondered if Christina would react the same way when she finally confessed to what she'd been hiding.

"Well, the reason I was calling was to see if you wanted to join us for a bonfire tonight at the old tow yard," Emily said. "I think it'll get your mind off everything. I already talked to Pen, and she's on board. I mean, she's expecting you to be there. I think maybe it'll allow us to reclaim the summer."

Christina hesitated. "I don't know. I'm not really in the mood."

"I'm sure it'll make you feel better, Chris. You know how much we love people-watching!"

"I don't think I'd be the best company right now." Christina sniffled again, and Emily realized she was about to lose her chance to fix everything.

"Sitting at home isn't gonna make you feel better, girl. You know that," Emily insisted.

Christina sighed.

Emily felt sick listening to the sorrow in Christina's voice. "It'll be so fun, I promise." Emily insisted.

"All right. What time?" Christina asked.

"They said around nine. Does that work?" Emily asked, spitting the bitten nail from her mouth.

"Yeah. You need a ride?" Christina asked.

"No, I have one set up already. I'll meet you there at nine."

"OK, I'll see you then. But I might not stay long."

"Totally understandable," Emily said.

"See ya soon," Christina said before hanging up the phone.

Emily's remorse deepened as time passed, gnawing at her from within. She couldn't pinpoint why this bonfire was so important to her. Yes, she wanted to tell Penelope how she really felt, but the timing was off. Emily had broken Christina's heart, but all she could think about was getting this secret off her chest. It was the secrets that were splintering their friendship, and she realized they had to start being honest with each other, if they were going to save what they had.

CHAPTER 36

Present
Christina

"Christina?" Chief McCormack asks.

I look — wooden desk, computer, Chief McCormack. I listen — ringing phones, police radios, hushed voices. I move — biting my lip, tapping my fingers, cracking my knuckles. *You are safe. It's all over now.*

My eyes meet his. "I'm sorry. My mind was on something else."

"Did Jeremy explain what will happen over the next few days?" Chief McCormack asked, tapping his pen on his desk.

I glance next to me. Ryan is sitting beside me, and beyond him, Jeremy is leaning against the wall. "He did, but I think it went in one ear and out the other. I'd be lying if I didn't admit everything has been a little overwhelming."

They all smile in unison. "Understandable. I'd be more worried if you weren't feeling that way. It's been crazy the last few days. So, we had enough for a search warrant of Bonnie Solace's residence, which you already knew," Chief McCormack says.

"Meaning, we had probable cause that she was related to the crime," Jeremy adds.

"Thank you for that," Chief McCormack adds, rolling his eyes. "The search warrant was enough for us to go to her house, which led us to the remains. Of course, this was enough for an arrest, along with some of the other things found at her house. However, that doesn't mean it's just a slam dunk. The arrest has been made, but now it has to be proven in court."

Ryan places his hand on mine. "Obviously, you have enough that she will be found guilty. Right?"

"It's pretty damn solid," Jeremy says, crossing his arms and standing erect. "However, we are still waiting on DNA confirmation of the remains, which can take a few months."

"A few months?" I say, surprised.

"Yes. Unfortunately, this isn't Hollywood," Chief McCormack says.

My shoulders drop as I shift in my chair. "So, will she be kept in jail, or is she out on bail? How does this work?"

Jeremy walks over, kneeling to my level. "She already posted bail."

My jaw drops in disbelief. "What? How is that possible? She's wanted for murder!"

"She has money. She wasn't a flight risk. The judge didn't deny it," Chief McCormack says. "Plus, I don't put it past the judge to have a sweet spot for her, being that she was the former mayor and all."

"So, if you have money, it doesn't matter if you're wanted for murder? They just let you out? That is insane!" I say.

"Well, you know how it goes. Everyone is presumed innocent, right?" Jeremy says.

"Am I in danger?" I say, looking at Jeremy.

"I don't think you have to worry. She would be crazy to hurt you now," he says.

"I didn't bring this up earlier, but I was getting threatening notes at my rental," I explain. "Someone threw a Molotov cocktail through the window—"

"What? When?" Jeremy exclaimed. "You didn't tell me!"

"I was with her. It was fine," Ryan chimed in.

"I know I should've said something, but it seemed silly at first. I didn't think they were actual threats. Plus, I didn't want to bother you. You were busy chasing down leads." I drifted off, trying to choose my words carefully.

"That changes things. Damnit!" Jeremy paces, frustrated. "We could've pulled surveillance and seen if it was her. That would've kept her ass in jail."

"Let's not jump to conclusions, bro," Chief McCormack says. "We don't know it was her."

"Who else could it have been, then? Don't we *want* it to be her?" Ryan asks.

"I'm just saying we can't jump to conclusions. But I wish you would've said something sooner, Christina," Chief McCormack says, with a slight condescension. "We can't protect you if we don't know what's going on."

"I'm sorry. It's just all so . . . overwhelming," I say. "There's not a better word for it."

Jeremy walks over and places his hand on my shoulder. "I understand. You don't have to worry. It's a slight setback, but we can patrol the area around the clock. Maybe we can get some extra security at the rental," he says, shifting his focus to his brother.

Chief McCormack clenches his jaw. "We can try, but with two people out with pneumonia, we are short-staffed."

"I can do it, then," Jeremy says.

Before Chief McCormack can agree, Ryan interjects. "I can watch her."

"I don't need to be watched," I protest. "I should just get out of town and let things cool down."

"That came out wrong," Ryan says. "What I meant to say is that I can accompany you while you're still here. If we need help, I'll call Brandon." His tone turns snide. "Does that work for you, Jeremy?"

Jeremy grinds his teeth. "Yeah, that'll have to do for now."

"So, what happens now?" Ryan asks.

"A murder trial will take a few months," Chief McCormack says, "because Bonnie's out on bail and waived her time for a speedy trial. So, try to get on with your life. Pretty soon, this will all be over. For real, this time." He smiles.

I look at Ryan, biting my lip. "But she didn't do this alone. Someone helped her. I know there were at least a couple of guys. What about her accomplices?" I make eye contact with Jeremy, and his face turns pale. *Was I not supposed to say anything? Does he already know who the accomplices were?*

Jeremy's eyes meet mine, calming me. "We're working on that. Chances are, she will start singing as much as she can to get a sweetheart deal. Trust me, she won't be the only one going down for this."

"Well, we will be in touch. I'm glad this all worked out. It made this little town look good," Chief McCormack chuckles. "Christina, how long do you plan on staying in Tranquility Ridge?"

My eyes shift from Ryan's to Jeremy's, landing on Chief McCormack's. "I'll take off tomorrow. My neighbor is doggy-sitting, and I don't want him to overstay his welcome at their house. Plus, it's really time that I move on with my life."

"Good," Chief McCormack says. "I'm glad that you came, and that you got the justice you deserved. But I'm sure it'll be nice to be back home and away from all this nonsense here."

Ryan and I stand up, shaking his hand and thanking him for everything. Ryan shook Jeremy's hand, and then I did the same, but he pulled me in for a hug. The embrace was comforting, yet unexpected. Somehow, I knew he would ensure all the parties involved would end up behind bars for this.

As we walk out of the office, Ryan says, "I didn't know you were close to Jeremy."

"I'm not."

"I'm sure they don't always hug their victims," he says.

I laugh. "Are you jealous?"

"No. Not at all. I just wish you would've been honest about him."

I stop and face him. "What do you mean, 'honest about him'?"

"You just seem closer than you are letting on."

I roll my eyes. "Seriously, I think he's just happy he cracked the case. I mean, I had to share some pretty crazy things with him. It's refreshing to see an officer show compassion. Plus, it looks good for his resume. I'm sure he'd like to get out of this town, too."

I walk again, leaving Ryan speechless.

As we exit the police station, the media is still waiting for a statement. It is chaos. They rush me, taking photos and bombarding me with questions. Ryan shields me as best as he can as we rush to his car.

Quickly, he puts the car in drive, and we take off. Anywhere is better than here.

* * *

I am taken aback when I realize he is driving us to our spot. We found it by accident one day when we took a wrong turn on the way to the lake, and the car broke down. We weren't dating then. The other car I was supposed to ride in was full, and I had no choice but to ride with him. It was the first time we had ever been alone, with no distractions or interruptions. It was the catalyst that started everything.

"This place hasn't changed. It's wild," I say.

He smiles at me. "Do you ever think about what would have happened if we hadn't made that wrong turn that summer?"

I chuckle. "Well, I don't think you would have ever given your little sister's friend the time of day, that's for sure."

"It's crazy, right? How things work out. The only time it was just you and me, I took a wrong turn. We ended up in this beautiful spot, and the car broke down. Kinda seems like fate," Ryan says.

"Sounds like it was set up," I say. "Did you really take a wrong turn?"

He chuckles. "I guess we'll never know."

I touch his hand, wrapping my pinky finger around his, still staring at the lake. "I don't regret it, you know? I never got to tell you that summer. We had that huge fight because Emily saw us, and then everything happened. I said things I didn't mean, but I never regretted our relationship."

He places his hand on my cheek, bringing my face toward his. "We were kids. We were young and reckless. But I don't regret it, either. I loved you as much as a teenage boy could understand." He pauses. "I just — I just wish I would have handled everything better."

* * *

Ryan texts me later that day:

Are you sure you have to leave?

> *Yeah, it's time for me to live my life. I can't do that if I stay here. Too many bad memories.*

How about you come over later? I am having some people over for a little party, but I'd love to see you before you leave.

> *A party so close to Emily's funeral?*

I know, the timing sucks. It was planned before everything happened. I just moved into my house so it's a combo housewarming party and early b-day celebration for Maddie. I thought it would be nice to lift everyone's spirits.

I stare at the text. I should cut my ties and go back to my life. What good could come from being around his family?

It'll only make me want to stay. I write back, but then erase the message.

He knows me too well.

I know you are thinking of reasons you shouldn't stop by. Please come.

> *Fine, but not too long. I have to leave early in the morning. I have a long drive.*

I know. I'm not ready for you to go yet, but I get it.

> *I can't stay for long. I'm so tired.*

I get it. You'll be in and out. I promise.

> *Fine, you convinced me. I'll see you soon.*

I put my phone down, only to feel it vibrate once more. It's Jeremy.

You did great today.

> *I can't believe it's really over. I feel you haven't told me everything yet.*

I haven't. It's very complicated.

> *Have you made any progress with the other involved parties?*

That's why I was texting. I'd rather talk to you in person.

> *That bad?*

Maybe. What are you doing later?

I have this thing at Ryan's, but I can meet up with you after.

You two seem pretty close again. It's like déjà vu.

Oh, it's nothing like that. He's just trying to be a good friend.

Just be careful, at least until we figure everything out.

I will be, I promise. I'll let you know when I am done at Ryan's.

Perfect. See ya soon.

I should pack my things and go. This is getting complicated. Ryan and I already did too much. I need a clean break. Nothing good can come from holding onto the past now. I should slip away without a farewell and leave Tranquility Ridge behind for good.

CHAPTER 37

Before
Penelope

"You seem quiet," Christina said as Penelope drove toward the bonfire.

Penelope turned to her, smiling. "No, just a lot of things going on in my mind."

"I was surprised that Emily called us, to be honest. I didn't tell you, but we had a huge fight a few days ago," Christina said.

"You did? About what?" Penelope said.

"I was kinda dating Ryan."

"You little whore! Are you for real? How did I not know this?" Penelope chuckled.

"I didn't think it was gonna turn into anything."

"I did not expect that! Holy shit! How long were you guys *dating*?" Penelope said, with air quotes.

"I dunno. Like a year—"

"A year?" Penelope exclaimed. "No fuckin' way! How did Em find out?"

Christina peers out the window. "She caught him dropping me off at my house."

Penelope cackles. "Poor Emily. I can't believe you got caught. When did this happen?"

"It's not funny. It was a few days ago."

"Maybe she invited us here to kill you," Penelope said, bringing her finger across her throat.

"Oh, my God! Shut up! No, she didn't," Christina protests.

"You never know!" Penelope jokes. "I didn't know you had it in you, Chris! I'm proud of you. That's something right out of the Penelope Solace playbook! You have to tell me how big he is! I bet he's huge!"

"Penelope! I'm not gonna talk about that," Christina said as her cheeks reddened.

"You can't hook up with one of the hottest guys in Tranquility Ridge and not tell me how big his junk is. It's girl code!"

"I said we were dating — not sleeping together," Christina whispered.

"Don't lie to me, you little trollop!" Penelope laughed.

"Oh, shut up!" Christina said.

"Trust me! You're gonna tell me before the night is over!" Penelope demanded. Christina turned up the volume on the radio as "Crush" by Jennifer Page played. "How fitting," Penelope joked.

They didn't talk for the rest of the drive as Penelope continued to navigate the deserted streets of Tranquility Ridge. By 9 o'clock, the small city resembled a ghost town, with only a handful of people out, their dogs trotting alongside them in the glow of the dimly lit streetlights.

Penelope pulled into the driveway of the abandoned tow yard, where none of the cars were in good condition. It was a chaotic sea of rusted metal, worn-out tires, and shattered windshields.

"I don't like this. It feels creepy. Are we early?" Christina asked.

"Maybe there's parking out back, so that it doesn't draw attention to the cops."

"Oh, that makes sense, I guess."

Penelope backed out of the driveway and went around to the alley. The rear gate was slightly ajar, and she entered the premises with caution. The back lot contained a handful of cars as well, their hoods popped open and engines silent, a somber reminder of the bustling activity that once filled the now-abandoned space.

"I don't see anyone," Christina said.

"Oh, look. I think they are inside the building. Doesn't that look like a fire inside?" Penelope said, pointing toward the windows.

Through the boarded-up window slats, an orange light flickered from within. "Yeah, they must all be inside, I guess," Christina said. "I would have assumed the bonfire would have been outside."

"Maybe they just don't want to get caught, since we're trespassing," Penelope murmured.

Penelope parked the car, and they exited, suddenly feeling very vulnerable and exposed. They scanned the yard for evidence of life. "I don't know, Pen. Maybe we should go? Something doesn't feel right," Christina said as the fluorescent pole light flickered in the yard.

"Well, let's check it out. If it's lame, we can go somewhere else. I mean, we're already here."

"I don't know. I don't like this."

"Stop being such a coward. It's just a party. We're just early," Penelope teased.

They walked to the building, their eyes darting around, hoping to glimpse something that would confirm they were in the right spot. Opening the door, Penelope was greeted by the gentle drumming of music playing in the background.

"I guess we're in the right place," Christina said. "Still feels off, though."

The closer they got to the music, the more they recognized the unmistakable sound of Blink-182's "Dammit" blaring from the speaker. Penelope opened the door to where the music was emitting, and they walked in.

"What the fuck?" Penelope said. A trash can sat in the center of the room, smoke and flames rising from it, yet the room remained devoid of any occupants. The music was coming from the speakers attached to the walls.

"I don't like this," Christina said, frightened. "This is weird. We need to go."

"I agree! Fuck this!"

Before she could turn to leave, Penelope was seized by an unknown person, who lifted her and silenced her with a hand over her mouth.

CHAPTER 38

Present
Christina

In a daze, I blindly follow the car's GPS to Ryan's house.

A blend of crackling and hissing noises draws me back. I scan for another radio station to quiet the static. After a few moments, the radio lands on a woman talking.

"I don't think I'll ever get enough of this story," the radio host says. "Isn't it, like, rule number one when investigating to start with the family?"

"You would think so," a male chimes in.

"So, how did they not realize the girl's mom was behind—"

I press mute on the radio. "None of that today," I mutter.

With a quick glance at the GPS, I realize I'm only two minutes away from my destination. Tranquility Ridge used to be a peaceful haven, but now it feels like a cage, and I long to escape. Each towering tree, gnarled and ancient, mocks me with its silence, a constant reminder of how they hid the house from my search team. The sight of every crumbling house, the walls scarred and overgrown with weeds, triggers memories of the worst three weeks of my life. Every passing car is a reminder that one of Bonnie's accomplices could be behind the wheel. Where any normal person falls in love with the peaceful solitude of this place, all I see is the evil hidden in the shadows.

I see the house, and the driveway is filled with cars, so I park on the street. As I walk to the front door, I feel my phone vibrate. It's Nicole.

I just saw you all over the news. How come you didn't tell us what was going on? Mom is freaking.

I sigh.

> *Everything blew up within the last twenty-four hours. I didn't have time. I swear.*

It would've been nice to have some warning.

> *I know. Trust me. Tell Mom not to worry. I'll call you in a little bit and fill you in. I just have to do something first.*

All right. Don't take too long. It's not good for Mom.

> *I promise. If you don't hear from me in a few hours, send a search team! Haha.*

That's not funny!

> *Sorry. Too soon. Talk later!*

I put the phone back in my pocket.

I look — brown craftsman house, white door, rocking chairs. I listen — laughing, faint music, wind chime. I move — cracking knuckles, rolling my shoulders, walking to the door. *You are safe. It is all over now.*

When I knock on the door, a girl about twelve years old answers. She smiles and lets me in. Most people have settled out back, where the tables and food had been set up. So, I remain inside, keeping my distance for obvious reasons. Eventually, Ryan enters from the backyard and sees me.

"CJ! I didn't know you were here! You should have come outside," he says, leaning in and kissing my forehead.

"Stranger anxiety. Remember?" I shrug my shoulders.

"Oh, shit. But these are old family members. Hardly strangers."

I smile at him, but it strikes me he will never understand the complexity of being with someone in my condition. "Don't mind me. I'll hang out here, if that's all right with you."

He looks disappointed. "Well, let me at least tell my mom you're here. She'd love to see you, I'm sure."

He walks outside, and I stay in the kitchen. I stand there looking at the photographs on the fridge of him and Maddie and their life together. In every picture, Maddie's smile lit up the room — cheeky and gummy, eyes up at Ryan. I couldn't help but applaud his dedication and his ability to be such a good father to a child that requires so much extra care.

"You haven't changed at all, Christina," a soft voice says from behind.

I see a woman with short, white-streaked blonde hair smiling at me. "Mrs. Henderson," I lean in and hug her. "It's so nice to see you. How are you holding up with everything? I can't imagine what you've been going through."

She reaches for my hands, holding them in her delicate grasp. "It hasn't been easy. She had been such a pillar of strength when I found the courage to leave her father. And after all those years of trying to have a baby, and then adopting—" Her voice cracks as she peers through the window into the yard. "She never forgave herself for what happened to you girls that summer, Christina. I don't know why, but she always felt like she let you down somehow."

"That's ridiculous. How could she have known?"

"I know, dear. I know." She releases my hands and places her hand on my cheek. "I saw the news, and I am so grateful they caught who did it. I'm so sorry for what happened to you girls. You deserved so much more than that," she says.

"Mrs. Henderson—"

"Please, Christina. It's Donna. We're both adults now." She smiles.

"Donna," I say. "If it weren't for Emily, I would have never returned here. I would have never gone to the police and asked them to look into it. She is the reason they caught Bonnie. She is the reason justice was served. I owe everything to her."

Her eyes swell with tears as she brings her hands to her heart. "That's my Emily. Even in death, she is doing good."

I hug her again, this time holding on much longer. "I'm sorry I didn't stick around. I would have liked to see her in all her successes."

"Well, maybe now that everything seems solved, you don't have to leave. You were such a big part of her life; it would be nice to have you around."

"I'll see what I can do, Mrs. — I mean, Donna."

She smiles and places her hand on my cheek. "All righty, I'm gonna head back outside, but please come join us. My nephew, Johnny, is smoking some tri-tip, which will be done soon. He makes the best BBQ."

"Of course. I'll be right out there," I say, as she walks away. "Oh, Donna. Where is the bathroom? This place is enormous."

"This is my first time here, actually. Ryan just moved in a few weeks ago. I'd imagine it's down the hall," she says.

"Leave it to Ryan to have a housewarming and not show everyone the house," I joke.

"You want me to help you find it?" she asks.

"I'm sure I'll be OK," I say. "If Ryan asks where I went, tell him I'm probably lost in this gigantic house of his."

She smiles, and I walk toward the other side of the living area. I glance down the hall, surprised at how many rooms are down the corridor. Systematically, I check each closed door. Every room has been filled with boxes and moving materials. Finally, I get to the end of the hallway, where there are two opposing doors. I open the left one, which leads to the garage. A fluorescent light automatically flickers on. As I am about to shut the door, something catches my attention, tying my stomach in knots.

No, Christina. You are being paranoid.
Close the door and walk away.
Don't do it.

I am about to shut the door, my fingers brushing against the handle, when I stop and open it again. It'll put my mind at ease. If I don't, it will eat away at me.

I walk into the garage. The fluorescent light hums, drowning out my beating heart — deep breath in and deep breath out. It's just paranoia. Slowly, I get closer to what drew my attention. There before me is a vehicle covered with a large blue tarp. The tarp is caught, barely exposing the bumper, which was dark in color.

All I see in my head is the article about Emily's accident. *Dark-colored four-door sedan, window tint, front-end damage. No further information.*

Stop being so suspicious of everyone, I think. But why is it covered in the garage?

I walk around to the front of the car and lift the tarp.

The sudden dizziness causes my knees to give way and the room blurs. The windshield is shattered — blood and hair stuck in the shards of glass, and the hood still has the imprint of a body.

Ryan killed Emily.

I look — blue tarp, dark vehicle, blood. There is so much blood. I listen — humming lights, drumming chest, intensified breaths. I move — place my hands on my knees, tap my fingers, take deep breaths. *You are—*

A voice behind me disrupts my thoughts. "You just couldn't leave it alone, could you?"

I turn, shocked I didn't hear him come in. "What did you do, Ryan?"

Before he could answer, he strikes me with something. Suddenly, all I see is blackness.

CHAPTER 39

Before
Christina

Without warning, a powerful force came from behind, lifting me and clamping a hand over my mouth. In a frenzy, I flailed my legs and tried to scream, but my captor's overpowering strength rendered my efforts futile. As I turned my head toward Penelope, all I could hear were her panicked, muted shrieks in the darkness. Suddenly, a rough material was placed over my eyes. Tape firmly pressed against my mouth made it impossible to scream.

My heart thudded violently against my chest as my shallow and rapid breaths made me lightheaded. I attempted to scratch my captor, only to realize that he had taken precautions by wearing gloves and long sleeves. The vice-like grip of his arm constricted my body, and it felt impossible to move.

I was terrified.

I felt the cold, unforgiving restraints placed around my wrists. In that moment, the gravity of the situation became all too clear.

I was being kidnapped.

As they brought me outside, the air shifted from warm and stuffy to a crisp chill. There was a soft purr of an idling engine accompanied by Penelope's muffled cries. They were taking both of us.

I continued trying to kick, but nothing worked. Another person grabbed my ankles as someone else, holding onto my shoulders, laid me horizontal. Out of nowhere, I was catapulted into the air, feeling a momentary loss of gravity, before crashing down onto a hard surface. I grunted.

A strong vibration shook the ground beneath us, and tires rotating against the pavement signaled we were in motion. Penelope was screaming, and I tried to roll until I felt her. As we huddled in the truck bed, our bodies pressed against each other, the sense of urgency grew, the seconds ticking away, unsure of how long we had left.

For the first time in my life, I felt legitimate fear. My breaths became shallow and rapid as adrenaline flooded my system. My muscles tensed, my hands were clammy, and my thoughts were hijacked by every single worst-case scenario possible. Penelope's cries were muted, and while our bodies were touching, I felt like she was a million miles away. I knew something was off about that place, but I never could have predicted this.

Time ceased to exist for me. I was completely absorbed in the present. Every bump and jolt of the rough terrain reverberated through my body. The wind rushed past, whipping my hair, and carrying the scents of dirt and pine kicked up by the tires. Should I try to jump?

I felt paralyzed. I should try to escape, but what if this was just some kind of cruel joke? What if it's not what it seems, and I accidentally get run over after escaping from the bed?

The truck turned, and I rolled and struck the truck's side; I grunted again. The truck halted. Everything was quiet. *What's happening?*

My body tensed with the shutting doors. Footsteps rushed toward me. Suddenly, powerful iron grips pulled me from the truck bed, hauled me up, and carried me into the unknown.

I trembled with fear, my tears caught in my blindfold. Each footstep was heavy and deliberate and reverberated in an enclosed space, making me think this place was empty inside.

After a few moments, they stopped, and their footsteps were replaced by a gentle creaking. Without warning, I was heaved into the air and landed on the hard floor, knocking the wind out of me. The door slammed, followed by a sharp, mechanical click.

I am locked in here. This isn't a joke. I have been kidnapped.

CHAPTER 40

Present
Christina

My eyes adjust to the dark room. The floor is littered with dirt and leaves and smells like mold and decay. I know this place.

How the fuck did I end up back here?

I try to move, but I am handcuffed to a rod on the ground. I lean closer to the wall. While they're faint, I can see the etchings from when I was here last.

I am back in the white house in the woods.

I hyperventilate. I look — etches on the wall, door, wooden floor. I listen — silence. I listen again — breathing, heart racing, metal clinking against metal. I move — pull on the handcuffs, pull my body forward, roll my body back and forth. *You are not safe. How did this happen?*

I scream as loud as I can, but it is useless. I know no one can hear me. I have been down this road before. How long will they keep me in here this time?

Ryan? How could Ryan be behind this? I thought he loved me all those years ago.

Why?

How can I be so stupid?

How could he kill his sister? Did she know he was involved somehow?

I scream again.

In the distance, there is a howl of an engine and tires on the dirt road. I am seventeen again; that foreboding sense of dread returns. I'm sweating; my pulse is racing. I know what's coming.

Please, don't take me back to the torture room.

Only now, I know who he is. I don't think I'm escaping this time.

The engine stops, and the car door slams. I listen.

Thud. Thud. Thud. Those footsteps. It was the same walk. The same gait. It had always been Ryan.

The door opens, and he stands there.

Whatever feelings I had for him have disintegrated. No longer can I see Ryan's sweet smile or remember the way he made my heart flutter. The memories of how he'd tuck my hair behind my ear or wrap his pinky around mine have disappeared. All I see is the dark shapes beyond the blindfold, accompanied by the electronic voice of the modifier.

How did I fall in love with a monster?

There is a vulnerability now, being chained in this room. No longer am I an adult, but a kid waiting for her punishment — her torture. He stands over me as I wait for the unknown.

"Talk about déjà vu. Am I right, CJ?"

"Well, I could never look at you, so this is a first for me," I say.

"You got a point there," he says. He turns and sits on the floor, some distance from me.

"Why? How could you do all that to me, Ryan? You ruined my life!" I yell.

"It's complicated."

"Complicated? There is nothing complicated about it! You're a fuckin' psychopath!" I scream.

"There's no need to call me names, CJ. After all our history, I think we can be civilized toward each other."

"What about Emily, huh? How could you kill your sister?"

He brings his legs to his chest, hugging them with his arms. "To be honest, it was never supposed to happen this way. You can blame Penelope for all of it."

I scoff. "Bullshit. She would *never* contribute to this."

"Oh, precious little Penelope. She wasn't a very good friend, you know. She was willing to let you suffer to benefit her. Isn't it convenient that she was never found?"

"Wh—What?" I stutter. "They just found her body at her mom's house! You don't know what you're talking about."

He laughs. "Did they, though? Was that really Penelope? Hmm? Maybe she wasn't so innocent after all."

"No. I still call bullshit. There's no way they would have arrested her mom if it wasn't her!"

"I guess we'll have to wait and see."

"No!" I yell. "She was with me here, being tortured. I heard her screaming, too."

His gaze is mischievous. "But were those screams real? Now, that is the real question!"

The room seems to tilt and spin, leaving me disoriented. I want to vomit, cry, scream — all of it at the same time. I never saw her because they kept us apart. There were those few times she yelled to me from down the hall when no one else was here, but there were days on end I could have sworn it was only me in here. Was she part of this entire plan? Was I the only victim?

I feel like someone had gut-punched me. I can't breathe.

"But why?" I mumble.

Before he can answer, his phone rings. "Oh, gotta take this," he says, putting his pointer finger up. "Yeah, I know . . . Bro, it's not my fault . . . You're just as much to blame as I am." He listens for a while before muttering and hanging up. "Sorry about that. Where were we?"

I yank on the restraints — the handcuffs rattling violently as I twisted my wrists, trying to escape.

Ryan laughs. "It's no use, CJ. You're not getting out of here. So, where were we?"

"You were trying to convince me that Penelope was involved," I say, breathing heavily.

"Ah, that's right. Seriously, CJ, it's not rocket science. You're a smart girl. If you wanted to disappear, wouldn't someone need to be an actual victim? Have someone to corroborate the chain of events?"

The bile rises in my throat, but I choke it down. "I still don't believe you. She wouldn't let you guys torture me. We were best friends."

He laughs. "You act like friendships prevent people from doing what's best for themselves. It's no different from you running around with me behind Emily's back. You knew it was wrong, but you did it anyway."

"That's different," I mumble.

"Is it, though?"

"Yes, it is!" I scream at him.

"Whatever makes you sleep at night."

"I was fucking waterboarded. That seems pretty excessive," I yell. "There's no way Penelope would have allowed you to *waterboard* me, Ryan!"

He nods his head in agreement. "Okay, you're right. I agree. She didn't know about that part. For that, I will apologize."

"How could you do that to me? After all we had been through that summer! I could've *died*."

"You're right. It was a terrible thing, but it's in the past. Time to move on," Ryan says.

"I can't believe you. You're a fucking monster," I say, shaking my head.

He looks down, almost as if he is disgusted at realizing his actions. "It was never meant to happen. That was never the plan."

I yank on the handcuffs, the clinking startling Ryan. "What the hell, Ryan? What happened? What made you do that to me?"

He doesn't answer.

"What you did to me is deplorable. Someday, I could forgive you for that. But Emily? Your own sister? How do you look yourself in the mirror? You stole Maddie's aunt from her to cover your own ass."

He pulls his knees to his chest again, and as he tries to speak, he breaks down. Tears stream down his face. He exhales. "I tried to get her to stop. Every time she brought up your kidnapping, Christina, I tried to redirect her. I'd tell her it was in the past, and what good would it do? But she kept saying she was responsible, because Eric told her about the bonfire, and she wanted you all to go. She was tired of all the secrets, and wanted to share hers with you guys."

"What secret?" I say, trying to remember what she was going through that summer.

"Apparently, she had a thing for Penelope."

"A thing for Penelope?" I say, puzzled.

"Yeah, she thought she may have had feelings for Penelope, I guess. She told me Penelope had kissed her one night, and she wanted to confront her about her complicated feelings. That's why she all wanted you guys to go to the tow yard. She just didn't realize Penelope had other plans for you guys that night."

"Wait, what? Penelope kissed her? I thought she was in love with her neighbor, and that she was jealous of Pen and him hooking up?" I ask, trying to put the pieces together in my head.

"Stick with the story, CJ," he says, sarcastically. "She liked both of them. She was confused."

"But why didn't she tell me? That's something I could've helped her with."

"Because you were too busy running around with me that summer, remember?"

"I had no idea," I whisper, disappointed in myself for not knowing any of this.

"How could you? She never got the chance to talk to you guys about it," he said, wiping his cheeks.

The world feels heavy. I can't fathom how lonely it must have felt for Emily. She must have been so scared, confused, and alone. It all makes sense how she pulled away when I got back — this whole time, she thought she was the reason we were kidnapped.

"You still haven't explained one thing," I say.

"What is that?" he asks, annoyed.

"Why did you kill Emily?"

"Isn't it obvious, CJ?" Ryan's voice cracks.

"No. Enlighten me," I say.

"Because I am all Maddie has in the world, Christina! She needs me! I can't abandon her like her mother did. I can't go to prison. I couldn't let Emily keep digging into it. I did it for Maddie!" He buries his face into his hands.

I shake my head. "So, you committed murder and set up an innocent person instead?"

"Oh, she was hardly innocent, and you know that. She was a fucking bitch. The minute she knew Penelope was missing, she used that for her career — a career that went nowhere! Bonnie knew Penelope was a political liability, and was fine if she never returned."

I shake my head. "What the fuck is wrong with everyone in this godforsaken town!"

"I think people just look out for themselves. Survival of the fittest, you know."

I sigh, overwhelmed by the revelation overload I've just received. "So, what now? What if I just drop it? Leave town? I won't tell anyone. I'll take it to the grave."

He laughs maniacally. "It's too late. I tried to do the same thing with Emily, and you guys couldn't take a hint. I can't let you go. I have to do what's best for Maddie."

"Did Emily know you were behind this?"

"Of course not! But we did this shit as kids. She would have figured it out if she kept digging. I couldn't risk it! Don't you see that?"

"So, you're going to murder me?"

He stands up. "I told you before. I will do whatever is necessary to protect my family."

I can't believe I am going to die in this house. "How are you going to do it?" I whisper.

He leans down so that I can feel his breath on my lips. "There's a part of me that still loves you. I always will. I will do this so you don't feel pain."

"I don't get it! Why did you insist on trying to help me and keeping me in town? I could've been gone! Why did you ask me to come over?"

"I don't know. At first, I was just trying to mislead you and distract you. But the more I was with you, I liked your company. I mean, *now* I regret inviting you, but with so many people at the house, I never imagined you'd go snooping around. I assumed you'd be done with that. My bad," he says, shrugging.

"Ryan, I mean it. I'll go back and disappear. You're right. The case has been solved. I can let it go now. I'll just hide. No one has to know," I beg, tears forming.

"But I'll know. I'll never rest knowing that you might come back for me. For Maddie. I can't risk it!"

"Please. I beg of you. I don't want to die in this house. I'd never let anything happen to your daughter. She's innocent in all of this."

He leans in, kissing my cheek. "It's too late. You made your choice when you decided to be nosy," he whispers in my ear.

"I'm sorry," I plead. "You don't have to do this. You can right your conscience."

His temples bulge as he grinds his teeth. "I'm done talking about this." He releases me from the rod, leaving one wrist handcuffed, but my arms dangling freely.

This is the only chance to escape. I know once he gets me inside the torture room, it will be over. Gratitude engulfs me as I realize the blueprint of the house is deeply ingrained in my subconscious, leaving me with just one opportunity to flee.

As he pulls me down the corridor, I notice the flickering lights above, casting a haunting glow on the worn wooden floor.

I have one shot at this.

Don't get scared now.

Quickly and forcefully, I lift my leg and step down on his foot as hard as possible. He loses his grip on my arm just enough for me to raise my elbow and strike him on his chin. He is dazed, so I run. I sprint for the door, seeing it like I had twenty-five years before.

I reach for the door and pull it open; looking behind me, Ryan is so close.

Run, Christina!

I face forward, ready to propel myself to freedom.

Out of nowhere, a man appears in the doorway, bringing my momentum to an abrupt halt.

CHAPTER 41

Before
Emily

Emily walked the deserted streets, feeling a haunting sense of solitude surround her as she neared the abandoned tow yard.

She had meticulously applied layers of makeup, styled her hair, and chose an outfit with a revealing crop top, skirt, and a cute jacket to combat the chilly air. She had spent her entire life being more introverted than her friends, but now she was ready to branch out and show them a different side of her.

The closer she got to her destination, the more nervous she became. She chewed on her fingernails even though there was nothing left. She hadn't planned on how she would confront Penelope, or how she would reveal what she was feeling. All she wanted to prevent was a catastrophic failure like she had when she made her move on Eric.

After speaking with Christina and Ryan, she realized she had overreacted. She tried to put herself in their shoes, which was easier to do than she thought it would be. She would be devastated if someone had come between her and someone she cared for that much. That was the problem, though. If Pen and Eric were already a thing, then she missed her chance. It was now or never.

Emily didn't want to do adult things anymore. Instead, she wanted to be a regular teenager. She wanted to be someone who had crushes, sneaked around after curfew, and tempted danger with rebellion. She was tired of her life and all the chaos that came with it. For the first time, she wanted to have a normal life with everyday teenage problems. She didn't want to be excluded anymore because she couldn't relate to the girls' relationship woes.

Tonight, her life could change for ever.

The air felt cooler as Emily got closer to her destination. A shiver ran down her back; she wasn't sure if it was from the cold or the nerves. She crossed her arms and rubbed her hands to fight off the anxiousness.

"Time to be brave," she said. "Don't wuss out now."

The tow yard appeared abandoned as she approached, with rusty chain-link fences and faded signage. "Perhaps they're in the back," she mused.

As she walked through the rear alley, she scanned her surroundings for any signs of other people. As a chill traveled down her spine, she realized the unnerving silence surrounding her in the abandoned alley.

When she reached the rear gate, it was locked. Could it be possible that she had gotten the address mixed up? The silence was deafening as she walked the entire exterior perimeter — not a single soul in sight. Each footstep reverberated against the walls, exacerbating her nervousness.

I should've had Ryan drive me. Maybe walking here alone wasn't such a bright idea.

She stood there wondering where everyone had gone. With disappointment in her eyes, she turned around and started her trek back home. Maybe it was good that no one was here — perhaps it was a sign that this secret wasn't meant to be shared.

As she walked through the alley, something caught her eye. As she inched closer, she noticed it sparkling in the streetlight. She bent down to examine it further, and when she grabbed it, she realized it was a layered choker very similar to the one Penelope always wore when they went out.

"That's weird. So they were here. Did they ditch me?"

Emily tried to maintain her composure, but with every step back home, her walls were crumbling. One summer had ruined everything, and she was feeling completely alone.

She threw herself onto her bed and sobbed. She blamed Penelope for complicating their friendship and kissing her. She blamed Christina for falling in love with Ryan. Most of all, she blamed herself for believing their friendship was real. She trusted these girls with every embarrassing detail of her life, and now they ditched her?

Emily got up and looked at the collage of photos on her wall. The longer the stared, the more the fury boiled within in her. Forcefully, she ripped the photos from the wall, tearing them to pieces as their betrayal sunk in.

"I hate both of you!" She screamed as she fell to the ground, crying harder.

For the first time, Emily felt like her life was over.

"How can things get any worse?" she mumbled.

* * *

Emily awakened early, still upset about the chain of events the night before. Did they really ditch her, or had it just been a miscommunication?

She stared out the window, her gaze fixed on the empty driveway, waiting for Eric to appear and confirm if the girls had showed up, but he never did.

Later, she walked into the living room and saw her mom watching the news.

"Hey, Mom," she said.

Her mom's face was white when she turned to greet her. "Emily, I think you should sit down."

"What? Why?"

"Please. Come sit," her mom said, patting the cushion beside her.

Something felt very wrong. "What is it, Mom?"

She put her hand on Emily's knee and pointed to the TV.

Emily turned her head and was sickened when she saw the headline: *TWO LOCAL GIRLS MISSING*.

She watched as the reporter broadcast from Penelope's house. There was a frenzy of police walking around the property. Emily sat tall, feeling her heart beating faster in her chest.

"Thanks, Jane. I'm standing here in front of Mayor Solace's residence. Her team has advised that her daughter, Penelope, and her friend, Christina, went out last night and never returned.

"According to the Mayor, the girls may have attended a party or get-together at an abandoned property in the industrial area of town. While Mayor Solace acknowledges that the girls were trespassing and she would have never condoned that behavior, she was made aware of the event only after Penelope missed her curfew, and she came across the address written down in her daughter's room.

"Authorities have indicated that there was no evidence of foul play at the site. However, they are treating this as a high-priority potential kidnapping case, and are not viewing them as runaways."

The reporter fades away as a photograph of the three girls appears on the screen, with Emily's face blurred out. "Please look closely at this photograph," the reporter continued. "Penelope is on the left, and Christina on the right side. Mayor Solace advised that this picture was taken within the last few weeks and accurately depicts the girls' current appearance.

"Authorities are still trying to track down why the girls were going to the location and identify any other attendees. They ask that if you have any information, please get in touch with the TRPD as soon as possible.

"There will be a press conference later this afternoon, but we're being told that a large-scale search team is being recruited to search for the missing girls—"

"Turn it off!" Emily cried.

"I know, sweetie. I'm sure they are fine. I'm just so relieved you weren't with them."

Emily felt nauseous, realizing she was the one who had told them where to go.

She jumped up and ran out the door to Eric's house. She pounded on the front door.

He opened the door, yawning, wearing no shirt and baggy sweatpants. "What's up? It's early," he said, yawning once more.

"Why did you tell me about that party? The girls are missing! I went there, and no one was there."

"What party?" he asked, confused.

"The bonfire! The one you told me to go to last night."

"Bonfire? That wasn't last night. That's next weekend."

Emily felt like she was going to vomit. "What do you mean? You told me it was last night!"

"Emily, I don't know what you're talking about. I told you it was next weekend. There was no bonfire last night."

The world began spinning, and Emily fell to her knees.

"I — I told them it was last night, and now they are missing."

* * *

Knock. Knock. Knock.

Emily walked to the door and saw two officers standing there.

Cautiously, she opened the door. "Can I help you?"

"Yes, hi. I'm Detective Whiteman, and this is Detective Saunders. Can we come in?"

"Sure," she said.

They walked into the living room. "Mind if we sit?" Detective Whiteman asked.

"Sure," she said, as she picked up beer cans scattered on the floor. "I'm sorry. I guess my dad had a rager here last night." *And every night*, she thought.

Detective Whiteman smiled. "Is your dad here? Or your mom?"

She sat down across from them. "Dad is at work and my mom stepped out for a bit."

"Normally, we don't like to talk to juveniles without their parents present. Do you know when they will be back?"

Emily felt her stomach turn. "Dad won't be back until tonight, and I don't know about my mom."

"Is there a phone number to call, so we can get their permission to speak to you?" Detective Saunders asked.

"My mom is running errands. She doesn't have access to a phone," Emily said.

"Ah. I see. Well, do you mind if we ask you some questions? You're not in trouble or anything."

Before Emily could answer, she heard her mother's voice. "Why is there a police car in the driveway?" her mom yelled as she ran into the house.

Everyone stood up. "Ma'am, I'm Detective Whiteman, and this is Detective Saunders. We are here regarding the missing girls. I'm so glad you are here, so we can ask Emily some questions."

Her mom rushed over to shake their hands. "I'm so relieved. With all the commotion, I was afraid something bad happened to my kids."

"Oh, that's normal, ma'am. Things like this don't happen a lot around here," Detective Whiteman said.

"I'm so worried about the girls. It's so tragic," she said, placing her hand on her heart.

"Well, we're not giving up hope yet," Detective Saunders said.

"But I thought they said on the news it was a kidnapping," Emily said.

"Well, that was a little exaggerated. We don't know what happened. There was no indication of foul play, but it doesn't seem like they would be runaways, either," Detective Whiteman advised.

The door slammed open, startling the detectives; they turned and placed their hands on their pistols. "Is it true,

Emily?" Ryan shouted as he ran to her. The detectives released their grip from their guns.

"Is what true?"

He put his hands on her shoulders. "Christina is missing?" he exclaimed.

"Christina and Penelope are missing," Detective Whiteman said. "And you are?"

"I'm Ryan. I'm her brother," he said, pointing at Emily.

"You seem very concerned about Miss Johnson," Detective Saunders said, writing notes in his notepad.

"No, well, yes. Shouldn't we all be concerned?" he said sarcastically.

"Did you have a relationship with Miss Johnson, son?" Detective Whiteman asked.

Ryan's face turned pale. "No. We are not in a relationship," he lied. "I just know that these girls are my sister's best friends, and I was worried about my sister."

"Is that so?" Detective Whiteman said, placing his hand on his chin as he studied Ryan. "Wait, do I know you? You look familiar."

"Yes, sir. I'm friends with your son."

"Which son?" Detective Whiteman asked.

"Brandon."

"Brandon McCormack is your son?" Emily asked, surprised.

"Stepson," he advised. "I thought you looked familiar. Do you play football with him?"

"No, he's just around a lot."

"Excuse me, I'm sorry," Emily's mom interrupted. But what does this have to do with Christina and Penelope? And with Emily?"

"I'm sorry, ma'am, you're right. It has nothing to do with that. The reason I came here was to ask Emily some questions, if that's all right with you."

"She doesn't know anything. I already asked her," Emily's mom said.

"I'm sure, but do you mind if we ask her some things? It may help us find them," Detective Saunders said.

She looked at Emily. "Are you willing to talk to them, sweetie?"

"Yeah, definitely. Anything I can do to help."

"How about we take a seat," Detective Whiteman said, and everyone complied.

"Emily, Mayor Solace said you were one of their best friends. So, we were hoping you could help us out," Detective Saunders said.

"I don't know how I could help."

"Well, first, do you know where they were going? Mayor Solace said she found a note with an address that ended up being an abandoned tow yard. Did you know anything about it, why they'd be going there?" Detective Whiteman inquired.

Emily hesitated, feeling nauseous. "Um, no. I hadn't heard anything about it."

"Is there a reason you weren't with them?" Detective Saunders asked.

"No, I just was tired," Emily said.

"When did you last hear from either of them? Was there anything going on at home?" Detective Whiteman asked, writing notes.

"Uh, I talked to them on the phone that day, but nothing seemed out of the ordinary."

"What about boyfriends? Anything going on with either of them?" Detective Whiteman asked.

She looked at her mom, wishing for an escape. If she tells them about Eric and Ryan, they will immediately become suspects. That was the last thing she wanted. "Uh, no. Not that I know of."

"Mayor Solace said that she saw a Black male jumping out of Penelope's room a few days ago. Any idea who that might have been?" Detective Whiteman inquired.

A Black male? Emily immediately envisioned Eric and knew it was him. "I don't know anyone she was dating. That's news to me."

Emily's mom grabbed her hand and squeezed it, comforting her. "I don't know what this has to do with Emily. She said she doesn't know anything," her mom said.

The two men looked at each other. "Well, if you think of anything, please let us know. We are arranging a search party, so if you're interested, it'll kick off in the town square at 1500 hours this afternoon," Detective Whiteman said.

They all stood up. "If I think of anything, I'll let you know," Emily said.

* * *

"Penelope! Christina!" a voice yelled.

It had been a week since the girls went missing, and there was still no sign of them. Wearing a high-visibility vest and holding a flashlight, Emily was part of the hundred-person search team.

The streets within the town had already been combed through, leaving no stone unturned. The bloodhound dogs had led them to the tow yard, where Emily knew they would have been. But the trail didn't last long, because the dogs lost their scent in the alley. The last update from Detective Whiteman was that they believed the girls had been thrown into a getaway vehicle behind the tow yard, which the bloodhounds' behavior indicated.

The guilt gnawed at Emily day in and day out, a constant reminder that she was the one who proposed the idea of going there, for her own selfish endeavors. Ever since the night she learned they were missing, Emily had this recurring nightmare. It always started the same: she was walking with the search party when a dog picked up a scent, and they all followed behind. The dog rushed to the lake, the group not far behind, and suddenly, everyone saw two bodies floating in the water. Each time, Emily startled awake, sweat pooling on her pillow.

Regardless of what emerged about the missing girls, Eric continued to deny that he had told her the wrong date. Initially, Emily questioned herself, but as the days progressed, she was confident about her recollection. Although she had her suspicions, she didn't want to accuse him without concrete evidence. Her biggest fear was that he would be falsely implicated in the abduction of two white girls, causing irreparable damage.

"Penelope! Christina!" another voice shouted.

Emily walked in her designated area of the grid, looking for any sign of their whereabouts.

"Hey," she heard from behind her. She turned to see Ryan approaching.

"Ryan, what's up?"

"No luck?"

"Nope. It's like they disappeared off the face of the planet."

"They'll find them. I know they will," he said.

"But what are they going to be like when they get back? What if someone is raping them? Why else would they kidnap them?" she cried.

He stopped walking and hugged her. "You can't think like that, Em. I'm sure there's an explanation."

"It's all my fault."

"What do you mean?"

She looked around, ensuring no one would hear her. "I'm the one that told them about the bonfire. Eric told me to come! But he swears it was gonna be a different day. I'm the reason they are missing."

He looked at her. "Did you tell anyone about that?"

"No!" She took a deep breath, getting her feelings under control. "I was afraid I'd get in trouble."

"Good! Keep that between us. No one can know that."

"But what if it helps find them?" she asked.

"It won't. Look, they already found where they went missing. Changing your story now will only make you look involved. Keep this between us."

"Okay," she sniffled.

"Come on, let's keep searching."

With a sinking feeling, Emily realized that the longer it took to find them, the more likely they wouldn't be found alive. Every day, she weighed the option of revealing the truth to the police. The thought of betraying her best friends gnawed at her conscience, leaving her with an indelible sense of remorse. Regardless of what Ryan said, she knew that if they came back alive, they would never be the same. The weight of the situation hit her, leaving her feeling lightheaded and dizzy with worry. Her friends were kidnapped, and there was a chance they were already dead, because of her.

CHAPTER 42

Present
Christina

It took a moment for my brain to process the disruption, but relief overcame me.

I throw my arms around him. "Help me! It was Ryan! He was behind it the whole time!"

He looks down at me, his gaze meeting mine and his hands caressing my cheeks. "Don't worry. It looks like I got here just in time," he says, smiling.

His hands quickly drop to my arms, forcefully turning me around and re-clasping the handcuffs to my wrists. "You're really fucking lucky I got here when I did," Chief McCormack says, directed at Ryan. "She could have escaped."

Immediately, a heavy weight settles in my chest, and a cold sweat appears as I realize what is happening. Jeremy was right — there was police corruption. He didn't want me to say anything because he was investigating his brother.

I am going to die. There's no way they'll ever let me go now.

Be strong.

"I would have caught her," Ryan proclaims.

"Yeah. Doubtful," Chief McCormack says, as he pulls me toward the hallway.

I let the weight of my body fall to the ground, forcing them to drag me. I kick and scream — something I wish I had done more when I was younger.

"You got a little fight in you now," Chief McCormack says. "It's not gonna change anything, though."

They pull me into a large room and handcuff me to a metal chair bolted to the ground. I look around. It must have been the primary bedroom at one point. It looked different in my imagination, from behind the blindfold. The windows are covered with a thick, porous foam-looking material, which I am assuming is to soundproof the room. When I look down below the chair, I notice a layer of plastic ready for quick and easy clean-up.

I can't believe this is where it will all end: this house and this room. Looking back, I never left this place. The nightmares plagued my existence — constant reminders of those few weeks, the torture, and the fear. It's like I never left, and I regret I could never move on and live my life. If I somehow make it out of here, I'm never looking back.

"Can you just get it over with?" I plead.

Brandon exchanges a glance with Ryan. "Well, it's not that easy. Because we can't just kill you and make you disappear now. You had to make us bring everything up. Now the media is involved, so we can't just get rid of you."

"You never should've helped me then! You're the one who gave me the case files!" I scream.

"No, I didn't. My jackass brother found them and went to you behind my back," he said with disdain. "I would've burned them, if I could have without raising suspicion."

Shocked at the revelation, I wondered how much Jeremy knew this whole time. "What are you going to do with me?" I hiss.

"You should've just stayed away," Chief McCormack says. "Let sleeping dogs lie. We were fucking kids. You came back and risked ruining everyone's life. For what? For Penelope Solace? That whore set you up! She didn't care about you, and now you have to die because of it." He balls his fists, paces back and forth, and punches a hole in the wall. "Dammit!" he screams.

"Bro, calm down," Ryan says.

"I will *not* calm down. I thought we were done with this shit after you handled your sister."

"You don't have to take care of anything. You are choosing to do the wrong thing," I protest.

"CJ, stop," Ryan says, running interference.

"Why? You're just gonna kill me anyway."

Chief McCormack turns to me, his eyes filled with rage as he walks to me and slaps my face. "Did I permit you to speak? Or did we forget the rules of this house?"

My cheeks tingled as if his hand were still there. I open my mouth to speak, but his words reignited a paralyzing fear that existed. I look — Ryan cowering behind Chief McCormack, Chief McCormack pacing, open door. I listen — footsteps, arguing, heart beating. I move — pulling on the handcuffs, biting my lip, leaning forward. *You are not safe anymore. You're going to die here.*

Chief McCormack and Ryan leave the room, but I hear them arguing in the hallway.

"How the fuck did you let this happen?" Chief McCormack screams.

"It was an accident. Somehow, she found the car."

"How did she find your car?" Chief McCormack yelled.

"It — it was in my garage."

"*Your garage?*" Chief McCormack screamed. "Are you fucking kidding me? Why was it in your garage?"

"I haven't had time to get rid of it," Ryan muttered.

"You are so stupid! I told you to get rid of that weeks ago! Why was she at your house?"

"It was a family thing. I didn't realize she'd be snooping around."

"You are such an idiot," Chief McCormack yells.

"It's your fault. You wanted me to seduce her!" Ryan yells back.

"Only you could screw that up. If you would've done what I asked, she would've never been in your house to begin with."

"I don't know what you want from me. I have done everything you told me to do! I killed my sister to protect us! What more do you want from me?" Ryan yells.

"I should have never been involved with this shit! I still can't believe you fucking blackmailed me into kidnapping your ex to begin with! I knew this would blow up in our faces!" Chief McCormack howls. "And you know what, Ryan? I don't want to keep killing people for some high school bullshit. That's what I want!"

"Oh, don't give me that shit. You were the one who came up with what to do with her! Don't start trying to act all superior now. I know who you are, Brandon."

"Because you blackmailed me, asshole! I had no other choice. Of course, if I was stuck helping you, I was going to give us some insurance to make sure this didn't happen!"

"No, it was because you were already a sick fuck! Don't forget I knew your secrets and your obsessions!" Ryan yells.

"If I was already a sick fuck, like you say, I would have wanted to do more than your PG-13-rated torture. I would've actually hurt her," Chief McCormack shouts.

I realize that this had happened before, and it was Ryan who wanted to keep me here against opposition. They are cracking at the pressure of having to finish what they started. There is desperation in their voices as they try to determine how to fix this.

I still have a chance.

It's not over yet. I continue yanking on my handcuffs, trying to free myself from the chair.

"I'm done arguing with you. Let's just get this over with! How do we do this?" Ryan says in the hallway.

"I'll put in a radio call of a trespasser. When I get here, it'll be a scuffle. She was drunk, lost it with all the media coverage, went for my gun, and I had to shoot her in self-defense," he says.

"Will that work?" Ryan asks.

"It'll have to look like it was a hell of a fight because of our size differences, but it's buyable. I'll put out a backup, the whole nine yards."

I pull on my restraints once more, but it's unsuccessful.

"Do you have anything to give her to drink?" Ryan asks.

"In the cruiser. I'll meet you back in the room."

Tick-tock. Tick-tock. Tick-tock. Time is running out.

* * *

My throat still stings from the harsh liquor being forced in my mouth against my will. They pulled me into the kitchen, and we all sat in an awkward silence as I awaited my fate.

Chief McCormack sips the whiskey from the bottle before handing it to Ryan, who takes a large gulp.

"You drunk yet?" Chief McCormack asks, looking at me.

"Fuck off," I say.

"Language, language! I am an officer of the law. Show some respect!"

I spit in his direction. "Respect is earned, not given, asshole."

He smiles. "I gotta admit, Christina. This version of you is much more satisfying. It got depressing before. You were always so sad. But now, you're feisty. It'll make killing you a lot more fun."

"So, what do I do?" Ryan asks.

"Well, I need you to fight like a bitch. You know, slap me a few times and scratch me, like a girl would fight."

"Well, that's kind of sexist," Ryan says.

"When did you become such a pussy? Having a girl has made you soft," Chief McCormack says, irritated. "What I meant is that it has to look real. Most women scratch and slap. It can't look like some dudes fighting in a bar."

"Fine," Ryan says. "How do you want to do this?"

"Come over and hit me!"

Ryan stands up and raises his hands. He looks at them as he figures out what to do first. Like a cat, he slaps Brandon multiple times on both cheeks, causing his head to bounce between his hands.

"Enough!" Brandon yells. "It still hurts."

"Sorry," Ryan says. He drops his hands.

"Scratch me. But do it fast. If you hesitate, it won't look real."

Ryan raises his right hand and motions downward. "Oh yeah, that'll work. You're already bleeding a little."

"That shit stings, man. It better not get infected," he says, applying pressure to his face.

They walk toward me. Chief McCormack takes my fingers and scratches his hand, ensuring his DNA will be under my fingernails.

Chief McCormack stands there looking at me. "It's still not right." He takes his hands, dishevels my hair, and rips my shirt. "That's better."

"Don't forget the gun!" Ryan adds.

"Oh, shit! You're right." He grabs my hand as much as he can, since I am still handcuffed, and wraps it around the butt of the gun. He places his hand on top of mine and squeezes it tighter. "Okay, let's do this."

"Are we doing it here?" Ryan asks.

"Yes. Clean up the plastic in the other room and throw it in your car."

This is it. My time is out.

Game over.

I am out of options; this is where it would all end. I regret so much. I should have let this all go and tried living my life. I held on so tight to this place it sucked me back in, and now I will forever be a victim.

I stand in the middle of the kitchen, and a tear rolls down my cheek — a prisoner awaiting her execution. My hands are still cuffed behind me, and there is nowhere to go.

"Any last words?" Chief McCormack asks.

"Someone will figure out what you did. You won't get away with this."

He scoffs. "Get on your knees."

Slowly, I lower myself to the ground. My eyes meet Ryan's, and I can't tell if it is the alcohol or my imagination, but I think I see tears glistening on his cheeks. Chief McCormack wraps a cloth around the butt of his gun and removes it from the holster.

"Wait!" Ryan yells. "Wait!"

He walks to me and kneels. "I am so sorry for what I did to you when we were kids. I am sorry for this, right now. I have to protect my family." He leans in and kisses me.

I bite his lip. He pulls back, wiping his lower lip with his hand and revealing the blood.

"Are you done now?" Chief McCormack asks, annoyed.

"Yes," Ryan answers, distraught.

I watch as McCormack raises the gun. I close my eyes. Take a deep breath.

The last thing I see is a memory of Penelope, Emily, and me in my backyard. They are both laughing. The sun's rays illuminate their smiles, and for a moment, the bright light makes me feel like I'm in heaven.

BANG.

CHAPTER 43

Present
Christina

Am I dead?

I open my eyes just as Brandon turns around and falls to the ground. Standing in the doorway in the living room is a silhouette, the gun still raised as smoke emerges from the barrel, obscuring the face of the shooter. As the pistol lowers, I realize it is Jeremy.

I look down at my body; I don't see any blood.

I'm alive. Jeremy has saved me.

Jeremy walks across the threshold, and behind him is Dan Swanson. It transports me back to the day I escaped — my savior rescuing me once more.

They both enter, guns still drawn, and I've never been so relieved in my life. Somehow, I am going to make it out of here alive.

"Don't move yet," Jeremy tells me. "It's not safe!"

Another gunshot rings out, followed by a loud thud and more gunshots. I bury my head, trying to avoid being struck. There's a brief lull between the volleys of gunfire, so I look up to get a better grasp on the situation.

Chief McCormack is cradling his shoulder, smoke billowing from the barrel of his firearm. Jeremy has made his way to one side of the room, but Dan is on the ground beside the doorway, not moving.

"Dan!" Jeremy screams. He ducks behind the couch, as Chief McCormack kicks the table. It falls perpendicular to the floor, providing him cover as he reloads his gun.

What do I do?

I look over at Ryan. He is standing against the wall with eyes wide open and a dropped jaw. His skin is pale, with a frozen expression. Their plan is failing, and shock is setting in.

The shooting starts again, sounding like a firing range, but with glass breaking and wood splintering. Ryan's eyes dart toward mine. He stands erect with his hands covering his ears, looking from me to the chaos in the living room. His mouth opens to speak, but then he just turns and rushes toward the hallway.

"You're not getting away this time!" I yell.

I jump up, nearly stumbling, but regain my footing and run full speed to avoid getting struck by the ongoing gun battle. With my hands still restrained behind my back, I bend over, put my shoulder down, and charge into his lower body like a defensive tackle in football. He loses his balance and goes headfirst into the wall, knocking him unconscious. I jump on his back, my weight holding him down. I pray he doesn't wake up.

"Someone come help me!" I yell.

I hear the commotion in the other room — loud grunts, thuds, shouts, and heavy breathing.

BANG. BANG.

I hide my face in Ryan's back. Furniture crashes as male voices yell expletives at one another.

BANG.

Thud. Thud. Thud. The footsteps grow louder in my direction.

A shadow drowns the sliver of light from the living room. I look up.

Am I dreaming? Standing before me is the same woman from the photograph.

Penelope. Penelope Solace. My Penelope.

She's alive.

I found her.

As she helps me up, Jeremy is behind her. He unlocks my handcuffs and puts them on Ryan, who is still unconscious on the floor. Jeremy rises, throws his arms around me, and all the stress leaves my body.

"How?" I say.

He releases his embrace and pulls back. "Are you okay?"

"I'm fine," I say. "But how is she here right now?"

"She came to us after seeing you on the news. She was with us when I saw the tracker I put on my brother's car heading this way. I knew something was up, and she wouldn't let us check it out without her."

He lets go of me, my eyes meet Penelope's, and we are transported to 1998. We aren't two adults that had spent twenty-five years apart. We are two best friends who hadn't seen each other over the weekend.

"What's up, Chris?" Penelope says, smiling. "I'm glad you're safe."

"I was supposed to rescue you, not the other way around," I say softly.

She wraps her arms around me; we hold onto each other tightly. I sob, surprised by the depth of my emotions, and cling to her, unwilling to let her go. An overwhelming sense of dread washes over me, making me question if it is all just a figment of my imagination. I fear that none of this is real. What if I really had gotten shot, and I'm dying?

THUD.

We all jump — the sound bringing me back to reality as we all look toward the entrance to the hallway. Dan is leaning against the wall. "Sorry, guys. Didn't mean to startle you!"

"I thought you were dead!" I exclaim, running toward him and throwing my arms around him as he winces in pain. "Oh! I'm sorry!" I say, releasing him.

He chuckles. "Me, dead? No way. Just a flesh wound. Through and through. I'll be fine."

I sigh in relief. "You did it! You kept your promise and brought her back."

"I can't take credit for this, kid. This was all Jeremy and Penelope. I'm just so happy you're safe," Dan says, with a sparkle in his eyes.

Jeremy pulls his handheld radio from his belt. "Dispatch, this is Officer Jeremy McCormack. I need EMTs at 1350 White Pine Way. We have a suspect down, not conscious, and not breathing. We have an additional suspect, not conscious, but breathing. We also have a former officer with a flesh wound to his left arm. I will also need additional units for a crime scene and contact the DA's office. This is related to the Solace case."

"*1A2, copy. Verify you need three RAs?*" the voice over the radio says.

"Roger. Actually, make it four. I'd like them to check out our victim, too."

"*Roger that, sir.*"

"Roger. Thanks." He looks at me. "I'm so sorry about all this. Let's get you out of here. For good this time."

CHAPTER 44

Present
Christina

Sitting across from me in a corner booth is Penelope Solace.

Somehow, she is a stranger, but familiar at the same time. Her perfect skin now has soft lines around her eyes and mouth — from years of laughter that I never got to experience myself. Her lips have lost their youthful fullness and her cheekbones are pronounced, casting shadows below. Her hair is no longer overly processed and dyed but is a gentle auburn with specks of gray peeking out. I have been waiting for this moment since I ran out of those doors all those years ago, and now I'm speechless.

I tap my fingers around my glass, biting my lip. Unsure of where to start. Jeremy told me I could give my statement another day, because it was more important that this conversation take place. *Investigations can wait*, he insisted, *a reunion of this magnitude supersedes everything else.* Who am I to not listen to the law?

"So, I guess I'll start. I thought you were dead," I say, breaking the silence.

She looks down. "That was the point."

"I thought *I* was the reason you were dead," I say.

"Oh, Chris, I never meant—"

I interrupt her. "Where have you been all these years?" My knee bounces uncontrollably beneath the table.

She sips her water. "Here and there. Made a nice little life for myself nearby, once I was ready to settle down."

"Must be nice," I sneer. "Did you know Emily was looking for you, too?"

"I had no clue," Penelope says, reaching across the table, but I pull my hand before it reaches mine. "If I did, I wouldn't have let it get to this. It just got so out of hand, I couldn't face coming back."

"Our lives were ruined, Pen. She *died* because of this."

"Don't do that. It's not fair," Penelope mutters.

"It's not fair? Please! I spent my life thinking I was the reason you were dead. *Dead*, Pen!" I say, throwing my hands in the air. "How could you let me go through that?"

"I didn't realize it was gonna turn out the way it did. I was committed. If I had come back, could you imagine what people would've said about me?"

Some things never change. Typical Penelope, only caring about herself.

"I want to know what really happened. I deserve to know, because I have had a fucked-up life because of it. Tell me the truth!" I yell. "And no half-truths. I want to know what part you had in this entire thing."

Her eyes water, and she crosses her arms. "I didn't know until later what happened to you. Until I saw it on the news."

"Bulls—"

"Please. Let me explain," she continues. "You asked for the truth, so let me try to explain. You know how terrible my mother was. Probably still is. I had to get away. I was young and immature. Honestly, I thought it was the only way out. Eric had this plan, and then Brandon jumped on board. Next thing you know, Ryan agreed to help. But it was supposed to be stupid stuff. You weren't even supposed to be taken at all when we initially talked about it. It just all went so wrong. Eric told me later about Ryan, and how he went crazy. He insisted they all tried to stop him at one point, but he went full psycho. I swear I didn't know!" She pauses, her hands fidget on the table. "I fell for Ryan's bullshit. He convinced me you had to be taken too, but I would've never allowed them to hurt you. That was never part of the plan. I swear! I cried for days when I saw you."

"Penelope! I talked to you while I was there! You knew I was being hurt!"

"I — it was too late. We were already knee-deep in it. I didn't know how to fix it!" Penelope cried.

"So, Ryan was being honest? It was your plan all along? I was just some pawn to make it look real?"

"No . . . well, yes. But they were our friends, Chris! I had no idea what they were capable of."

My lip quivers. "You knew they had to do something to me to make it seem like a real kidnapping."

"I know, but not what they did for real," she exclaimed, reaching for my hand once more. "They said they were gonna do frat stuff. Like make you drink too much, feed you weird stuff, stupid hazing shit. Brandon said it was harmless, because they use that stuff during hell week in college. I didn't know any better."

"Did Eric know what was really going on?"

"No, I swear! He said he confronted them one day when he saw your condition, and they got into a huge fight. After that, we tried to move up everything, but they tried to take away Eric's access. They got so weird with everything."

"So, who did you attack that day?"

"That was always part of the plan," she says. "Once there was enough attention to make my mom look bad, we would stage an escape. You'd be the girl who survived, and I'd just disappear."

"Was that Eric?" I ask.

"Yes."

"But I saw you stab him!" I say, pointing at her.

"It was a movie prop. One of those fake knives that retracts, to make it seem like it went in."

"Jesus Christ, Penelope," I shake my head in disgust. "I can't believe you guys thought you were gonna get away with it!" I sigh. "Let me ask you this. Did any of you consider, just for one millisecond, that I'd have long-lasting trauma from being kidnapped?" my voice quivers.

"We were kids, Chris. We thought since you escaped, you would have gotten over it. I thought you being an instant celebrity would make up for it. Maybe get you a *Lifetime* movie or book deal or something."

I slam my hands on the table, spilling my water. "That I'd just *get over it*? I couldn't leave my house for years! *For years!* I blamed myself, Pen. I thought you were dead, and it was my fault because I left you behind! I was a fucking child. How could you do that to me?"

Tears stream down her cheeks. "I know! I'm sorry," she buries her head in her hands. "Nothing I do can fix that."

I lean back in the booth and cross my arms in front of me. "So, what now? Are you going to come clean?"

"I already did. I told Jeremy everything. When I saw you on the news, and I heard about my mom's arrest, which was bullshit, I knew it was time to make things right. It was time to stop running."

"I don't get it. They found human remains on her property. Who is it they found?"

"You have me there," Penelope says.

"You're not lying to me? This wasn't part of your plan?"

"I hated my mom, but I would never set her up that way. I just wanted to get her out of my life. I have no idea who or what they found there. I was just as shocked as you are."

I scoff. "You guys are all fuckin' sick. I don't even have the words for how reckless and irresponsible you all were. Well, selfish, really. You were willing to ruin my life 'cause you had mommy issues. Un-fuckin-real," I say, slamming my hand on the table.

I sit there in silence, taking everything in. It was as if my entire life had been a lie — a cruel joke everyone was in on but me.

I lean forward, crossing my fingers on the table, and stare at her. "Did you know about Emily?"

"Not until I got back—"

"No, not her death. Did you know why she wanted us to go out that night?"

"It was summer. Why wouldn't she want to go out?"

"Penelope, did you kiss her?"

"Kiss her?"

"Yes. Did you hook up with her that summer?"

She rolls her eyes. "Maybe. I don't really remember."

"Apparently, she was all twisted 'cause you guys hooked up, and she wanted us to meet her there 'cause she wanted to tell us her secret."

"What secret?"

"She thought she had feelings for you — romantic feelings for you, I guess."

Penelope's eyes widen, and her jaw drops. "What do you mean she had feelings for me?"

"Typical Penelope. You act without thinking. Emily wasn't some skank who went around hooking up with people. I'm pretty sure that was her first kiss ever. No wonder why she was so confused. All she wanted was to figure out everything, and you had us kidnapped the same night!"

"I—"

I interrupt her. "It's not fair that you messed with her like that. How could you do that?"

"I was having a rough time. I was searching for something. I was a dumb kid. I didn't mean to hurt her."

"Well, you did."

We sit in silence for a few moments. "Can I ask you one more question?" I say.

"Of course. No more secrets," Penelope says.

"Was it worth it?" I ask.

"What do you mean?"

"You know what I mean. Was it worth it?"

Her lip quivers, her shoulders sink, and her eyes swell with tears. "No. It was the biggest regret of my life. I was so alone. I had lost my two closest friends — my soulmates. Things fizzled with Eric pretty fast, and he ended up getting killed in an illegal street race not too long after. I thought about making a miraculous return, but I couldn't bear the thought of facing you. So, I stayed away."

"Did you ever think to come back and make it right?"

She reaches across the table for my hands wrapped around my glass. "Chris, I can't tell you how many times I was in my car ready to drive back. But I was a coward. I couldn't face you. I was so embarrassed."

"You were embarrassed? Once again, you didn't take my feelings into account."

She sniffles. "I know. I am so sorry. Nothing I say can make up for what happened. It was selfish and immature. I suck."

I shake my head. "So, what do we do now? Where do we go from here?" I ask.

"I don't know. I want to make things right. I'd love to get to know you again. Maybe we can even be friends someday, if you forgive me. I know that will take time."

I take a deep breath. Emily wanted me to find Penelope, and I did. The mystery has been solved. One suspect is dead, and the other will end up being in prison for the rest of his life. It took twenty-five years, but I got the closure I sought. I don't want to be scared anymore. I want to be free from this purgatory. And sometimes, people don't deserve second chances.

CHAPTER 45

Seven Months Later

Transcript Excerpts from "Echoes of the Missing" Docuseries on Investigation Discovery.

Episode 1

Narrator: *In this episode of Echoes of the Missing, Penelope Solace and Christina Johnson disappear on August 16, 1998. When someone vanishes without a trace, it is often the details from the days or months leading up to their disappearance that hold the key to understanding what happened. Little did the girls know that their actions and secrets that summer would set in motion an incredible plot, one that would take a quarter of a century to unravel.*

* * *

Episode 2

Officer Jeremy McCormack: *I don't think anyone could have foreseen how this entire incident would play out. Even the most twisted mind couldn't have fabricated what took place.*

* * *

Episode 3

Narrator: *In this stunning conclusion, it is twenty-five years later, and the defendants are on trial for their roles in the kidnapping and torture of Christina Johnson.*

Penelope Solace: *I guess it was crazy, the whole plot. I mean, what do you expect? We were kids. Eric and I thought we could stage the entire kidnapping, but we never realized how out of control it would get.*

Producer: *So, what was the plan?*

Penelope: *Christina was supposed to be a witness. But, as it got closer, the boys kept saying that she had to be taken, too, to make it believable. But they promised me she wouldn't be hurt. I would have never allowed that to happen.*

* * *

Episode 3

Producer: *How does it feel knowing your family was involved?*

Officer Jeremy McCormack: *It's hard to believe that both my brother and stepdad could be part of something so evil. So, I don't really know how to feel. What made me feel a little better was realizing it wasn't until my stepdad saw Christina's injuries that he started putting everything together. At least he wasn't an active participant for the entire thing. But he knew no one would believe that he wasn't involved, with his equipment being used, so he made a terrible decision to help cover up the incident with Brandon. I finally had him cop out to me how it all went down. Really, he was just lucky. Mayor Solace approached him and asked him to stop investigating. Then, within a few weeks, the Widowmaker serial killer required all hands on deck, which allowed him to reallocate the resources. It was easy to make the whole investigation disappear.*

* * *

Episode 3

Narrator: *At the trial of Detective Whiteman, the true identity of the body located at Bonnie's house was revealed. He had taken a Jane Doe who had died from exposure around the same time the girls went missing, removed all of her teeth, and burned her remains. The plan was never to frame the mayor unless she double-crossed him, because he didn't trust her.*

* * *

Episode 3

Producer: *How did Emily get involved?*

Jeremy: *When Emily saw Penelope and started digging, she came to me. We started working on the case together, and I think that is when Ryan tried to stop her. He casually tried to dissuade her, knowing how many people were involved. He didn't want the past to ruin everyone's present, and he freaked out, which led to a series of wrong decisions. I don't condone his behavior one bit, but I empathize with his feelings of desperation to protect his daughter.*

* * *

Episode 3

Producer: *How did Emily's death lead to unraveling your kidnapping?*

Christina: *When I came back to town, the dominoes were set in motion. Ryan befriended me to ensure I didn't figure out the whole plot. He figured he could control the investigation and steer me in the wrong direction. Ryan and Brandon were behind the threatening notes and the Molotov cocktail, but I couldn't stop. He tried to persuade me romantically, thinking that would help, but I was too determined. Brandon asked his dad what to do, and they let Jeremy be the hero, not knowing it would lead to Brandon's demise.*

* * *

Episode 3

Producer: *So, what happened with Eric?*

Penelope: *I was dreading this question. I guess the best way to describe what happened was that I was not mentally capable of loving someone at that age. I had abandonment issues, and I was constantly in need of attention.*

Producer: *Did you use him as a means to an end?*

Penelope: *Sheesh. In a way, yes. It wasn't his fault. He was great to me, and I felt like he loved me the best he could for our age. He did everything he could to keep me grounded as I settled into my new life, but I was still me. I didn't want to be tied down.*

Producer: *Weren't you scared he'd go to the police about what happened?*

Penelope: *No, he was in too deep. He was just as guilty as me. He let me move on with my life and we stayed friends. Well, until he was killed in the street racing accident. I always told him that damn car would get him killed someday.*

* * *

Episode 3

Narrator: *Former Mayor Solace was released after the incident at the house, and all charges were dropped. Former Detective Whiteman was arrested and charged with conspiracy, desecrating human remains, and interfering with a police investigation. He was found guilty and is currently serving fifteen years in prison, and is eligible for parole in seven years. Ryan was arrested and charged with conspiracy, kidnapping, false imprisonment, and torture. He was found guilty and is serving a life sentence in prison without the possibility of parole.*

* * *

Episode 3

Producer*: So, what happens now?*

Christina: *I start living again.*

Producer: *What about Penelope? Have you been able to reconnect and make up for lost time?*

Christina: *I take it day by day. I'd like to forgive her, but only time will tell. I spent twenty-five years thinking she was dead. That's not something that goes away overnight.*

CHAPTER 46

One Year Later
Christina

With each movement, the unforgiving hardwood floor causes a jolt of pain to travel up my knees and through my entire upper body. Even with the chill in the air, sweat tickles my brow.

Kneeling here, I fixate on the cold steel of the pistol's barrel, my hands tightly restrained behind my back, and the realization washes over me that I am about to die.

I close my eyes.

BANG.

I look — book, sand, lake. I listen — laughter, splashing, boats. I move — rolling my head, rolling my shoulders, wiggling my toes. *You are safe. It is really over now.*

As I lie on the sand, looking at Lake Tahoe, I am still consumed by the memories of what happened. While they are less frequent, a panic attack will strike when I least expect it. The trauma of what happened to me will never go away, but knowing who did it — as well as the reasons behind it, however ridiculous — helped with the healing process. The monsters aren't so scary anymore.

Penelope's return made headline news for weeks — not in a good way. Suddenly, I was the sole victim, which was hardly what I wanted. The press excoriated her, but she owned up to it. After a long discussion with the District Attorney, she agreed not to file charges against her. I had just gotten her back, and I didn't want to lose her again. I knew people wouldn't understand, but they didn't have to — it was my life and I was ready to move on.

Once the District Attorney's office realized there was possibly police corruption, they immediately notified the Office of the Inspector General, who ensured an outside agency came in to do the official investigation of what happened. In the end, Tranquility Ridge Police Department was gutted with those involved in the corruption and cover-up, and Jeremy became the new police chief. It took months, but finally, I got the answers I deserved — and it was crazier than I could ever imagine.

It turns out that Jeremy always suspected some collusion between the mayor and the police department, which was why he was the host of the *Terror in Tranquility Ridge* YouTube series. He partnered with Dan Swanson, and they tried to work the case out together, hoping to give me the justice they felt I deserved. With no other means to find me, they hoped I'd come across the series and come back to town. After everything came out in the press about Penelope's return, the series took off. This led to Jeremy getting a show on the Investigation Discovery Channel, *Echoes of the Missing*, where he highlights missing persons and cold cases — mine being the first case they featured.

When all was said and done, Brandon was dead, and Ryan and Detective Whiteman ended up in prison, where they belonged. Ryan's daughter, Maddie, was sent to a great home for kids with special needs and has an adoption pending. When the Department of Children and Family Services got involved, I ensured they would take special care of her. She deserved to be taken care of, which doesn't always happen. It wasn't her fault her dad was a psychopath. She will be loved, and that is all that matters.

During the search warrant of Ryan's residence, they found a manuscript he had been writing. It turns out that he used my story to get a publication deal without my consent. He had been contracted to write a "dark, twisty, edge-of-your-seat thriller about the harrowing escape of a girl held in captivity." When Jeremy told me about the manuscript, I called the agent to let him know what happened, and he was much more interested in reading about it directly from the source. So, in addition to spending a lifetime in prison, Ryan lost his daughter and six-figure contract — the final nail in the karma coffin. Finally, everyone was where they belonged, and I could move on.

"Want some?" Penelope says, raising the chilled Chardonnay from the cooler.

I smile. "Yes, please!" I lean to her with my Yeti wine tumbler and she pours. I sit back in my chair, looking at the lake while sipping my wine. "It's such a nice day out here today."

"It is. We need to do this more. We can't just slave our lives away. We have a lot of time to make up for," she says, turning to me and smiling.

It took me a long time to forgive Penelope. I know if some people had endured what I had, they would never speak to her again. I wanted to be that way, but I had already lost so much in my life. I knew I could never move on carrying so much hatred in my heart, so I left the past where it belongs. Our friendship will never be the same, but I'd like to think that we're new people, and this version of ourselves would never do that to each other.

My phone vibrates. A message from Nicole.

Mom and I are about ten minutes out. Need us to grab anything at the gas station?

No, we have everything here. See you soon.

"Mom and Nicole will be here in ten minutes," I say.

"Oh, good! Is this your mom's first outing since going into remission?" Penelope asks.

"Yes. She's such a strong woman. The doctors are confident that she beat it for good this time!"

"What a relief. We gotta take her somewhere to celebrate!"

"Somewhere tropical, for sure!" I smile, diverting my attention to Thor rolling around in the sand with his newest companion— a seven-month-old rottweiler puppy we named Emily.

"Thor, Emily!" I yell. "Come here!"

They both run toward us, Emily losing her footing and landing in the sand. Thor ignores her, rushing to me and licking my exposed toes. Emily runs to Penelope, who pets her on the head, causing her to lie on her back and expose her belly to get additional scratches.

My phone rings. "Hello?" I answer.

"Mrs. McCormack, what are you doing?" a deep voice says. I smile, still getting used to the title.

"Playing with Emily and Thor, enjoying a delicious glass of Chardonnay with Pen. What are you doing, Police Chief Jeremy McCormack?"

"Oh, you know, important police stuff. Highly confidential."

"I bet," I say.

"Guess what came to the station today?"

"Is it here?" I say excitedly, slapping Penelope's arm.

"It sure is! It's beautiful! I'm so proud of you. Let Curtis know we got it!" Jeremy says.

"Please send me pictures! I can't wait to hold it in my hands!"

"I will," he says sweetly. "Tell Pen I said hi! Have fun at the lake. Don't forget to reapply your sunblock!"

I smile. "I won't. See you later, babe. Love you." I hang up the phone. "It came to his station today!"

"Shut up! Your very first book! This is cause for celebration, Mrs. Author!"

My phone pings and I open the picture. Jeremy is smiling gleefully, holding the first copy of my novel, *The White House in the Woods*.

"I can't believe it's real," I say, showing Pen the photograph.

"After all those years, you deserve to enjoy every moment of this," Penelope says, pouring more wine into our glasses. "Cheers," she says, raising her glass. "To the baddest bitch I know, and all you've had to overcome because of my dumb ass!"

We clink our glasses and take a sip — looking at each other and smiling. We were missing Emily, and our friendship would never be the same without her, especially after everything I had endured. However, if it hadn't been for Emily, I would have spent the rest of my life searching for this feeling, this moment. In the end, it took twenty-five years to escape from the trauma of that house, finally finding peace in the last place I expected — with the very person who stole it from me.

EPILOGUE

Before
Ryan

Ryan laid on his bed, reading the letters Christina had written. One, in particular, he couldn't stop reading.

> *Dear Ryan,*
>
> *I was thinking the other day, and I realized we've been together for six months now! Time goes by so fast when you're having fun, right? I have to tell you, I'm so happy that we got lost together. Do you believe in fate? Because I do now. You have made my life so much better.*
>
> *I know we never really said what this is, but I can't hold it in any longer. I am way too shy to say this to your face, but I love you. I love you so much you have no idea. I wish we had gotten lost sooner so we could have experienced this together for longer.*
>
> *I know I am only sixteen, but I think this is the real deal. You bring out so much happiness in me and I wish we could tell Emily. I don't know how she would ever be ok with this, but over time, I think she'll understand.*

So, I'm hoping that you feel the same way too. If you don't, rip this up and pretend you never saw it, OK?
I love you! (Eeek! That's so fun to write!)
CJ

He ripped up the letter and threw it on the ground.

"All bitches lie," he said to himself. "Fuck her for choosing Emily over me."

***

Ryan walked to Brandon's front door — knocking hard three times. Brandon cracked the door, peering out, then opening it. "Damn, dude. You're knocking like you're the police. What's up?"

"There's a change of plans," Ryan said.

"What do you mean?" Brandon asked.

"Not here. Let's go to your room," Ryan said.

They walked down the hall in silence, Ryan following closely behind Brandon. They entered his room. Ryan looked up at the walls that were filled with posters of bands and girls — specifically Pamela Anderson in her red *Baywatch* swimsuit.

"Talk to me. What's going on?" Brandon asked.

"I know Eric had specifically laid out this fake kidnapping to not involve CJ, but fuck her. I think we make this shit look real."

"Why, bro? What did she do?"

"It doesn't matter. Penelope wants a kidnapping. I say we give them a kidnapping."

Brandon sat down on the chair next to his bed, which was filled with dirty laundry. "I'm all for fucking with people, but kidnapping her is a serious felony. I'm not tryin' to get ass-raped for the rest of my life."

"Bro, are you fuckin' serious? After all the shit I've done for you. Now you're not down?" Ryan snapped.

"Yes, I'm serious. My dad is a cop. Faking a kidnapping is one thing, but really kidnapping someone is serious shit. What the hell happened?" Brandon said.

"She broke up with me. She's a fucking whore. I want her to pay," Ryan muttered.

Brandon reached for Ryan's arm. "I'm sorry, dude. I really am. But there's—"

Ryan slapped Brandon's hand. "This isn't negotiable."

"Bro, c'mon. This is crazy."

"I didn't want to have to do this, but last time I checked, you were gonna piss dirty last year before I stepped in and helped you pass your drug test. You would've been kicked off the football team before playoffs, remember?" Ryan said.

"Whoa! Are you kidding me right now?"

"Let's just say I took out an insurance policy," Ryan smirked.

"What the fuck, man? Are you blackmailing me?"

"It's only blackmail if you make me follow through."

Brandon put his hands on his forehead, pacing back and forth. "This is so fucking bad. I can't believe you're making me do this. Are you sure you don't want to sleep on it?"

"Yes. I've never been more sure of anything in my entire life."

Brandon put his hand to his chin. "Somehow, I knew that would come back to bite me in the ass. At least I already started thinking of something if it came down to this."

"What do you mean?" Ryan asked, sitting on Brandon's bed.

"Well, we can't kidnap her and not have it look real. No one would ever kidnap someone and not do something to them, right? My dad always said that shit was for pedophiles. But what if we haze her?" Brandon said.

"Haze her? What is this? A fuckin' frat house? How do we not get caught doing that?"

"I mean, it's just an idea," Brandon said.

"What type of hazing?"

"My dad just got this new taser issued to him. I've really been wanting to try it out, so it wouldn't be terrible helping you out — at least it would make it fun. He always leaves his work belt on the table. What if we took his pepper spray, baton, and taser and used those on her? There's no way he wouldn't realize her injuries were from his own stuff, you know?"

"But then he'll know it was us," Ryan said.

"Well, yes. That's the point. He'll be in trouble. Maybe child endangerment for leaving his shit out, or even better, he'll be considered a suspect!"

"Would he cover up for us?" Ryan asked.

"Dude, for sure! There is no way anyone is going to believe two high school kids kidnapped some girls and had access to a bunch of police gear. He'd look so guilty; he'd have to help us."

Ryan laughed. "That's epic! See, I knew you were just as much of a psycho as me."

Brandon rolled his eyes. "I'm not a psycho, but if you're gonna blackmail me, I at least want to have a little fun with it."

"This is a way better plan. Should we let Penelope know the change?"

Brandon thought about it for a moment. "Yeah. Well, just spin it. She doesn't need to know about the hazing. We'll tell her it will make it more realistic if they are both taken. She won't actually stay at the house. We'll have her scream a few times so CJ thinks they are there together."

"That's so bomb," Ryan said.

"I'll talk to Eric and Penelope and see when they want this to happen."

"I say we do it tomorrow. Fuck that bitch."

"All right, I'll talk to them. But you know we take this shit to the grave, right? Whatever you have on me gets destroyed. My debt is paid off. Because these are legit fuckin' crimes that will put our asses in prison."

"I promise. It'll all be destroyed. But don't worry, we will never get caught. That's the whole point," Ryan said.

Ryan and Brandon exchanged a final glance, silent and resolute, as they realized their lives would never be the same after this.

THE END

ACKNOWLEDGMENTS

First, I have to thank Steph Carey for taking a chance on me to write this book! While I was querying my second novel, *The Girl No One Loved*, she asked me to pitch her some ideas! Knowing she was specifically looking for a new, twisty, psychological thriller, I was stoked to come up with one of my craziest plots to date! This book would not exist without Steph and the team at Joffe Books! I would also like to thank Kate Lyall Grant and Siân Heap for taking over as my editors when Steph was granted a new opportunity! Siân you helped me tweak this idea into the perfect thriller! It has been such a pleasure working with you, and being part of the Joffe team has been fantastic.

Next, to my BETAS: Tabitha, Kate, Catie, Madeline, Amber, Emerson, Michelle, and Lauren — your feedback was INVALUABLE! Many of you have been with me since book #1, and it has been such a joy to have you along for the ride! Every book I write, I grow and develop new twisted ways to keep you entertained, but I couldn't do it without you.

To my family and friends, especially my mom and best friend, Tiffany — thank you for always listening to me freak out about where I want my stories to go and reading multiple drafts! I know it's a pain to have a writer friend since you are stuck being our guinea pigs! But every time you love one of my new stories, it makes the temporary insanity worth it!

To Bruno, without your support, none of this would be possible. I love you, and hopefully, this is just one of many more books to come!

Finally, to my readers, your support has been absolutely incredible! I love the relationships I've built with you over the years and the amazing messages you send me as you read each one of my books. I recognize that it's not easy to give new writers a chance, but I am grateful to have wonderful people like you who have supported me since the beginning. I hope you enjoyed this twisted tale, and I can't wait to show you what's coming next! Love you all.

THE JOFFE BOOKS STORY

We began in 2014 when Jasper agreed to publish his mum's much-rejected romance novel and it became a bestseller.

Since then we've grown into the largest independent publisher in the UK. We're extremely proud to publish some of the very best writers in the world, including Joy Ellis, Faith Martin, Caro Ramsay, Helen Forrester, Simon Brett and Robert Goddard. Everyone at Joffe Books loves reading and we never forget that it all begins with the magic of an author telling a story.

We are proud to publish talented first-time authors, as well as established writers whose books we love introducing to a new generation of readers.

We won Trade Publisher of the Year at the Independent Publishing Awards in 2023 and Best Publisher Award in 2024 at the People's Book Prize. We have been shortlisted for Independent Publisher of the Year at the British Book Awards for the last five years, and were shortlisted for the Diversity and Inclusivity Award at the 2022 Independent Publishing Awards. In 2023 we were shortlisted for Publisher of the Year at the RNA Industry Awards, and in 2024 we were shortlisted at the CWA Daggers for the Best Crime and Mystery Publisher.

We built this company with your help, and we love to hear from you, so please email us about absolutely anything bookish at feedback@joffebooks.com.

If you want to receive free books every Friday and hear about all our new releases, join our mailing list here: www.joffebooks.com/freebooks.

And when you tell your friends about us, just remember: it's pronounced Joffe as in coffee or toffee!

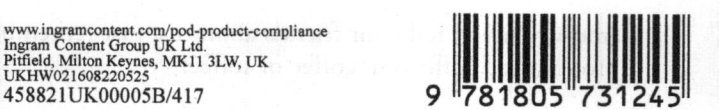

www.ingramcontent.com/pod-product-compliance
Ingram Content Group UK Ltd.
Pitfield, Milton Keynes, MK11 3LW, UK
UKHW021608220525
458821UK00005B/417